THE BLACK MASK LIBRARY

SOMEWHERE IN MEXICO

The Complete

Cases of Jerry Frost

1929–30

HORACE McCOY

---

introduction by John Wooley

illustrations by Arthur Rodman Bowker

cover by Jes Schlaikjer

BLACK MASK

2022

Table of Contents

Introduction

SOME AUTHORS, NO matter how many stories they've knocked out in their lifetimes, are destined to be forever linked to only one. So it is with Horace McCoy and his short novel *They Shoot Horses, Don't They?*

Although the book was a modest hit when Simon & Schuster brought it out in the late summer of 1935, selling four or five thousand copies stateside and starting McCoy on his way to becoming a darling of French critics, the major reason it's remembered now is because of the 1969 feature film made from the novel. Helmed by big-time director Sydney Pollack and starring another top Hollywood name, Jane Fonda, as the doomed female lead, the cinematic version of *Horses* grossed almost $13 million and garnered nine Oscar nominations along the way, with its sole win going to Gig Young for Best Supporting Actor.

In its way, this grim tale of the travails experienced by down-on-their-luck participants in a dance marathon—with Young playing the oily promoter and emcee—perfectly foreshadowed the hopelessly nihilistic movies that became popular in the 1970s, those pictures in which the main characters generally experienced death, or worse, by the time the end credits rolled. It was a story ahead of its time. Or perhaps its time had just come around again; after all, 1935 was the height of the Great Depression, a time of deep cynicism and demoralization, and the marathons—which were very popular attractions for a few years—in many ways symbolized what was going on across the country, as dispirited couples dragged one another endlessly around the dance floor, simply trying to stay on their feet, hoping against hope to outlast the competition and earn a little money for all the suffering they endured. In the marathons, participants literally danced until they dropped, with the last pair standing, or shuffling, receiving the prize, often cash. In those hardscrabble days, there was no shortage of potential contestants, from anxious husband-and-wife teams with kids to support to would-be entertainers with no visible means of support who were looking to boost their profiles however they could. (In the Los Angeles area, several movie-business luminaries, including *Freaks* director Tod Browning, were marathon aficionados.)

McCoy himself had ventured to the West Coast in the early '30s with the hopes of carving out a career in films. By this time in his life, as we'll see shortly, he'd made a mark as both a writer and an actor—albeit many miles away from the West Coast—so he was better equipped than many to launch himself toward the studios. However, the frustration, bitterness, and dark fatalism expressed in *Horses*, as well in as another of his Southern California novels, 1938's underrated *I Should Have Stayed Home*, give the reader some pretty good ideas about what McCoy really thought about Hollywood.

While his acting opportunities proved to be limited, he was working more or less steadily as a screenwriter by the mid-30's, continuing in that profession until his 1955 death and knocking out the occasional novel along the way. His output tended toward westerns and other lower-budgeted efforts, B-pictures intended for the second part of a double-feature package. But there were exceptions. He was one of the scripters, for instance, on Warner Brothers' Gentleman Jim, a 1942 biopic starring

Errol Flynn. He also shared screenwriting credits with Irving Wallace on 1953's noirish drama *Bad for Each Other,* featuring Charlton Heston and Lizabeth Scott. And he even saw one of his own novels, *Kiss Tomorrow Goodbye,* made into a James Cagney vehicle, released by Warners in 1950.

McCoy's first script credits dovetail with his disappearance from the pulps, where he had earlier found steady work, most notably as the creator of the flying Texas Ranger Jerry Frost for *Black Mask;* the first half of his 14-story Frost *oeuvre,* covering 1929 and 1930, appears in this volume.

COMPARED TO THE 20-plus years McCoy worked as a screenwriter, the pulp portion of his life was relatively brief. It began with a short called "The Tenderfoot" in the October 8, 1926, issue of *North-West Stories* and ended, fittingly enough, with the final Jerry Frost adventure—a novel-length tale called "Somebody Must Die"—in the October '34 *Black Mask.* By then, as was the case with several other talented pulpsters, McCoy had started cashing Hollywood checks and wasn't inclined to look back. He may have been destined to toil mostly in low-budget efforts, but even small pictures (and small studios) paid better than the pulp houses—although the skills, subjects, and storytelling needed to succeed in both pulps and movies were often quite similar. Take a look, for instance, at McCoy's first screenwriting credit, as per the online movie database *IMDb.* It's for a 1933 Columbia B called *Soldiers of the Storm,* in which Regis Toomey plays an aviator who goes undercover for the Border Patrol. That storyline certainly echoes the exploits of Jerry Frost, as does another McCoy-written Columbia release from the next year, *Speed Wings.*

The final Frost tale, "Somebody Must Die" (to be collected in our second volume), came out not quite a year before *They Shoot Horses, Don't They?* So even if he hadn't established himself with the studios by then, it was likely McCoy wouldn't have returned to the pulps anyway—especially when you consider that writing novels was another way of extricating yourself from, as Frank Gruber referred to it in the title of his 1966 memoir, *The Pulp Jungle.*

Before he went on to movies and books, however, McCoy crafted an intriguing group of tales that blend hardboiled detective fiction—a relatively new concept when Jerry Frost first appeared in the September '29 *Black Mask*—with elements of the aviation-pulp genre. It was a hybridized approach that attracted the attention of both *Black Mask* readers and the magazine's editor, Captain Joseph T. Shaw, as Frost and his Hell's Stepsons compadres flew and fought their way through 14 high-octane adventures, the first seven (reprinted here) appearing between September 1929 and August 1930—a rate of more than one every two months. Clearly, Shaw thought he had something with Frost.

And he certainly had something with Horace McCoy.

IN A RADIO-SHOW review that appeared in the June 10, 1928, *Dallas Morning News,* critic "C.H.B." penned a few lines about a local program on station WRR called *The Trou-badours,* describing its announcer as "a sort of *enfant terrible* of journalism and amateur theatricals in Dallas."

He was writing about Horace McCoy, who was 31 years old at the time. And the *enfant terrible* tag gives an indication not only of McCoy's personality, but also his reputation as a local star on the Dallas scene.

McCoy was not a native Texan, having been born in 1897 "in a dog-trot cabin near Pegram (or Pegram Station), Tennessee, an isolated rural whistle-stop on the Nashville, Chattanooga and St. Louis Railroad Line, twenty miles due west of Nashville, in hilly Cumberland plateau country." That's according to a 1966 doctoral dissertation by John T. Sturak titled *The Life and Writings of Horace McCoy, 1897–1955.* McCoy's deeply religious father worked for the railroad, while his mother, an inveterate reader, was a descendant of once-wealthy forebears who'd left her with little more than the family name.

In order to help with the home finances, McCoy, wrote Sturak, "was selling newspapers at six, and by the time he was sixteen had quit school to work—perhaps first as an automobile mechanic, more certainly as a traveling salesman." Sturak mentions that McCoy, along with his father, sold Jewel Brand coffee and tea door-to-door throughout the Southeast until the fall of 1915, when the family moved from Tennessee to Dallas, Texas. The World War was raging overseas, and in 1917, young Horace—whose education had only gone as far as his freshman year of high school—enlisted in the Texas National Guard.

"By July of 1918," noted William F. Nolan in his trailblazing pulp-story collection *The Black Mask Boys* (Morrow, 1985), McCoy "was overseas as a member of the American air service, stationed near Romorantin on the Normandy plain of central France. During that same month young McCoy saw action over German lines as bombardier and aerial photographer in a bomb-laden De Havilland."

On August 5th, according to Nolan, McCoy was riding in one of those De Havilland observation planes when it was attacked by a quartet of German Fokkers. McCoy not only took over the controls after the pilot was killed, but also managed to shoot down one of his pursuers on the way back to the French home base, even though he was wounded. This incident led to his receiving the Croix de Guerre.

Returning to Dallas after seeing four months of combat, McCoy worked his way into the newspaper business, and by 1920 he'd become sports editor of the *Dallas Journal,* which was then the afternoon publication of the *Dallas News.* A few years later, he began acting in productions staged by the Dallas Little Theater. Reviews of the time indicate that he was a major part of that city's theatrical scene, taking lead roles in the likes of Ferenc Molnar's *Liliom* (later adapted by Rodgers & Hammerstein into the musical *Carousel)*, Philip Barry's comedy *The Youngest*, and Sidney Howard's *They Knew What They Wanted*, among others. His experience on the Dallas theater scene would inform one of his novels, *No Pockets in a Shroud*, published in England in 1937 and debuting in America as a Signet paperback in 1940.

The idea of someone combining amateur theatrics with a career in sports reporting may seem unusual, but Horace McCoy was an unusual guy who tried his hand at a lot of different things. In addition to acting, and writing and editing for a paper, he also could be heard as a radio sports reporter. One of his higher-profile radio jobs was announcing the opening game of the 1924 Texas League season, which pitted the Dallas Rangers against the Fort Worth Panthers.

It was during this time that he, like many other newspapermen across the nation, began looking to the pulps as a way to supplement his income. That was something of a logical progression for many newspaper writers, who worked at a profession that demanded economy of style and direct subject-verb sentences, just like those in the pulps—especially the ones that took a cue from *Black Mask* and embraced the kind of tough, swift storytelling that was well on its way to becoming a major characteristic of the hardboiled-detective genre.

Given McCoy's experience as a flyer, coupled with his newspaper background, his creation of Captain Jerry Frost seems logical. His theatrical background even comes into play with Frost's sidekicks, known collectively as Hell's Stepsons; they're first seen as Hollywood-studio contract players who get fed up with moving pictures and return to the air.

McCoy, with only a handful of pulp credits at the time, had cracked *Black Mask* in the December '27 issue, with a non-series story called "The Devil Man." It was a tale of the South Seas that, as Sturak noted in his dissertation, McCoy may have been working on for some time. A little less than two years later, in the September '29 *BM*, "Dirty Work"—the first Jerry Frost tale—appeared. It was followed in swift succession by three novel-length Frost adventures: "Hell's Stepsons" (October '29); "Renegades of the Rio" (December '29); and "The Little Black Book" (January '30). The December issue would've probably been on the stands on October 24, when the event that came to be known as Black Thursday signaled the start of America's Great Depression.

A month or so earlier, however, buoyed by his *Black Mask* reception, McCoy apparently ditched the newspaper business for good to take a stab at the freelance life. "As the story goes," wrote Sturak, "McCoy quit his newspaper job that day in September 1929 that he received a check from *Black Mask* for

600 or 650 dollars." Sturak speculates that this money represented payment for "Dirty Work" plus, perhaps, an advance on the next one or two Frost yarns.

Of course, editor Shaw was continuing to hire and encourage writers who reflected that "hard, brittle style" and "authenticity in characterization and action" that he would mention later in the introduction to his anthology, *The Hard-Boiled Omnibus* (Simon & Schuster, 1946). And clearly, he saw something in Frost and McCoy that he wanted to cultivate.

It should be noted here that for whatever reason, Frost didn't make the cut for *The Hard-Boiled Omnibus*. And this may also be a good place to mention that, some four decades later, William F. Nolan thought it advisable to do a rewrite on "Frost Flies Alone," the McCoy story he chose for *The Black Mask Boys*. (The original is included in this collection; those so inclined can make their own comparisons.)

Still, McCoy was clearly one of Shaw's "boys," visiting his editor in New York during the winter of 1929–30 and continuing to sell the Frost tales to Shaw with regularity. In his dissertation, Sturak gave a hint of the connection between writer and editor during McCoy's *Black Mask* years.

"McCoy... in a letter written in 1952," wrote Sturak, "reminded Joe Shaw of 'the good old days when I would frantically wire or phone you for $100 of *Black Mask* money so I could pay the rent.'"

McCOY WAS STILL several years away from Tinseltown when he left the newspaper business to begin his pulp career. And he was in Hollywood when he abandoned pulps for good, despite the fact that his Jerry Frost was still a popular attraction for *Black Mask* readers. In 1935, for instance, when editor Joseph T. Shaw sent out questionnaires to the magazine's subscribers, asking them to name their favorite *Black Mask* character, Frost came in twelfth—not bad considering the plethora of contestants for that title and the fact that the survey was published a year after the final Frost story ran.

But Horace McCoy, Dallas theater's *enfant terrible,* had caught Hollywood fever, and westward he went. How and why he got there depends upon whose version you choose to accept.

In *The Black Mask Boys,* for instance, Nolan wrote, "Impressed by one of his stage performances, an MGM talent scout offered to set up a Hollywood screen test. McCoy eagerly agreed, driving out to Los Angeles in May [1931] for a go at the movies."

However, McCoy's *Dallas Morning News* obituary from December 17, 1955, said that McCoy got to L.A. because "Oliver Hinsdell, director of the Dallas Little Theater from 1923 to 1931, was engaged as a speech and acting coach for MGM studios. McCoy drove Hinsdell's automobile from Dallas to Hollywood."

The least likely explanation of McCoy's breaking into the picture business comes from a Consolidated Press Association wire story from May 1932. In it, writer Jessie Henderson claimed McCoy had been "selected as the nucleus" of what was called the "college writer unit" at RKO, put together by H.K. Swanson, described as "a magazine editorial director, who is acting as a story editor at RKO during a leave of absence from his magazine duties."

According to the article, the idea, credited to RKO executive vice president David O. Selznick, was to elevate the quality of the scripts by using screenwriters fresh out of college.

"What Hollywood wants is fresh ideas," wrote Henderson, "and the rumor is that the colleges have 'em."

RKO, wrote Henderson, had already contracted McCoy, "a graduate of Vanderbilt University, whose stories have appeared in many a magazine and whose name is found in the authors' blue book for 1931."

We must, of course, take this press-agent fantasy *cum grano salis*. The fact that McCoy was hardly a college graduate, not even making it past his freshman year of high school, pretty well throws everything else into question.

However, panning through this frothy piece may yield some small nuggets of truth. *IMDb*, for instance, has McCoy as an uncredited "script assistant" on RKO's *King Kong*, which came out in '33. In '33 and '34, a man named H. *N.* (not *K.*) Swanson was an associate producer at RKO who'd worked with Kong producer Merian C. Cooper, so it's just possible Swanson could've gotten McCoy the uncredited gig. (A former editor of *College Humor*, Harold Nordling Swanson later became an agent, representing F. Scott Fitzgerald, William Faulkner, John O'Hara, and many former pulp writers.) And then there's the true statement that McCoy had appeared "in many a magazine," even though the vast majority of them were pulps.

Just as he'd used the writing skills honed in the newspaper business to jump to the pulp mags, McCoy called upon the narrative skills—and subject matter—from his pulpwood days to end up writing pulp-like stories for the movies. In between, with the encouragement of a legendary editor, he created one of the most unusual series ever published, serving up high, hardboiled adventure that took *Black Mask's* "hard, brittle style" and "authenticity in characterization and action" and launched it into the skies above Texas, with a memorable character named Jerry Frost at the throttle, fronting a group of two-fisted ex-movie actor wingmen collectively, and colorfully, called Hell's Stepsons.

This collection will never be confused with *They Shoot Horses, Don't They?* But in its own way, it's every bit as memorable.

> — John Wooley
> Foyil, Oklahoma
> 1 June 2022

(My thanks to John Locke and John McMahan for their assistance with this introduction. I also want to acknowledge the helpfulness of the online resource *The FictionMags Index* at philsp.com)

Dirty Work

CAPTAIN JERRY FROST walked through the rotunda of the Texas State capitol, past the oils of Crockett and Houston and Hogg, and into the deep-toned offices of the Adjutant-General.

"What's on your mind, General?" he said, dropping himself into a chair and stretching his long legs.

"This Jamestown business." The Adjutant-General drummed on the desk with his incredibly long fingers. "It's quite a mess." Plainly he was just a little irritated.

Frost grinned. "Yes, sir. It's quite a mess." But the Adjutant-General didn't think it was so funny. He was quite serious.

"Jerry, for the life of me I can't understand why all police act so stupidly. This purely is a local case, but they can't handle it. They bump their heads against the wall and cry for the Rangers. I'm sometimes sorry we've got such a thing. Now the bigwigs are kicking." He held up a small packet. "Know what these are? Got any idea what they mean?"

Captain Frost confessed he hadn't.

"They're clippings from newspaper editorials in which the people who sit in the offices of the daily gazettes tell us how to run our great commonwealth. The robbery is up to us. I'm sorry, of course, you had to be ordered off leave. You know what that means, don't you?"

Jerry nodded. Did he know what that meant? Indeed! And since when had the Adjutant-General become so obtuse? He was tempted to laugh. Did he know what that meant? Hell,

of course he knew. What did trips to this office usually mean? Dirty work—that's what. Dirty work.

He was not offended; he was too much of a soldier for that. It was that he just didn't have any illusions about the romance of criminal work. That was a lot of applesauce that looked good in print and nowhere else. He had spent two months in the Border Patrol on some tough work and had been promised a week's leave. He had got but two days of it. Two days on the Galveston beach, and when the messenger boy found him with that fatal telegram from the Adjutant-General he was waiting on a fair young person who would be due in ten minutes.

That annoyed him no end. He had earned a rest, why couldn't he get it? Now there was more dirty work to be done. That's all he had ever done, it seemed. God knows, there had been plenty of it in the old Lafayette Escadrille, where he won his wings, and that crazy hitch with the Kosciusko Squadron over in Poland hadn't been any pink tea. And those four years down in the Guatemalan banana country hadn't made a dilettante out of him.

Go into any Latin-American country and mention Captain Jerry Frost and nobody would have the slightest idea of whom you spoke. But mention El Beneficio to any *soldado* and he was all attention. In those countries where men still die for illusions and assume musical names, they tell you that El Beneficio was a bold, roistering Americano who could handle women and a machine-gun like nobody's business.

No, he was no stranger to dirty work.

"Well," the Adjutant-General interrupted his reveries, "you can take the pick of the staff. You can do anything you want to. Forty years ago a train robbery in Texas might have been ordinary, but this is 1929. This infernal publicity is bothering me. It's up to you and the men you name."

"I'd rather look around a bit first," Frost said, as he rose to go. "If I need anybody, I'll let you know."

"Good luck to you."

He accepted the hope with a nod of his head and walked out.

CAPTAIN FROST EXPECTED little information from the chief of police of Jamestown, and he was not disappointed. The chief pointed out that he and his men were after all merely humans, and that they were doing everything humans could do. That this had availed nothing was not his fault. Captain Frost could see that?

Very frankly, Captain Frost said he couldn't. "It beats me," he said. "Here it is, the high-powered twentieth century—a scientific age. And a gang of bandits sticks up a passenger train in orthodox Wild West manner and gets away clean with a fortune. Every copper in North Texas is caught flat-footed. I'd like to have the opportunity sometime to get in on top of a case instead of waiting two or three weeks. I sure would."

"Well," the chief observed pointedly, "maybe we can arrange that just for you. It's a funny thing, but criminals never invite us to their parties. However, they might make an exception for the Rangers."

"Never mind the wisecracks! Didn't anybody in North Texas make any reports or anything after the robbery? It looks to me like a correspondence school sleuth could have done that."

"Ain't I been telling you they didn't? There wasn't nothing to report! My God, don't say that any more to me! It makes me sore all over. Every newspaper in this town has been plastering stories all over their front pages about it. It's got me goofy!

"Now, listen while I go over it again. Then you'll know as much as we do—or anybody else does. That train carried $300,000 in torn money that was going back to Washington. It left Jamestown, going east, at 8:45 and when it got to Reddy, about eight miles out, it was flagged down by a man on the track with a lantern. A moment later the engineer and fireman looked into the muzzle of a sub-machine-gun held by a masked robber.

"While this one kept the engineer and fireman covered, another went in the express car, blowed open the safe and got the coin. They slipped in on the messenger, tied him up, but when Cummings, the brakeman, ran through the door, they dropped him with a slug of lead in the forehead. Before anybody else knew what it was all about, the train started. It stopped a little farther on, but the bandits had disappeared.

"It happened right beside the highway but they had put red lights half a mile apart to stop the traffic. It's the general opinion that they are hiding out somewhere, but we've got the numbers of some of the bills and sooner or later we'll nab the men. Nobody can beat the law!"

It was the sort of a preachment Frost could expect from the chief. He was a man who had been in the chair for twenty years, and was slightly antiquated. One of the old school, as the newspaper boys liked to say.

"Now you know as much as we do."

"So that's all, eh?"

"All? Ain't it enough? It's been plenty to keep these newspapers in copy. It ought to be enough for you."

"Are you worried about what they think?"

The chief glared. "Ain't you?"

"Not particularly."

"Well, *I* am; you're damn well right I am. We got an election coming off here next month and unless the right guy gets in, I go back to pounding a beat. Damn if these crooks can't pick fine moments to pull big jobs! So, you see how much I'm for you. Personally, I'll let you have my moral support and hope you have a lot of luck. *But I don't think you will!*"

SOMEBODY ONCE WROTE that clever crime detection is one-third luck, one-third hard work and one-third intuition. Great detectives rate luck and intuition as a standoff, which is to say they reckon one as important as the other.

Jerry Frost was not a scientist, he was not a criminologist, he was not, in the technical sense of the word, a detective at all. But he had had a fair amount of luck thus far, he was perfectly willing to work hard, and he knew his intuition had stood him in good stead before.

And he was going to be able to use it this time. He realized that an hour after he had left the Jamestown chief of police.

He saw something that clicked in his mind—and would not be shaken. The very incredibility of the thing was what sold him.

He had dropped into the Secret Service offices of the government in the Federal Building, for, after all, it was their case. His conversation with the inspector had not been especially productive. But his eye caught a picture on the desk. It was a wrecked airplane, and he naturally was interested.

"This was a sweet one," he said. "Where'd it happen?"

"That," replied the inspector, "is an old one. It happened about a year ago. I was rummaging around my desk the other day and found it."

"Nasty spill."

"Yea, Charlie Cox got killed in it. You ought to remember that. The air-mail pilot. He crashed up in the Red River country. We lost a registered pouch in it."

"Oh," said Frost. "I do remember now. Never got anything on that case, did you?"

"Nope, never did. None of the bonds ever showed up."

"Ever have any ideas about it?"

"Well, not exactly. Charlie just crashed, that was all. Somebody came along and took the pouch. Anybody'd know the difference between registered mail and ordinary mail. We figured some farmer had got it, but we watched that country for a long time. None of the bonds ever showed up. Just another one of those mysteries."

It was at that moment that Jerry got his idea. But then it was too ridiculous. His intuition kept trying to tell him something, but he wouldn't listen. The voice was too faint. A little later the idea came bounding back again. And he couldn't lose it. The air-mail job. What made him think it was connected with the train robbery?

He wondered. Still, there had been innumerable baffling crimes solved by leads much more absurd than this. The air-mail job. Well, the idea was there to stay. He couldn't get rid of it.

He slept on it all night. Or tried to. Writing people and artists know how that is. You can't tear those things out of you. They weigh you down like an anvil. Sometimes you can't breathe comfortably. You think of it for hours and then very suddenly it comes, clear and clean, like big handwriting. All you have to do then is sit down and copy it.

Frost was like that. In the morning, it took definite form. It wasn't nebulous any longer. That air-mail job hadn't been an accident. It was premeditated. Everybody thought it was just one of those things that have to be a part of any new field of endeavor when man pits his brain and brawn against nature. But Jerry was willing to bet his life it had been premeditated.

Once, down south, when they were having a lot of fun with Salazar and Madero, a grizzled veteran had said, "Kid, when you get a hunch—*ride it!*" Well, that wasn't always so easy. The odds were big. No matter if you had a strong body, the odds were big. But Jerry Frost had a hunch. And he was going to ride it.

It all depended on one thing, and he went out to see about that. He wasn't the least bit surprised when he discovered the spot where the train had been held up was but a few hundred yards from Withers Field, the municipal airport. He had expected it.

He telephoned the Secret Service chief and the Jamestown chief and made the same request of both. It was for them to forget they had seen him.

Irrespective of the theories of the investigators, and their verdicts, Jerry was convinced the mail plane had been tampered with. To do that required cold nerve and daring that not every criminal possessed. Find the man who conceived that idea and you had the brains behind the train robbery. And he was a man who would need and who would have a sound knowledge of airplanes.

That afternoon he reported to the hangar of the Mid-West Air Transport Company at Withers Field with a letter of introduction to Captain Eads. An hour before Captain Eads had been telephoned that one Thomas Femrite, a name Jerry adopted for obvious reasons, was to be given employment as a mechanic and test pilot.

He knew, of course, that there was little chance of any of the bandits being at the Field now. But that flying field once had been the center of their operations. That wasn't much to work on, but it was something. It was considerably more than anybody else had decided.

"Captain Eads?" Jerry asked.

A man seated at the inside desk turned and looked. Before him in the door stood a man six feet tall and as brown as a nut. He had long arms, long legs and good eyes. He looked every inch a flyer. There is something about a new man who comes to a flying field that compels attention. You immediately size him up and wonder how much stuff he's got, and whether he's going to be a heel or a good fellow, and whether or not he can fly. Captain Eads decided this lad would do.

"Mr. Femrite, reporting for duty."

"Come in, Mr. Femrite. An old army man?"

"Yes, sir."

"I thought so. What outfit?"

"The Forty-seventh."

Captain Eads lifted his eyebrows. "Oh, yeah? Pretty good gang of crate-busters. The downtown office telephoned me about you. How many hours have you had?"

"Oh, six or seven thousand."

"Whoosh! That's plenty. Well, you've come to the right place if you're a seven-thousand-hour man. We need men who can assemble motors and who aren't afraid to fly those same motors. Know what I mean?"

"Yes, sir."

"All right. Red!"

An oily individual who escaped being a dwarf by a few inches shoved his auburn head through the door.

"Take Mr. Femrite around and make him acquainted. He's going to work for us."

Getting acquainted with the Mid-West crew was the work of but a few moments. Red was short, Jerry learned, for Fred Walker, and apart from him the only other veteran was Slimmer King. There were a couple of youngsters but they didn't count. They hadn't passed the prop-spinning stage.

Going over big was simple with Red and Slimmer. Jerry spoke their language. The kids were aloof, but after he had stunted one of the rickety Travelairs one afternoon, they warmed up and immediately made him a model.

Nor had his maneuvers hurt his prestige with the old-timers. Jerry had all but knocked the knob off St. Peter's gate. That particular day he went crazy. What he didn't do with that old bus hadn't been invented.

"Gee, you looked great!" Red beamed. "But I thought once or twice we oughta kissed you good-bye before you left the ground."

"Stop kidding, Red. I bet you can do things with a crate I've never thought of."

"Naw," Red confessed. "I ain't much of a stunter. I can get 'em up there and get 'em down and that lets me out. I wasn't born to kick no rudder bar. My head belongs in a motor."

After that, things came easier for Jerry. The ice had been broken. He came to know something of the other fellows on the Field. He was particularly attracted to the bunch in the No. 6 hangar. They were commercial men.

He sensed a sort of rivalry between the Mid-West fellows and the bunch in No. 6. There was no particular reason for it, but he did. Ostensibly, they just about had the commercial business at the field sewed up. The Mid-West wasn't in competition with them, yet they growled and glared every time Jerry got close. He spoke to Red about it.

"They're just a gang of five-dollar-a-lick boys," Red said. "Don't pay them any attention. They haul passengers, but personally, I wouldn't let one of 'em push me in a wheelbarrow. I just don't crave their company."

"There's no reason for them to be sore at me," Jerry said.

"That's their way. They're sore at everybody. The farther away from those guys you stay the better off you'll be."

But he had no intention of staying away. He was curious. So the next day, under the pretext of borrowing a porcelain, he invaded their hangar. He went up to the fellow who had been pointed out as Casey.

Casey gave him the porcelain. He was stocky and careless in his personal appearance, even for an airplane mechanic. "Where you come from, feller?"

"Oh, all over," said Jerry.

"I saw you yesterday doing some fancy flying. Looked like you'd wobbled a stick before."

"Yep—I've wobbled 'em before."

"You a new air-mail pilot?"

"Nope, just a mechanic."

"Well, there ain't many mechanics can fly like that."

"Oh, I dunno."

"A guy like you is wasting his time meddling with spark plugs and pushing a gasoline truck over a flying field. You'd ought to get in the big money. Commercial stuff."

"Sounds pretty good."

"It is good." Casey was positive. "Any guy what can bust clouds like you can is wasting his time drawing two hundred bucks a month. Interested?"

"Maybe. Much obliged for the porcelain."

THAT NIGHT CAPTAIN Jerry Frost reported to the Adjutant-General by telephone. He reported that he had become established and that the outlook was promising and that something possibly would happen soon.

The Adjutant-General, still annoyed, retorted that something would happen soon—to the entire force. "They're still raising hell," he said bluntly. "Let me send you some help."

"Now, listen," said Jerry firmly. "Any outside interference will gum the whole works. You sit tight and stop worrying. And don't send anybody! Forget all about it."

The Adjutant-General grumblingly agreed, and then told himself he was glad Frost was on the job. If anybody could do it, Jerry could.

Jerry was convinced the gang in No. 6 hangar wasn't all everybody thought it was. He had been made an overture, and he expected another. To bring it about, he spent the next few days in direct defiance of all the laws of flying. He was either a plain damn fool or the sweetest pilot who ever brought a bus down on one tire. He almost tore the ships to pieces. All this time the gang in No. 6 looked on.

One night Casey and another man, of a distinct continental air, visited the Transport hangar.

"Meet Mr. Crouch," said Casey. "He's the boss of our outfit."

Jerry shook hands with him.

"I'm glad to know you," Crouch said. "I saw you the other day and I wanted to congratulate you. I've seen a lot of flying in my time, but I don't think I ever saw the equal of that."

The man spoke with a slight accent, and a high voice. It was an unusual tone. Something in Jerry's memory stirred. He looked into the face closely. Gray mustache. Black eyes, sharp and deep-set. A small mouth and thin lips.

He had seen that face somewhere before. But where? The panorama of his life passed swiftly. It produced nothing.

"Thank you, sir," Jerry said. "I sometimes think I was born with my feet on a rudder bar."

"You were," Crouch agreed; "and that's just the point. You are the type of man commercial flying needs. Would you consider a change?"

"Well," said Jerry, "a fellow always needs—"

"Exactly. And you're worth just twice as much to us as you

are to the air-mail people."

Jerry debated for a moment. He had no idea of refusing; he just didn't want to be too anxious.

"I'll take it."

"Good! When can you leave?"

"When do you want me?"

"Tomorrow. We're opening a hangar at Waco. You'll be on hand in the morning?"

"Yes, sir. I don't think they'll hold me."

"Of course they won't! If necessary, tell 'em to go to hell!"

Getting his release was simple. He merely got in touch with the home office, where the officials knew his mission and identity, and explained the situation. They in turn notified the Field. There was little comment. There seldom is. Young flying men are notorious nomads.

Waco was but an hour's hop from Jamestown, and as Jerry was eager to get there he left at once. During that hour he rolled his memory before him, seeking to pull from its kaleidoscope the face of the man called Crouch. That high voice rang in his ears above the drone of the motor; and gradually the years fell away.

Flying now, as he was flying then, the slender threads of memory were picked up more easily.

Once more he was in the air over Bapaume with the 47th. This was Richthofen's old stamping ground and the Boche knew it like birds. Jerry was flying a Camel at 8,000 feet. They were climbing in close formation. He looked ahead and to the right. There was Bapaume in all its raggedness, half-obscured in the mist. On his left were a couple of youngsters. They waved. They were going through the agony of their first patrol. He had gone through it two months before. But it hadn't wrecked him. He hadn't a lot of imagination. He was sure of himself. But he knew it must be hell on the youngsters. He thought he'd better keep an eye on the eaglets.

There were clouds above—gray blanket clouds that came together in a solid roof, with only a gaping hole here and there to reveal the blue. Bad stuff. The squadron leader knew. He kept them climbing. Jerry glanced again at the youngsters. It bucked him up a bit to think about them. They were green. He squinted his eye and put up his thumb to have a look around the sun. They were up above now. He warmed his guns. The chatter reminded him that he was tired. So this was war. Well, they could have the damned war for all he cared. He was tired. He wished… And then he caught himself. A fellow couldn't do that. It wasn't decent. He was in it, no use wishing he was out. Then he saw he was straggling. Straggling was suicide. They were out in Richthofen's country. The Baron's men were devoted to stragglers. They ate 'em alive. He looked up. His intuition again.

His throat closed abruptly and his knees melted. An Albatross was coming down fast. His wing fabric was ruffling into lace and the wood of his camber ribs was splintering. He pulled up sharply and pressed his trigger. Both guns vomited. He was firing wildly. The Albatross slipped under him. Oh, for a fast bus! His Camel would do 100. An S.E. would do 135. A Spad would do 140. And an Albatross would beat that. A butter-fly-winged Albatross. *Rat-tat-tat-tat-tat. Rat-tat-tat-tat-tat.* Sping! A shower of gasoline. His motor conked. He fell over in a dive. The Albatross followed him down. The Spandaus were rattling. He could hear them above the bite of the motor. A hundred red-hot needles hit him in the shoulder. Her dammed something warm back with his lips. Something warm and wet. The dirty, lousy swine! Fine stuff! What the hell? He was done… he was falling. The Spandaus rattled *fortissimo*. A drumlike roar, blackness swept, swirled over him…

A high-ceilinged room. The penetrating smell of anesthetics. A face that bent over and shut out the depth of the room. An enormous face by contrast. He slowly made it out. He moved his body and winced. Bandaged. The face grinned. It spoke.

"Never," said a high, irritating voice, "break formation. How did I hit everything but your head?" The face came closer. The *Pour le Mérite* swung out on its ribbon. "Byfield, my name is. You're my personal prisoner…"

Jerry tried to laugh. Instead he fainted…

That had been eleven years ago. The vision passed and its present significance came upon him so suddenly he went into a *renversement* that almost popped his neck. Byfield! The German Ace! Crouch! By God! There was dirty work somewhere. His first vague hunch, even so soon, assumed the form of reality. There could be no doubt that he was on a trail that would lead somewhere.

Out of the mists loomed the Amicable Building, perennial landmark, sentinel of the Brazos, gaunt and lonely for want of companionship. Bearing to the left, he came over the field and settled down. He was trembling as if he had been out on his first patrol.

Byfield!

A luxurious cabin plane idled down and disgorged two men. One was Casey. The other was Crouch, né Byfield. It was all Jerry could do to keep his hands off the man's throat.

"You must have been in a hurry," said the high voice.

That voice! There was no doubt of it now. Von Byfield. Every step of the way now was fraught with danger. He half hoped Crouch wouldn't see it in his face.

"I was," he said finally.

"Well, there's a lot to do. We'll brush up and visit the newspapers."

They brushed, breakfasted, visited. Crouch planted all his ideas. But that was simple. He had them talking about it already. There were a dozen pilots coming in from New Mexico and Arizona to take part in the circus. A dozen men who, Jerry knew full well, were bums. And then he thought it was funny that he should be walking beside this man in such a placid way... the man who called himself Crouch, who had shot him out of control and then followed him down. He had prayed to meet him a hundred times—and now he had. And he was helpless. Funny.

That afternoon the pilots dropped in. That afternoon they were not an impressive collection. Just as Jerry thought, they were tramps. He thought they were a tough-looking bunch of eggs to be pilots. Had it come to the point where there was as much evil in the air as on the ground? God forbid. The air was the last outpost of chivalry. Of romance. It was dead as hell everywhere else. And it wouldn't be long—

But his big shock came later in the afternoon.

HE DISCOVERED A portion of the hangar falsely constructed. From the outside it seemed all right, but from the inside it seemed shorter than it should be. He opened a door and stepped into semi-darkness. A ghostly form confronted him. And another.

There is nothing quite so ghostly as to come across an airplane in a poorly lit hangar. Even if you are expecting it, you are half startled. There is something weird about it, even if you are an airman. It strikes at the roots.

Jerry recovered from his shock and opened the door wide.

The light revealed two planes. Two planes so lovely, so trim that his breath came in a swift intake of admiration. Two tiny planes that seemed unreal. Watch fob types. He moved closer. And stopped.

He saw they weren't so lovely. They were grim. Trench mortars looked like that. They looked like playthings—until they belched. Then they were hideous. On the cowling of each of the planes was mounted a machine-gun, its squat muzzle merging almost indistinguishably into the background.

He was amazed. He hadn't, in his wildest fancies, anticipated anything like this. He hadn't seen a plane like this since he had left the Polish front. Not even then. Those things were hayracks compared to this. Before him stood two of the highest products of scientific civilization.

"Good-looking, eh?"

The voice cracked through the hangar like a sputtering electric wire that has found a ground. For a moment Jerry was disconcerted. Only for a moment.

"I'd give a month's salary to fly one of them!" he breathed.

"Yes?" It was evident Crouch didn't know whether to be angered or amused. He decided on the latter course. "Maybe you will. They're patented. I'm trying to sell them to the government. I wouldn't like for *anybody* to know I had them."

Jerry caught the faintest hint of a threat in the words. Of course, it was a lie. It wasn't even a good lie. He knew that, and he knew that Crouch knew he knew. Crouch must have thought he was several different kinds of a prize fool to swallow that one. But he was just as anxious to repair the damage as his employer.

"Not a word. You can trust me."

When they went out, Crouch locked the door with a padlock. Jerry looked back over his shoulder and decided the compartment was well hidden. And he decided something else. To dally with this thing was to play with T.N.T. Crouch and his gang were dangerous. One man couldn't stand in their way. They had too much to protect.

But what had the air circus to do with it? Jerry felt that everybody knew more than he did. The flyers knotted into little clans and got their heads together. He stumbled around stupidly. It made him, for the first time since he had won his wings, terribly self-conscious.

He stopped Casey later in the day. "Say, I guess I stumbled onto a little family secret this morning."

"Yeah?"

"Yeah. I saw two of the sweetest little battle wagons—"

"Easy, feller." Casey turned on him and glowered. "Don't go around popping off your face. They're inventions. The old man's a nut. He's afraid somebody might steal his plans."

Jerry gestured disdainfully. "Don't make me laugh. I wasn't born yesterday. How come I don't rate some of the secrets."

"Listen, you! If there are any secrets, the old man'll let you in on them. In the meantime, keep your trap shut—*tight!*"

For the second time that day, Jerry was tempted to crown somebody. But that would have spoiled everything. He had been acting; he could continue.

"Now, now; ain't I one of the outfit? You pulled me away from a good job—for why? I don't even know what I'm supposed to do."

Casey melted somewhat. Maybe the kid was right. Maybe he ought to rate a few secrets.

"Well," he said, "I can't tell you nothing but this: if there hadn't been something big doing, the old man wouldn't have wanted you. He's a pretty good student of human nature—and he figured you'd been in a jam somewhere and wasn't too particular what you did as long as it was in an airplane. There's something about an airman that's written all over his face. He's like a schoolboy in love. He doesn't know it's there, and even if he did he couldn't do anything about it. You sit tight."

Jerry made up his mind to sit.

THE AIR CIRCUS came off as scheduled. Good advertisement. It packed the field and roads for miles around. The spectacle of fifteen pilots in the air doing all manner of stunts was appealing anywhere—especially in Waco. They hadn't seen anything like it since the training days of the war.

Crouch's business acumen was sound. The trade rolled in. There were innumerable hops. Everybody wanted to fly. The young men visioned themselves not as Foncks and Guynemers and Bishops and Lukes, for they belonged to another age. It was Lindbergh now. The old people grinned as they came in contact with the onrushing age. Jerry caught a passenger to Austin one morning. He had gone on a rush call. He had an hour to wait.

He visited the capitol and found the Adjutant-General in another rage. This was getting to be the best thing the Adjutant-General did.

"What's the big idea?" he bellowed. "We're wasting time. I've had to fight with myself to keep my hands off. From your reports, we've got enough on those fellows to get a conviction now."

"From my reports—yes," Frost replied. "But my reports wouldn't convict them because I haven't got one single fact. It's pure hunch. But I'm going to nail them to the cross, and it won't be long. This is the toughest, nerviest outfit I've ever run across in my life. They'd stick up the National City Bank in New York with a little encouragement. But something's in the wind. I need help."

"Take anybody you want."

"It isn't that kind of help. Listen."

For five minutes he talked, all the while the Adjutant-General nodded and drummed on his desk top. Hardly had Frost left the office when the state official reached for the telephone and placed a call for the commandant at Kelly Field, the army base.

And thus, that night, one of the new A-3 battle planes, carrying six thousand rounds of ammunition and mounting six machine-guns, dropped out of the darkness at Withers Field and was quickly rushed into the hangar of the Mid-West Air Transport Company and covered with a tarpaulin.

Given that impetus, Jerry felt more confident. Nothing was likely to happen at Waco. If anything broke, it would be at Jamestown. And something was going to break—soon.

Riding his hunch, Jerry was sure Crouch and his gang had wrecked the air-mail plane a year before. They had held up the Rio Grande express. God knows what else they had done. Jerry felt it had been plenty.

He had fitted himself up a bunk in one corner of the hangar on a collapsible cot that was hidden away each morning. He didn't want to jeopardize the confidence Crouch might have in him.

A few nights later, as he lay there and stared into the darkness, and made up his mind to force the play within the next twenty-four hours, he heard the low drone of a motor. He rolled over and strained his ears. It was faint, then louder, then faint again. Then he heard another sound—a drone. There was enough noise to make him think it was a bombing raid.

Jerry looked at his watch. Four o'clock. Of course, it would be an hour like that. Something was up. Something was going to happen. He slipped into his pants and boots, knocked down his cot and shoved it under a fuselage and strapped on his guns. He went to the far corner of the corrugated hangar. There was an opening there wide enough for him to see. If there was anything to see. Right now it was black night.

Louder and louder the drones came. They were directly overhead now. Jerry wondered how Crouch expected to get away with anything like this. It amounted to pure suicide. And then it dawned that perhaps this was the very reason they had held that air circus. Adjacent residents might not be so curious if they heard motors at night. Or could Crouch have been that much of a psychologist?

Staring through the aperture, Jerry was momentarily blinded by a flash of light as the field was illuminated by two great searchlights. The motors throbbed, clawed furiously as they lost traction, and then whistled as the ships landed.

One was a cabin monoplane. The other was a tiny battle plane.

Then the lights went out. The entire operation consumed not more than two minutes.

Presently there were footsteps. Shuffling footsteps… and low voices. Out of the low conversation his ears picked strange words. Chinese!

Then: "Keep those Chinks quiet!"

Under cover of night, Crouch was running in Chinese.

Frost lay there for ten minutes, thinking. Crouch seemed to have his hand in everything. He heard echoes of automobiles on the highway, the grind of gears coming loud and clear through the stillness; then two men walked back. The office door opened, and a faint glow appeared through the cracks.

He got up and moved closer. He recognized the voices of Crouch and Casey.

"God, I'm glad that's over." This was Casey. "Two more trips and then we're Europe bound."

"Thompson's waiting in Mexico City."

"You wasn't sap enough to give him the dough, was you?"

Crouch laughed shortly. "Certainly not! Nobody knows where that money is—nobody but I."

"What do you mean?" Casey asked.

"Well, I moved it."

"You mean you moved our dough from that train job?" He was incredulous.

"Yes. Remember seeing some guys working on those old asphalt tennis courts behind our hangar at Withers Field?"

"Sure."

"Well, you thought they were repairing them, didn't you? So did everybody else. But they were just putting the asphalt over a little hiding place I'd previously fixed up."

"My God!" Casey ejaculated. "Suppose we wanna get away quick?"

"That's all right. We can smash that stuff in five minutes. And it was the safest place—believe me."

"Maybe it was wise. By the way, this wild man we got off the Mid-West ain't so certain everything's on the level. He cornered me and asked a lotta questions. I told him if there was anything to say, you'd say it. Might not be wise to stall him. He looks pretty sharp."

"I don't intend to. I'm going to talk to him today and he'll run in the next batch of Chinese. I figure he's got the nerve to help us pull a sweet one down South pretty soon."

"Course, you know what you're doing. But I don't see the point in hiring him. Never did."

"Perhaps there wasn't. But I collect good pilots just like other men collect stamps and books. I like to have them around. But you don't need to worry about this guy. He's been in a lot of jams before. You can look at him and tell that."

"I dunno—"

"Help me get that Moth in." They moved out on the field.

Captain Jerry Frost came alive. He had them nailed. His suspicions were confirmed. They had done the train job. And unless he missed his guess, those bonds from the air-mail plane were in that cache Crouch spoke of. He moved up in the dark until the two men got into the hangar with their plane. Then he started off on a dog-trot down the road.

At dawn the law forces of the sovereign State of Texas swung into action. They had long been waiting for this moment. The great, ponderous, clumsy law, with its thousands of tentacles, got going. The tide itself was not more relentless. It struck here sometimes, there sometimes, in a circle sometimes—but eventually it straightened out and began to roll. It was inevitable.

The Adjutant-General sat at his desk and manipulated the controls. He was the puppeteer.

Shortly after sunrise, two state planes were in the air. There were six men in each besides the pilot. Six tight-lipped, grim men, who would shoot their way into hell and back again to get their men.

The Rangers were moving up.

In the hangar at Waco, the telephone jangled. Casey answered it.

"Yeah, Casey... all right, Tommy... What's that? I can't hear you... wait a minute." He handed the receiver to Crouch. "The goof is excited. Get an earful."

Crouch took the instrument. "Hello, Tommy... Yes..." A long wait. Casey moved closer. Something had happened. One look at Crouch's face told him that. Finally: "Who told you?... Hell!" He slammed the receiver on the hook.

"We're fools!" He spat the words out. "One of the Mid-West fellows told Tommy this morning that this guy Femrite is a Texas Ranger. Come on!"

"Where?"

"That's the trouble with you damned Americans," Crouch cried. "You lose your head in a tight place. We're going to get that money. Maybe we can make it. He's waited this long without tipping his hand, maybe he'll wait a little longer."

"But what about the others?"

"This is no time to think of them. We can be in Mexico in five hours. Come on!"

They moved quickly to the hangar door, swung it open. They

wheeled their tiny, speedy planes out into the starting line. They swung each other's props, the motors barked into life, and dust and pebbles swept into the backwash and puttered against the side of the hangars.

Crouch was first off. Casey followed. Tails whipped up and wheels bounced lightly on the uneven ground. They zoomed into the air in broad climbing turns. Casey saw Crouch was loading his guns.

They didn't know it then, but they were to be disappointed. Jerry already was at Withers Field, had been there when Ranger reinforcements arrived. And, of course, a perverse fate decreed they would start at the wrong end of the tennis court.

To see a half dozen apparently intelligent men digging into an asphalt tennis court in the early morning is not a sight calculated to be passed without stopping for a moment. Mechanics stopped, workmen stopped. There was a great textile mill near the field, and a crowd begets a larger crowd.

Jerry was trying to direct the traffic and the Rangers at the same time. Three young men in handcuffs, late of the No. 6 hangar, looked on in undisguised amusement.

Then a shout. Somebody had the pouch. Jerry grabbed it and, with a single movement, slit the side. A handful of currency was extracted. Torn currency.

"That's it!" he said. "That's it! Take those men and this pouch into the office. Those other fellows are coming here sooner or later. We'll make a reception out of it."

The news swept about the airport like wildfire. The textile mill was all agog. For the first time in many of their lives, they were sitting in the middle of a big event. "The train robbers have been found!" The doorman at the textile mill told the switchboard operator, and the switchboard operator told the secretary. The secretary thought the police ought to know so he telephoned them.

Eagle-eyed news hawks caught the message the moment the desk sergeant finished his yawn and copied it. They flashed their papers. Editors stirred their stumps, called circulation managers, engravers, operators and pressmen. Reporters on the city staff got going, the rewrite man lighted a fresh cigarette off the butt of an old one and rammed copy paper in his mill. He pulled the telephone close. And muttered: "I hope to Gawd this is as big as it looks!"

The word got about Jamestown. Sirens shrieked through the traffic carrying enough police to take Mont Sec. In thirty minutes, the highways leading to Withers Field were choked. Some of them knew what was going to happen, but most of them didn't. This was the Great American Public.

SPEEDING NORTH FOR their plunder before seeking safety, neither Crouch nor Casey was aware of the plans being made for their welcome. Crouch, being of higher mentality, probably thought he had pushed his luck too far, but that was all.

He couldn't see Withers Field, he couldn't see Captain Jerry Frost beside the A-3 single-seater, positively the finest thing in battle planes. If Crouch's ships were lovely, there was no superlative for this. Jerry stood there, his eyes glued on the southern heavens, his propeller swinging idly.

He seemed just a little ridiculous to himself. He couldn't, for example, grasp that this was 1929. Imagine such a thing with so large a gallery? It was like an *opéra bouffe*. Still, he tingled. He almost, once, half admitted he liked it.

From out of the distance came a drone. Two planes were seen; they roared onward, still unaware of what awaited them. One dipped downward, the other, which was higher, began a long glide.

The cordon of police started forward.

"Wait a while," Jerry shouted. "Those ships have got guns on 'em! Take your time!"

But the police disregarded the command. They, too, had waited long. And neither were they self-conscious before the crowd.

Casey was in the first ship, and no sooner had his wheels touched the ground than he realized all was lost. He shot the throttle to his ship and the smoke belched from the exhaust. A policeman fired. The bullet whistled through the fuselage.

Then Casey either tried to zoom, or he lost his head. He later claimed he didn't know his finger was on the trigger. His guns barked through the propeller and two policemen pitched forward, twitched and lay still. A second later a shot got Casey and his plane dived into the ground.

Crouch had seen and heeded. He had gone into a climb— and he was going south.

Jerry throbbed and pinched. It was the old feeling. Something in him seemed to say, had always said: "Enjoy this, for it may be your last one." Not fear—and yet it might have been.

He swung his arm out for the chocks to be pulled. His motor whined and then caught with a roar. Something throbbed in his hands and feet and played along his nerves like tiny electrical impulses. He was talking to himself, and there was something terrible in it—prayer and hatred intermingled.

He opened his throttle and his propeller disappeared in a thin circle of light. Like a living thing his ship bounded forward. For a while he bounced along and then he went straight up like an elevator. He climbed 500 feet before it began to stall, then drifted his stick forward and presently flattened out at 140. His bus never even felt it. Tight. Solid. Maneuverable.

He warmed his guns with a burst of twenty. He rather hoped he wouldn't have to fight. Still, never could tell. Everything was different in the air. Once before, he had been in the same air with Crouch. He had remembered. Maybe there would be a fight after all.

He climbed to 7,500 and buckled on his straps. He had done that before, too. But this was something new. No straining the eyes to the right and to the left and above looking for black specks. No wondering if that was an L.V.G. two-seater—a decoy—with a half dozen Albatrosses lurking above. His man was just in front. Only one.

He crawled up on Crouch's tail and motioned for him to land. Crouch climbed to the left and got into fighting position. Jerry motioned again. His answer was a burst that raked through the A-3 ailerons.

"O.K.," Jerry bellowed. "Here we go!"

He half rolled to get on top, so did the other. Jerry touched the trigger and pulled up, dived again. Crouch Immelmanned and straightened out on Jerry's tail and another burst ripped through the fins. Jerry kicked it off into a slip and leveled out. Crouch was diving away. He was going to run for it. No doubt of that.

Jerry pushed his stick forward until the rush of air gagged him. The rattle of his guns came through the chatter of the motor. Crouch went into another Immelmann and Jerry dived by him. The German was a flyer. But he was not matching skill with the kid he had knocked down that day at Toul. This was another fellow.

Jerry pulled up and went into a climb. He banked sharply and started higher and higher. That was Crouch's mistake. His ship couldn't climb with the A-3. Jerry was so close now he could see the wheels on the other's undercarriage spinning.

Well, there he was. He had him. The trim white belly of Crouch's ship glinted along the tip of his guns. There he was. There was von Byfield, the great ace. *The* von Byfield. The one who had followed him down. He could still hear those Spandaus clacking as they raked his body in a steel flail.

Jerry touched his trigger. He could see holes tearing in the linen. He kept his guns open. There was a fan of flame. He noticed his altimeter: 14,000. Too high. And yet… He stalled and whipped out in a spin.

Crouch's ship hung momentarily like a leaf undecided whether to fall this way or that. Then it dipped its nose and wabbled. The glide became a dive; the dive went into a lazy, aimless spin, wings flopping, to the floor. The plane flattened, whipped out upside down, stalled, snapped out again in a final effort, and then again went downward in that grotesque way. Over and over. Over and over. Jerry watched it, fascinated. It was only a dot now, flashing in the sun as it keeled over. It was coming closer to the floor—closer, closer.

Then suddenly a tiny sheet of flame lashed out, a puff of dust. That was all.

Jerry sideslipped down, landed and taxied slowly in. He climbed out stiff-legged. He looked down and saw his pants were slightly torn. There was a gash in his leather coat. He looked into his cockpit. The floorboards were splintered. He looked up. The center section was riddled. The linen on his fins was ribboned.

Far down the field a group of police and civilians was rushing to the wrecked plane.

"Cigarette?"

Somebody gave him one.

"Match?"

Somebody else struck it. Frost thought those fingers were familiar. Long… white… He looked into the face. The Adjutant-General. He had his arms extended.

"Hurt, Jerry?"

"Nope. Tired." Quite matter-of-fact. The curious crowded around. The Adjutant-General very plainly was ill-at-ease. It had stirred him tremendously. He wanted to say something nice, but he couldn't. Men are like that. Especially men who are suddenly overcome with pride. They try to say flowery things, but the words clog up in their throats. They think them right down to the tip of their tongue, and then strange words come out.

It was like that now. The Adjutant-General said: "Well, take a rest. California, Florida. Any place."

"Nope, Galveston."

"Galveston?"

"Yep, Galveston. Unfinished business."

The Adjutant-General nodded. He didn't understand; he didn't want to understand. Captain Frost had come through. That was the code of the Rangers. It had been that way when the Conestogas squeaked their way through the Indian country, and it was that way in the day of science and aviation.

When all else fails, when there is a knotty problem, when there's dirty work—the Rangers. Yesterday and today and tomorrow, to the ends of the earth—get him!

Hell's Stepsons

*The new "wing" of the fighting
Texas Rangers goes into action*

THE HEADQUARTERS ROOM of the Texas Air Rangers in the little town of Gentry held an oppressive, stifling silence. It was not so much due to the blistering heat of a blazing summer day noon in the Rio Valley Borderland, although that contributed its effect. It was rather from the absence of sound where men customarily moved, the lack of joke and banter and rough riding common to a fighting unit off duty.

The men were there—that is, all but one. But no one wanted to talk, to put his unreasoning dread into words, and they were too conscious of a feeling of tense unrest to speak of trivial things.

In one corner sat Chili Allen and Frank Hart in a lethargic game of checkers. On the porch "Doc" Barr gazed into the distance that was Mexico as if it held some sort of priceless secret.

Behind Barr, idly fingering a magazine, was Captain Jerry Frost. His eyes alternately went out to the tarmac and the battle planes of his squadron which shimmered in the brilliant sunlight. Their very stillness reflected some of the oppression. Mechanics moved slowly about in the blistering sun as if every step might be their last. Five hundred yards away lay the brown cicatrix that was the Rio, motionless too, so motionless it might have been a frayed ribbon dropped from the hair of a Valkyrie...

Captain Frost was no stranger to this country or to situations of dread foreboding fostered by enforced waiting and idleness and an unanswered question.

He broke the silence by ripping from the magazine a page that had caught and held his attention; he crammed it in his pocket and dropped the book to the floor.

The tension was shattered, Doc Barr got up, noisily scraping his boots on the porch.

"For God's sake, sit down, Doc!" Frost said petulantly. He also got to his feet. He knew what was worrying Doc. It was worrying the rest of them too, only Frost couldn't very well show his concern. "The kid's all right!"

Doc Barr shook his fast-graying head. "I ain't so sure, Jerry. I got a damned funny feeling."

"Hell, Doc," said Frost with an attempt at levity, "you're full of funny feelings. You make me feel guilty because I let the kid turn that tour of duty alone. Maybe I oughtn't—"

Barr nodded and cut in swiftly: "Maybe you oughtn't, Jerry." He looked into the eyes of his commander in a mild indictment. They stared briefly, and Barr smiled weakly. He realized this was no tone to take with Jerry Frost. Why Frost would— "Don't blame yourself, Jerry. I wanted to go, but you know how youngsters are. He said no."

"Sure, I know. Now stop worrying. That won't get you anywhere."

"I don't know but what you're right. Just the same I'd like to have a look-see down the river. Mind?"

"Certainly not; but you'd better turn in. You've had a long siege. Better get some shuteye while the getting's good."

"I couldn't. I kind of like young Pool. He's a clean kid."

"Better let me go with you then. You never can tell, you know."

Doc Barr grinned. "Reckon nothing's going to happen. I ain't

worried about myself. It's Pool. He's long overdue." He looked at Frost, a little wistfully, Jerry thought. Then he stepped off the porch and strode out to the starting line. Halfway out, he turned and waved his hand. That was funny, Jerry told himself. Doc Barr had never done that before.

He was perturbed, of course, and there was good reason for it. Even the veterans in the air wing of Texas' crack constabulary constantly were in danger. Over the nine hundred miles of the Border from El Paso to the Gulf there were all manner of scum who'd give a pretty penny to have an Air Ranger knocked down. The danger increased fourfold for a youngster, increased apace with his enthusiasm and his inexperience. Young Pool had both. Maybe that was what Doc Barr liked. He hadn't tried to figure it out.

Chili Allen and Frank Hart came out on the porch in time to see the tall, gangling form of Barr swinging across the field. They didn't know it, but Doc was cursing softly. It might have pleased them to hear it. There is something relieving about a fighting man's curses.

"Got his wind up, eh?" said Allen.

"Yes—it's Pool. Doc's worried."

"Well," Hart put in, "he's got a damned good reason to be worried. This Border ain't no picnic for nobody—much less a kid."

Across the field came the faint cry of *coupez!* and then the echo of the mechanic *coupez!* That was the war-time expression for switch off. Then—*contact! contact!* The motor caught in a roar, rose and fell as Barr revved it, and barked as he taxied out and took off. Five hundred feet up he ruddered around and streaked down the Rio.

"I'd hate to have a scrap with him now," said Allen. "When them old-timers get that catch in their voices, bee-ware! They're pure-dee hell!"

"We ought to go with him," said Hart.

"No." Frost said quickly. "You two stick around here. Might need you."

"Anything special?"

"Nothing special, only—I dunno," said Frost vaguely. "I guess I got the heebie-jeebies."

"We all got 'em!" Hart declared. "It's this damned quiet. Every time it gets like this, something busts. I don't know what's up, but I'll gamble my pay check it ain't nothing good."

"Maybe," Allen hazarded, "the Black Ship gang is figuring on running over some souvenirs for the Old Man. They're sort of playful these days."

Captain Frost's eyes narrowed. Something in him had clicked. His uneasiness had been vague, now it was definitely crystallized. That was it—that gang. "I'd like to have one more crack at that outfit—one more!" he half-whispered.

Allen and Hart suddenly became grim. The secret was out. Each had hoped this was not their fear, that this was not the reason for the nerve-rasping quiet. But it was and they all knew it.

Frank Hart had said the Border was no picnic, which probably is the most effective way to express it after all. No picnic. Not at any time. And lately the Black Ship gang had brought more trouble to the Border. Their vast workings had, as a matter of fact, been a sort of godfather to the Air Rangers. That wing of the law and order program was Texas' answer to the wholesale trafficking in contrabands.

But the answer was not very firm yet. The Air Rangers were young, and the Black Ship gang took no chances. It couldn't. It traveled with all the accoutrements of civilization. As science progressed, so they progressed. Witness that fleet squadron of battle planes, and the pilots of those planes. Where they came from, who they were, few persons knew. The backwash of war? Renegades? Perhaps. Call them what you may, still they were skilled performers. No doubt of that. Jerry Frost knew. He had brushed with them once—he and an Air Ranger named Yates—and there was a grave somewhere in Tennessee which silently attested the ability of the enemy. Yates was buried there.

Captain Frost had lived to tell the tale simply because he happened to be a young man of considerable discretion. It might have been the heroic thing after Yates came down to fight it out with them. Yes, that probably would have been heroic. But it also would have been absurd. He was outnumbered, he hadn't a chance, and a dead Ranger is a long time dead. A precious lot of good he could have done his State under the ground. So he turned tail and ran, biding his time.

The Border was a tough place. Those who think Port Said and some of those barbaric sounding South Sea ports are hard should take a fling at the Rio country. It demanded tough constabulary. It needed old-line flying men—not rookies. Rookies were courageous and ambitious and all that sort of thing, but they had little place here. Experience was the commodity on which the premiums were paid.

Captain Frost was the last person in the world deliberately to invite disaster. But he did have that peculiar fatalism so characteristic of fighting flyers, and he knew that some day there was going to be a battle with that gang—a hell of a battle. A showdown to the finish. And now he had but one man worthy of a place in such a scrap—Doc Barr. Doc had been through the war. Doc had had almost as much experience as Jerry Frost, and that was plenty. Frost had done a hitch with the Lafayette Escadrille, seen service with the Kosciusko Squadron over in Poland when the going was rather rough, and then for good measure had thrown in five years of professional soldiering in Latin-America. Those credentials would get him into any army in the world.

Doc Barr was the only man in the outfit on whom Frost could depend, and now Doc was gone. Where? Frost shook his head. Doc had been acting queer. He had waved a farewell, a gesture he never before had made.

"I'm going to look around," Frost said to Allen and Hart, as he started off the porch.

"Wait a minute," said Allen. "Let's all go."

"Nope," Frost said, "you two stick around. I'll do all the looking that's necessary."

He walked out on the field and beckoned to Johnny Rosenfield, a stubby little mechanic who had been kept at Romorantin during the late unpleasantness. He knew airplanes down through the middle and back again.

"Rosy, chuck me a thousand rounds in the pit."

"Sa-a-y," Rosenfield asked, "what's up? Doc goes off without saying a word and now you load up and go too. What's doing?"

"I wish I knew, Rosy," Frost said frankly.

Johnny Rosenfield understood. His round head bobbed in understanding and sympathy, and he stirred his stumps into the hangar. When he returned he divided his burden with another mechanic.

"My bus ready?" Frost asked.

"Okey!"

"Give 'er a yank."

Frost got in his seat and slipped on his helmet. Rosy swung the blade over a couple of times, yelled contact and then snapped it down savagely. It caught in a rush and Frost flipped down his goggles and waved his hand. The chocks came out and he bumped across the field.

Long after he had left the ground Rosenfield watched him. Pilots have no monopoly on premonitions; mechanics feel them too. Johnny Rosenfield had taken a good look at his commander. That was wise. In this country you never could tell if they were coming back.

FOR HALF AN hour Captain Frost roared along the south patrol, over the Rio, a crazy, crooked, unimpressive thing that separated two nations; and it was almost too fantastic to believe that such an unimportant stream could be the line of demarcation between people of different color, creed and tongue.

Only below him was there life. He was alone in the sky with his throbbing motor. There was no sign of young Pool or Doc Barr. For just a moment he was overcome by swift nausea. Something had happened. Pool and Barr were in a jam. He knew it.

He glanced at his board. 3500 altitude—good. 110 speed—good. 1450 R.P.M.—good. Wind, neutral. He stuck up his thumb to shut out the sun and took a look around. Nothing. He nosed his bus up and touched the trigger. His guns belched. A short burst to warm 'em up. Might need 'em.

He should have seen his men by now. Above was the sun, to the side were a few cumulus formations, below a country long ago burned into insensibility. He strained his eyes.

Humph! This was queer. Damned queer.

He dropped down to five hundred feet. There was that infernal Rio again. The Rio sort of got one. You hated it and yet you didn't hate it. Too bad it couldn't talk. It'd tell a wild tale or two, eh? But the Rio couldn't talk, so that was that. No use worrying.

There was a town. That'd be Espinard. Tough? Whoosh! Plenty! You could get bumped off down there for a dime and specify your weapon.

Captain Frost became aware that there was a shadow on his wing. He looked up quickly. It was a crate. A JN 4D. The pilot was signaling him. Jerry slanted his headland took a good look. The fellow was motioning for him to come down. Frost wigwagged all right and dropped back for the fellow to take the lead. He slipped into a slide over Espinard and made for the improvised flying field. Frost snapped off his switch and slung his automatic between his legs.

The pilot of the JN 4D came running over. "Something's happened the other side of the river!" he said.

Jerry lifted his helmet. He missed the words but he could tell by the man's manner that he was excited.

"What?"

"A little while ago four ships went over like bats outta hell! I saw one of the Rangers take in after them. About fifteen minutes later, another Ranger went across. Then I heard some shots."

Frost's heart did a loop. "What?"

"I'm telling you," shouted the fellow. "Them guys didn't come back. Four ships—"

"What kind of ships?"

"I don't know. Pretty fast, though. Painted black all over—"

"Black?" the word exploded.

"Yeh—they went that way." He leveled a finger.

Jerry Frost snapped back his helmet and locked the strap. His eyes narrowed. The muscles in his jaw knotted. Black ships! Well, it didn't take a genius to figure that one out. Pool had run across them. And Doc had got in on the tail end of the show.

Jerry was tight and cold. There was a spot in his heart that ached and throbbed like the first faint gnawing of cancer. Once before he had felt like this—the day Vic Chapman and Norman Prince had taken him over for his first look at the squareheads when the German skies in those days were policed by that magnificent hawk and the Baron's instructor—Boelcke.

Frost remembered how, on that spring morning in '15 on the Somme, his throat had tightened. Now it was tight again—only this wasn't fear. Something close perhaps, but not that.

"Give my blade a yank!" he shouted.

The motor roared. Peculiar how airplane motors absorb the personalities of their pilots. Peculiar and awful how their roars react in a near human way. The thunder from their exhausts are symbols.

Frost turned his ship around, glanced at the wind cone, and gave his bus the gun. It fairly leaped off the ground, quivered as it went into a zoom that almost was a stall, and then flattened out. The pilot on the ground stared in amazement. His thoughts were not complimentary. But what this man thought was of no consequence to Jerry Frost. He had forgotten the world. He was in the saddle again. Once he had met that gang and he had called off the fight.

Now he was calling it back on.

He drove across the Rio at a hundred and twenty. Mexico. The land forbidden. Texas had no jurisdiction here. No? What the hell did that matter?

He set himself on the course pointed out by the pilot in Espinard. Straight ahead. He looked out. Sage. Cholla thickets. Yucca. Cactus. A vast wilderness.

On and on he roared. The minutes were an eternity. The mountains loafed by beneath him. The illusion was weird. A railway line wound in and out of the valley.

His eyes finally picked up a glint. At first he thought it was a loop of the rails. Then he saw it wasn't. He got the sensation of looking into a mirror in which the sun was shining. He swung over and perceived it was the wreckage of an airplane. A silver airplane. Pool's ship, twisted and smashed.

Beside it was another. Not smashed. Standing alone as a sort of sentinel to see that the wreckage of its sister ship was not desecrated. Frost was not surprised. Of course not. That was Doc Barr's wagon. Doc had found his young buddy.

But where was he?

Frost looked around to see if he was clear and then he busied himself with landing. Ticklish job. Had to keep your head up. But Doc had got down and any place Doc could get down, he could. He felt a little heartened by that fact. He picked out a flat spot and pancaked in. Careful now. Wouldn't do to crack up here. Never would be found.

He bounced unevenly through the stubbles and came to rest. It was a sweet landing. Only he didn't think about that. His mind was going round like a dynamo. Thoughts were flying off in all directions. He left his motor going and climbed out to the ground.

Before him was tragedy. The tragedy of impetuous youth who asked no quarter and gave none, had no valuation of the odds. Pool's plane looked as if a giant trip-hammer had caught it dead center. One of the wings, rather a strip, was intact. From it glared a longhorn's head insignia of the squadron. The steer seemed as bewildered as Frost.

Jerry found the kid in what had once been the cockpit. Strapped to his seat and riddled with machine-gun fire. From the looks of things the gang had followed him down blasting to the finish. Frost thought he detected a trace of a smile on the youngster's face. He must have known he was going. And he had gone like a real airman. A pity that youngsters had to be caught in such a net—

Frost closed his eyes tightly, and snapped his head in a short, spasmodic convulsion of rage.

"God!" he groaned. "What's it all about?"

He moved slowly over to Doc's ship. Doc was lying on his back, his face turned to the pitiless glare of the sun. Frost saw at a glance that he was dead too. His automatic was in his hand.

He never got a chance to use it. One of that gang would have gone with him if he had.

What had happened was only too patent. Doc had seen the wreckage and had landed. And he had been ambushed. They had got him without a struggle. A hole through the temple as clean as a nail. A hell of a way for old Doc to go… after all he'd seen, after all the scraps he'd been mixed in… to get it like this.

Frost's eyes, the first impressions fading, welled with tears. He was no stranger to death. Men who live violent lives die violent deaths, and see others go the same way. Frost had strafed ground troops and seen them tumble like ten-pins; once he saw a whizz-bang get in a direct hit on a French corporal. Grisly things he'd seen in the tropics, too. But none of them ever got him like this.

Then the engulfing wave passed, and he bent to his task. He picked Doc's body off the ground. He didn't want to see Doc's face again. He hadn't the nerve—callousness—and—whatever it was. He had no illusions about death. Doc was a fighting man. When fighting men go, they go with tight lips and keen eyes. There is little beauty in death for them. They leave that to the poet. No angelic symphony, no fluttering of spirit, no singing heart—just plain, unvarnished death.

Somehow Frost got Doc in the front cockpit of his plane. Then he went to get young Pool. He unbuckled the straps that held his broken body and tenderly rolled him out. He saw that even had the bullets missed him, the crash would have been enough. Where Doc's body was bulky like a dummy, Pool's was unwieldy like a doll that falls in all directions. Frost thought it eerie the way Pool's head rolled from side to side.

He put the kid in Doc's lap and strapped them in. Had they

been able to talk, they would have asked for their last ride like that.

Jerry got in his pit, and turned his ship carefully. He would have liked to say something to his passengers. He thought about telling them it'd be all right now. He thought about a great many things. But he didn't say any of them. He believed that would sound rather silly. He told himself strong men didn't do that.

But if they were busting clouds for the last time, at least he could speak to them in a language they'd understand.

He touched his trigger.

Rat-tat-tat-tat-tat-tat!

They'd know what that meant.

A BRILLIANT SUNSHINE flooded the quiet room and seemed such an interloper that the antique statuary might have been frowning in disapproval. High-ceilinged and deep-toned, with a background of old chairs and old desks and a book cabinet that might have been Disraeli's, it seemed irritated at being thus subjected to the glare of the world. There was age in every corner of this office in the State capitol.

Sitting at the center desk was a man of fifty, gray, slim, and with deep eyes that were fixed on a page that had been torn out of a magazine. He swayed back and forth in his noiseless chair, his elbows on its arms, his hands clasped and his forefingers stroking the short ends of a stubby mustache. He was the Adjutant-General, and by virtue of that office, Commander-in-Chief of the Rangers of the sovereign State of Texas.

Before him stood a tight-lipped flying man whose name was a synonym for courage and action. He was Captain Jerry Frost.

"So, sir," Frost said finally, indicating the magazine page, "I ask permission to enlist those men. We have *got* to have them!"

The Adjutant-General fingered the page. It revealed four helmeted faces. The caption was "Hell's Stepsons."

"But," the Adjutant-General demurred, "these men are in the motion pictures. Are they fighters as well?"

"Yes, sir!" Captain Frost moved beside the desk and pointed his finger. "And some of the best of the war, too. That young one is Eddie Giles, who was in the old Royal Flying Corps before it became the R.A.F. He got half a dozen. That's Skipper Hinsdell, out of the 101st, the best dogfighter ever in the lines. And that one is Rowdy Perry. You must have heard of Perry. He got twenty or more. That Traub I don't know, but if he's with the others you can take a ticket on him to be just about as good."

"Well," the Adjutant-General nodded, "we'll grant they're good. But you forget they're probably making big money in the movies. Not only can they make more money there, but there is a possibility they won't be interested."

Captain Frost grinned. "Not a chance, sir," he said, positively. "You know, commander, air fighting is a funny thing. There's some kind of religion connected with it. You can't forget the rattle of the machine-guns. Those old-timers would swim the ocean to get it, sit in on some more action."

But the Adjutant-General wasn't so sure. He was wise. He said maybe Frost was getting sentimental. Maybe he was romancing.

That got under Jerry's skin. He heated up instantly. "I know what I'm talking about," he insisted. "We've got to do something! That gang murdered the Kid and Doc Barr in cold blood—and I won't let 'em get away with it. Look at us—the finest body of coppers in the world—helpless! Are we still as much in the dark as ever?"

"Oh, occasionally we pick up somebody about fifty cousins removed from a man who is in with them. But they never know anything. We do know they're running all manner of stuff across the Line. Now they've started making bad money." He opened a drawer and took out a hundred dollar bill.

"Ever see anything like that?"

Frost admitted he hadn't.

"Bogus. Came off a dead cop in Jamestown. They found him in an automobile with a slug of lead in his head. I guess you know what that means."

"Sure, I'll bet their filthy money's bought a lot of others, too."

"The Jamestown detectives found another one before the banks let out a yell. Somebody bought a lot of flying equipment with it."

"Sure," said Frost. "Those guys are gummed proper. All we've got to do is just land one of them."

"That's all."

"And," he went on conclusively, "if he's landed, *we'll* do it. The more I see of those detective departments, the more respect I've got for a country constable." He sat down on the edge of the desk and laid his hand on the Adjutant-General's shoulder.

"Commander," he said; "I'm running out to Hollywood tomorrow." He spoke as if it were across the street. "I'm going to bring back Hell's Stepsons." That was all. He went through the door while the Adjutant-General looked after his wiry form. He knew it was useless to expostulate.

HELL'S STEPSONS WERE glad to see their old buddy.

They told him if he had come a day later, he would have missed them. They were going East. The picture racket, they said, was all washed up; they had received a corking offer from a big firm to take a skywriting contract.

That got a laugh from Frost. He told them he had some sky-writing for them to do that *was* sky-writing.

He found they hadn't changed. Same old fellows. Hell-careless. Frost had known Rowdy Perry and Skipper Hinsdell intimately; Giles by reputation, Traub was a total stranger to him. But Hell's Stepsons, the three of them, vouched for the ex-Bavarian. They said he was a swell scrapper. He had worked down on the Piave with his own squadrons. And Hinsdell said when the hardheaded Bavarians turned you loose with your own squadron that was proof enough.

Hell's Stepsons were frankly skeptical of the tale Captain Frost told about the Border country and the crime syndicate which thus far had revealed no trace of the higher-ups. But Frost wasn't disappointed.

"Lissen," said Skipper Hinsdell, "we been shooting movies for a year and we've never heard one of these half-cracked scenario guys pull one as wild as that."

"Are you trying to tell us," broke in Rowdy Perry, "that these fellows are using battle planes?"

Were they? Frost grimaced. He had a fleeting picture of Yates going—and then the tragedy of young Pool and Doc—were they using battle planes? He passed his hand before his face as if to shut out the vision.

"Yes," he admitted quietly, "they've got battle planes. And they know how to use 'em, too."

Eddie Giles said, "Gosh! Where'd they get 'em?"

"Sandy Claws brought them," put in Perry. "Where the hell do battle planes usually come from?"

"Well," cut in the Skipper, "you gotta admit it's funny, Jerry."

"Maybe so," said Frost. "But if you'd seen what I did, you wouldn't think so. Lord! When I think of the mess they made of that young kid—"

"Lemme get this straight," said Hinsdell. "You want us to join up with your outfit to help patrol the Border. How long do we stay in?"

"Only as long as you want to, Skip. I need help. Otherwise, I wouldn't be here. I could get all the commercial flyers I want, but they wouldn't do. I've got to have old-timers; that Border has got to be cleaned up. And I've got to do it."

"Hell," said Giles, "that country'll never be cleaned up. Give it back to the Indians and move out here."

"That's an idea," Perry agreed. "We can get you in with this concern that wants us."

Frost shook his head. "Thanks, but I guess not. I've got my teeth in something else. I'm sort of anxious to see it through. I wish you fellows could see your way clear to give me a hand. I'll guarantee you the sweetest ships you ever rode."

Well, Hinsdell agreed, finally, in that case he supposed it might be a change. And a change of scenery was what he needed. If there was to be any action, of course that would be extra fine.

Skipper Hinsdell was like that. No matter if it was a parade or a war or a plain, old-fashioned brawl, he wanted a seat in Row A, Section A, preferably on the aisle. The trouble with Skipper Hinsdell was that he lived three hundred years too late. He'd been worth an empire to some of those French kings who needed a swordsman.

Rowdy Perry pitched in with Skip. That was certain to come. It was only a question of which was the first to decide and on what. The other agreed. Eddie Giles wavered and then said he reckoned he'd go too. Only Hans Traub dissented. Hans said he couldn't see where the gain would be.

"Certainly you can't!" Hinsdell snapped, good-naturedly. He was always kidding the chunky fellow. "You're like all the rest of the Krauts in the world—thick-headed. We whipped hell outta you guys in the war and now we're giving you a chance to get on a winning side. That ought to sell you quick."

"You didn't whip anybody," Traub declared. "We merely signed an armistice."

"Yeh? Well, right here in this little flat are three guys who knocked down about fifty of your ships. Laugh that off! And what's more—"

"Hey—*hey!*" shouted Rowdy. "You two pipe down! Stop fighting that damned war over again!"

"There's another war on," said Frost soberly. "And it's no cinch. Suppose a little action wouldn't suit you, Traub?"

"Hurry up, Heinie. Yes or no. You're stopping the parade," Hinsdell said. His eyes were twinkling. Everybody in the room knew what Hans Traub would say. But they wanted to make him say it.

"Very well," Traub announced; "I'll go!"

In that instant Jerry Frost experienced a swift rush of poignancy. A stabbing, exhilarating sort of thing. That was the camaraderie of the service. That was the bond that linked flying men together in a great fraternity. What mattered if four of these men had flown the Allied Circles and the fifth the Maltese Cross? It takes more than a contemptible little war to change men's hearts.

They came back to Texas the following day in a formation whose swift shadows rushed like a bad omen toward the evil-doers in the Rio country. At the point of the V rode Captain Jerry Frost, to his left were Skipper Hinsdell and Rowdy Perry, and to the right were Eddie Giles and Hans Traub, now a brother of the selfsame men he once hunted through European skies.

A strange squadron of fighting men with but one demand—action.

FROST BROUGHT HELL'S Stepsons back to Texas to learn that in the four days he had been away, the State had taken official cognizance of the existence of the Black Ship gang to the extent of moving a company of Rangers into Espinard under the command of Captain Jack Marvin, famed officer.

Newspapers which heretofore had scoffed at the Black Ship gang as the usual creation of disappointed police departments began to editorialize. Such editorials always are dangerous. They inflame the citizenry, roll on and on and, in general, put new obstacles in the path of the law enforcement bureaus.

Who were the leaders of the Black Ship gang? The people wanted to know.

So did the sovereign State of Texas.

Other counterfeit bills made their appearance. Federal sleuths took up the trail. The state constabulary was lashed into renewed activity. Local departments in Texas cities seethed. And the spotlight finally became focused on the Border.

This was the condition ninety-six hours after Frost had left. It seems unreal that such a widespread speculation could be born in such a short time. But it isn't difficult. Sheriffs always wonder where a mob comes from—out of the ground like Jason's soldiery perhaps. This was something like that.

He marched Hell's Stepsons into the office of the Adjutant-General and presented the great man to the four flyers. The great man was not even a little surprised. He had had no feeling in the matter one way or the other. Long ago he had learned the futility of anticipation with Jerry Frost.

But surrounded by men who had etched their names deeply into the scrolls of the air, he felt that his station, if nothing else, demanded a few words. He could not, by any stretch of the imagination, be called a sentimental person, yet he was visibly embarrassed.

"You gentlemen have no idea what you're up against," he said slowly. "For almost eighteen months we have tried to stamp out this gang, to no avail and with little advertisement. Now it seems to have gotten completely away from us. Three Air Rangers have been killed. The price is too great for Texas to pay," he said simply and cleared his throat.

"The newspapers are screaming about our ineffectiveness," he said and a shadow of a smile hovered over his lips; "but they are just about as correct in that as they are in other things. We know, but the public doesn't.

"Getting one man of that gang probably won't help. We have got to get at the bottom of it, and that will require time and patience. I give you gentlemen commissions in the Air Rangers, and because you are men and not children, I warn you now that you have undertaken a tough job. This is a fight to the death with a powerful syndicate that will stop at nothing.

"Captain Frost, you will return to your headquarters at

Gentry. I have ordered Captain Marvin to Espinard with a detachment. Battle planes will be delivered to you tomorrow."

"Tomorrow?" said Frost. "Then you knew—"

The great man nodded. "You told me you'd bring them back, didn't you? Gentlemen, good luck!"

He shook hands with each of them and sat down again, a motionless figure in that vast office, a little forlorn, a little weatherbeaten, Jerry thought. The commander, he said to himself, was a good egg. Well, Hell's Stepsons would show him their reverence.

On the broad street in front of the capitol Frost said, "See, I told you it wasn't a wild story. You guys are going to have plenty of fun."

"Suits!" said Eddie Giles. "It's been so long since I had any fun, I'd hop the Baron and Immelmann in the same afternoon."

"Well, it won't be like that right away," Jerry told him. "When there's hell on the Border—there's hell! And when it's quiet—it's quiet!"

That was a sort of prophecy, and Hell's Stepsons came to know it later. Now there is no particular thrill attached to patrolling the air lanes of a land after you have become familiar with its topography and its landmarks, not when you have so keenly anticipated something else. Air patrol to old-timers is comparable to guard duty for the fellow with three or four hash marks. Hell's Stepsons found themselves irked because they were compelled to sit under a burning sun and wait for action. They had been accustomed to rushing to meet it.

Things were being stirred up in the newspapers, and the reaction was not at all favorable. The press fired broadside after broadside at the officers and their methods. They accused them of being bought. They were inefficient. One country gazette with a college-boy editor likened the Black Ship gang to an octopus whose tentacles slowly were choking to death the greatest state in the union. Other editors with more trenchant pens were more to the point, but they all asked one question—who was the Black Ship gang?

HELL'S STEPSONS GATHERED in the headquarters room a week later on a dirty night. The rain fell in sheets, and there was only a yellow blob of light in the close darkness.

Frost spoke to them. He felt that somebody had to say something. "The Old Man's raising hell again. I reckon I've got to do something."

"What does he want us to do?" Perry grumbled. "Pull 'em out of a hat or something?"

"Well," Frost continued in the same tone. Hell's Stepsons looked up interestedly. "I've been thinking about that place where young Pool and Barr were killed, and I've about come to the conclusion that the country around there wouldn't stand close investigation. Maybe I'd better take a look."

There was loud disapproval. "Personally," said Hinsdell, "I've got a big bellyful of floating around this Godforsaken country, but I'm against any expeditions like that. We've got to stick together."

"Skip's right," said Perry. "It's too damned easy to get knocked down."

But Frost was insistent. The point was he wanted to do something. He was tired of waiting. He was highly irritated too. He couldn't say that, he tried even not to indicate it: he was their commander, but he must have felt his attitude was obvious. "I've got something to settle with those guys," he said in a flinty voice.

"Sure," said Giles; "we all have. But your way is no good."

"Maybe not—but I could find a starting point. Where'd they get the men for those ships? Who the hell is leading 'em? What about their counterfeit money? I want to know!"

"Don't be a damn fool!" Perry snapped, bluntly. "Cool down and you'll see you ain't got a chance single-handed."

Frost got up and walked to the window. There was a moment's silence, and then the roar of the storm. It seemed the flimsy roof would cave in from the incessant pounding of the rain. Thunder reverberated and through the window great, jagged streaks of lightning revealed a desolate land.

The telephone jangled. A Paleozoic night toppled. It jangled again, sharp and clear. The Paleozoic night crashed before the younger civilization. Hell's Stepsons jumped like nervous schoolboys.

Frost was first to recover. He went to the telephone. "Hello… yeh… Frost. Who? Oh, all right, Marvin… What's that? What?" his voice quivered. "Sure… all right… yeh… bring him right over, will you? Great!"

"That was Jack Marvin at Espinard," Frost announced. "He's got a fellow he said we might be interested in. His plane just fell over there—busted his arm."

"Well?"

"Yeh, one of 'em. He was flying a *black ship*."

It was a bombshell. It didn't seem real. After all their tedious waiting… now… They were constrained to laugh. But, of course, they did nothing of the sort.

"Turn in," said Frost. "It'll take 'em three hours to get through this storm. I'll call you."

They indulged in the luxury of a laugh.

"I ain't moving," said Perry. "I'm afraid I'll wake up."

"But," put in Hans Traub, "suppose he won't talk?"

Eddie Giles grimaced. "Oh, you squarehead! You can think of the most cheerful things!"

"Don't worry," said Frost grimly. "He'll talk."

"Sure and he ought to," added Hinsdell. "He's lucky to be living. I'd got killed if I came down in a storm like this."

"Maybe he's a better pilot than you," said Perry, who promptly ducked a magazine.

It took Captain Marvin five hours to reach headquarters at Gentry, ninety miles from his base at Espinard. He had a man named Murry with him, another Ranger, and between them marched the injured pilot. Water ran off them in little rivulets.

"Hello, Jerry," Marvin said. "Swell night, ain't it?"

Ranger Murry looked awkwardly around and thought it was time for him to say something. So he thought up a brand-new one. "Shore coming down, ain't it."

Frost rewarded the attempted wisecrack with a hard look and asked Marvin how badly the pilot was hurt.

"Arm's busted," was the reply, "and he's bruised some. Hell," he snorted, "these jelly-beans can't stand nothing. Why, I mind the time I got bit by a tarantula—"

"Yeah," said Frost quickly, "you told me that one."

"Anyway," Marvin went on, "this baby can sure swear." He reached in his pocket and took out a package of banknotes. "But he'll have a swell time swearing himself outta this. Look! More of that counterfeit money."

Captain Frost observed that it appeared as if the man was nailed. That, of course, was something. But not enough.

The pilot was not more than twenty-five—couldn't be. Nor

was he a rough-looker. Indeed, properly placed against the right background, he might have passed the most fastidious scrutiny. Frost went to the table where the fellow was sitting.

"Want anything?"

"No."

"We want to make you as comfortable as possible. Does you arm pain you?"

The fellow grunted.

"Now, listen," said Frost. "You loosen that tongue. This counterfeit money's enough to send you up for a long stretch. Open your face and maybe we might help you. Who do you work for?"

No answer. No sound but the rain. Hell's Stepsons looked on curiously. Did this man hold the key to the situation? They wondered.

"Who do you work for?" Frost's tone was harsh.

Still no answer.

Captain Marvin stepped over. "You talk, feller," he boomed. "I ain't gonna stand for no more monkey business. Come across and make it snappy! Who hired you?"

"I don't know his name," was the sullen answer.

"Where'd you get that money?" Frost put in.

"Jamestown."

"Where were you taking it?"

"Back to headquarters."

"Where's that?"

"Lamaraz."

"Well, where's Lamaraz?"

"A hundred miles south."

Frost thought that over. "In a straight line with Jamestown and Espinard?"

"Yes."

"I thought so. What kind of headquarters?"

"Just headquarters."

"What do they do there?"

"Make money."

"What else?"

"They got some dope there, too."

"How come you're taking the money back?"

"All I know is I got my orders."

"Orders? From whom?"

"Hoppy."

"Hoppy who?"

"Hoppy Douglas."

Skipper Hinsdell whistled. "So—Hoppy, huh? Well, well, well! Remember him, Jerry?"

Jerry nodded. He remembered Hoppy all right. Out of the 47th. And a bearcat, too. When he was sober, that is. When he was plastered he was an ugly customer. Hoppy got plastered one night and killed his major. Had to beat it out of the A.E.F. Nobody ever knew how he got away. There was a lot of stuff in the papers about it. You may remember it.

Captain Frost began to see the light. Little wonder the Black Ship gang had such a sweet outfit of flyers. Hoppy had been one of the best in the business and he must have taught them something.

"Hoppy teach you to fly?"

"No, I learned in the East."

"How'd you get in with that outfit?"

"Answered an ad. They gave me a thousand bucks and four hundred a month. Then I went from bad to worse. Finally, I had to stay."

Frost turned to Captain Marvin. "Can you leave this lad here until morning? We'll fly him over then."

Hesitatingly, Marvin agreed. "I wanna take him in as a personal souvenir," he said. "You know how much hell the Old Man's been raising lately—"

"Okey," said Frost. "You can cash in. Don't worry."

Marvin and the other Ranger left, but it was quite plain they did so against their wishes.

The moment he was out the door, Giles said: "Gosh, that guy gives me the creeps! Are all the others like him?"

"Not exactly," Jerry grinned. He was feeling better. "They're a queer brood, but they're damn fine bloodhounds. And not afraid of hell or high water."

They finally got the injured pilot into a conversation. He said he thought the business looked funny, and he swore he tried to get out. But that was impossible. They had him. He reflected bitterly that they'd fix him plenty for squealing, too.

"I don't care, though," he said desperately. "I'm ready to chuck the whole business."

"Now, listen," Frost reassured him. "Don't go worrying about what's going to happen to you. Those fellows aren't able to touch you."

"You don't know them," the pilot argued, and his expression was grim.

"Maybe not," Frost agreed. "But I know my gang. You come through for us and we'll do all we can to help you."

Well, the fellow said, they had headquarters at Lamaraz. He didn't know the leader, all he knew was Douglas. He guessed there were about ten men down there, some of them counterfeiters—two who had escaped prison—and some others who brought the stuff in from around Vera Cruz.

"Know anything about those two Rangers who got killed?" Frost said.

"Not a thing." They felt he was telling the truth. "All I know is Hoppy caught hell from the Chief about it."

"How'd you ever expect to get to Lamaraz in a storm?"

"I had to," the fellow said. "They've got it fixed up swell and I knew the police were pretty hot after us. So I tried to make it across the Border in the dark—that's why the ships are painted black—but my motor conked, and here I am." He tried to smile.

Frost spoke to his men. "We've got to get busy right now. Tomorrow this thing'll be all over the state and somebody'll gum up the works for sure." He went to the telephone and asked the operator to get the Adjutant-General on the wire.

"Say," Hinsdell demurred, "maybe the Old Man'll stop us. You know how he feels about us crossing the river."

"I know," said Frost. "But this is one time he isn't going to know anything about it. We'll shoot a load of regular guys over there and clean up the dump."

The operator got the call through in ten minutes. That may not be a record in some sections, but from the outpost to the capitol it constituted amazing speed.

"Hello, Commander!" Frost's voice filled the little room. "I want six men down at Espinard by noon. Get Charlie to bring 'em down in the big cabin job… with machine-guns. Sir? I say, send me down half a dozen men with machine-guns in the cabin plane… to Espinard… Important? Yes, sir… I'm expecting the Border to be run!"

Hell's Stepsons viewed the situation with what amounted to high glee. They had been waiting for action, and now it appeared they were going to get it.

The injured pilot said he personally thought it would be a bad idea. "They've got some good flyers down there," he said. "You'll lose some men, Captain."

"Yeh?" said Frost. He told his men to go to sleep. "I'll watch this fellow."

But they couldn't sleep. They couldn't do anything that even remotely approached sleep. Not with a sortie on the schedule.

They rolled out at dawn, wide-eyed. They strapped the injured man in Frost's ship, refueled, checked their ships carefully, got ammunition and went to Espinard. They made it in an hour. It was a fine morning. They noted, with great satisfaction, that the heavens were high and the visibility fine. There were no traces of the storm.

Captain Marvin was waiting for the prisoner and Frost admonished him to deal kindly with him. "He's helped us a lot," he said. He wasn't particularly worried about Marvin, even though that officer was an old-timer and therefore hardboiled. Still, prisoners often brought a lot on themselves.

They went out to the wreck. But the ship had not been equipped with a machine-gun. Frost said he thought that was funny; others had been.

"The ones I got mixed up with were armed," he declared. "No doubt about that."

"Maybe there won't be no show after all," Skipper Hinsdell complained.

"Don't worry. You just remember all those tricks you used to know. You'll find them handy."

"Okey."

The others nodded approbation.

SHORTLY BEFORE NOON a cabin monoplane landed at Espinard and disgorged six stalwarts. They were big and rugged like the country and in their eyes were the expressions men get when there are no buildings between them and the horizon.

One of them stepped up to Captain Frost and reported. "Old Man said you was gonna have a party," he announced. "So we brought our toys along." He meant machine-guns. His name was George Stuart and he was a veteran. He had a few notches on his gun, too, if he cared to display it.

"Yeh," said Frost. "A party. George—the squadron. Hinsdell, Perry, Traub and Giles. George Stuart, men—as regular as they come."

Frost then took him aside.

"You like the Old Man, don't you, George?"

Stuart blinked his eyes at the abruptness of the question, and then answered, "Hell, yes," in a rather blunt fashion.

"Then you can help me turn a trick for him," Jerry went on. "Game?"

"Sure—what is it?"

"Well," Jerry said, "I think maybe I got something on those guys who've been running all that stuff. They've got a place over in Mexico and I figured we'd pay 'em a visit."

"Okey." Stuart shrugged his shoulders. "I'd take a crack at the devil himself for the Old Man."

"But how about those others? This is a little out of line, you know."

George Stuart spat savagely. "They don't ask no questions. It ain't respectful."

"This may be a whole lot hotter'n we think it is," said Jerry. "We'll go over in a patrol and you'll land. The big idea is to get the house. They've got airplanes down there and we may get in a scrap. If we don't, we'll go down with you."

Stuart nodded. Jerry called the pilot of the cabin ship and spoke briefly to him in a low tone; the Rangers got into their planes. There was not a question asked; nobody speculated. It might be pleasure and it might be disaster. But you mustn't ask questions. That was not the creed of the service. Get him! That was it—no matter where, what, how—Get him! And if one of them fell, there'd be another to take his place and they'd follow—

Motors were roaring now, the field skimmed beneath—a bump and they were off. Jerry's ship swayed slightly but he pulled around in a left-hand climbing turn and circled the field until he reached a thousand feet. That would give them time to see if everything was in shape.

It was. Five minutes later Frost took a gap in the clouds at 7,500 in single file. Frost loaded both guns mechanically. He fired a short burst to warm them up. He tested both magnetos. Okey. There were metallic chatters to his right and left. He looked out. Hell's Stepsons were nosing up to warm their guns. Jerry grinned.

It made time seem such a petty thing. Why, it was only yesterday that they were riding above Mont Sec.

FOR AN HOUR they drove straight ahead, until Frost picked up the twin silver wire that was the railroad. He peered intently for the *hacienda* that was the home of the Black Ship gang, and suddenly it came into full view from behind a mountain peak.

The *hacienda* nestled in the valley; several hundred feet away were small buildings which Jerry knew at once were improvised hangars. He counted five black airplanes on the ground looking like so many lacquered moths.

He pointed below and wigwagged to the cabin plane, waggled his wings at Hell's Stepsons and went into a climb. The cabin monoplane was dropping rapidly down, the earth was rushing to meet it. It landed, bounded like a beetle whose legs have not been used for days; tiny-figures poured out and scurried into one of the hangars.

Captain Frost had hoped to get his ships down without attention. The cabin had landed; but now there was great activity on the field. Other tiny figures were tugging at the propellers of the black ships, and one by one they shot off the ground. Frost wondered why Stuart didn't shoot at them. But Stuart couldn't. Not from the side he had taken.

Frost counted the black planes. Four. He had five. Five to four. Okey. Fine. We've got the sun and the height. The odds are in our favor. Well, here comes a dogfight. Every man for himself. Hell's Stepsons had thought he was goofy, eh? Well, let 'em wait and see.

Hans Traub looked out, saw, and slithered off into the sun. Perry and Hinsdell were climbing. But Eddie Giles was doing neither. Lookit that baby ride! Whistling down to meet 'em at 200 easy! Out for meat, he was—to hell with a fight that paid a premium on maneuvers! That was all right for the story books. But not in war. Get 'em! Get him, or he'll get you! If you've got altitude, use it. Eddie was. Many an ace got his first five that way.

There go his guns! A livid streak cut through the ray of light that was his propeller. Frost could hear the chatter. And right there and then Jerry realized the Black Ship pilots knew what it was all about. This was old stuff to them. The ship in Giles' path Immelmanned just in time. Giles went dashing by, and another one got on his tail.

The leader of the outfit got off to Jerry's left and made him realize this was part his battle, too. He slipped over and got in position; the black ship climbed. Jerry saw it and laughed a little. He was climbing into the guns of Hans Traub who was lurking above like a stone image waiting to have his tumble. Then Traub nosed over and opened his throttle, and the wind whistled through his struts as he dived after his prey. But he held his fire too long. The black ship slid out of range.

The next thing Jerry knew one of the enemy was pecking away at his wing. He pulled back on the stick and soared up under Rowdy Perry. A black ship realized late that it was heading into danger, and banked sharply.

Jerry picked him for his own and raced over after him.

He let go a burst into his elevators, and the first burst ended that particular part of the fight at once. The pilot slumped, threw up his hands; the plane lost its traction and rolled lazily downward. Jerry reflected that it was rather a neat piece of work. There was another over at the right… and Prost turned to get in a shot at him.

The black ship vaulted into a wild split-air and Jerry took in after it furiously. He opened fire in short, hammering bursts. He let go five bursts on him; then the black ship flopped downward. Jerry grinned. Two in a minute! A piece of work even Huke would have applauded.

Skipper Hinsdell was away to the left and was having trouble. He let go a burst and ran his hand forward to clear a stoppage. He kicked his rudder, let go another burst and cleared another stoppage. He half-rolled; so did the black ship. They were maneuvering calmly. It might have been that they merely were sitting in on a game of chess or something.

Skip was in something of a jam, but Jerry could tell from hurried glimpses of him that he was not perturbed. That was where experience paid its premium. An impetuous finger might have cost him more than he would have cared to pay. A younger fighter would have been demoralized. This was exactly what had happened to Yates and Bob Pool—young. But those stoppages didn't bother Skip. Skip was an old-timer. A tight corner was nothing new to him.

Giles and Perry were diving to Skip's rescue. They had, of course, perfect confidence in him, but they were afraid he didn't realize his situation. Jerry saw it, too, and looked around to locate the other black ship and wondered what had happened to the one ship that had remained on the ground. Hans Traub was after the remaining ship in the air.

He was having no pink tea; just as he came out of a loop the black ship blazed away, and raked him fore and aft. Traub started up; then dived down to the right, swung around and leveled out. A black ring snapped off his exhaust pipes as he gave his bus its throttle.

The calm Bavarian had no intention of erring again in timing. Before he had held his fire too long. But not now. He pulled up under the black ship and carefully squinted through his sights.

The tail skid took form… the linen; he eased his stick forward slightly—then the landing gear. There! His guns blazed up into the cockpit, a vicious assault. The black ship was trapped. It flung itself forward; Traub recklessly pulled the stick back and kept his guns open.

It hurtled forward again, a final, spasmodic gesture, and flapped downward.

THERE WAS ONE left and it was on Skip's level, racing after him like a wild reckless comet. Giles and Perry were on their way, but they couldn't cut down the distance. They knew it; so did Frost and Traub, and so did Skip. It was one of those fights where life hangs on a split-second.

It was up to Skip.

When the black ship started after him, he had a thousand-foot lead. That is sufficient room in which to maneuver; but the maneuvering must be good. No, it must be perfect. The slightest fault in technique means the finish. Skip wasn't afraid of his technique exactly, but he resolved to wait and take it, and loop for his *coup de grace*. It required cold nerve and a steady brain.

Skip looked back. The black ship was closing up the gap fast. It was life or death for that pilot and he knew it full well. He was coming ahead. Seven hundred—five hundred—three hundred—two hundred. Close enough now. Skip wondered why the hell he didn't shoot.

Well, Skip reflected, he'll have to get me with the first burst. I hope to hell he's excited. He ought to be. I'd be if I was in his shoes. There comes old Jerry. Well, Jerry, you're too far back. You can't do any good now. Jerry. A swell guy. A swell scrapper, too.

Whoosh! Lookit that guy coming! Better'n two hundred. In a minute he'll—

Crack-crack-crack-crack! Crack-crack-crack-crack!

Skip felt the linen on his wings give before the hail of bullets.

Well, now or never. Here we go! Lookout, Satan, here I come! Sweep me out a corner and fix up my lodging!

He yanked on the stick with all his force. The terrific pressure threw him back against the seat and almost knocked him out. He nosed up and climbed over. The top of the arc passed and he started down. He caught the black ship through his rings, slipped the stick forward to hold the sight and let his guns go. The steel drilled through his target like a rip-saw.

Rat-t-t-t-tat! Rat-t-t-t-tat!

God, wouldn't he ever fall? What was holding him up?

Then Skip heard a new noise. Giles and Perry had caught up in that split-second and were spitting flame from each side. Their guns were chattering in a shrill falsetto.

All at once the black ship seemed to split in the middle. It buckled and fell.

Skip snapped out of it, and shook his head. He saw Frost waggle his wings and go into a long dive. He followed. He saw some of the linen on his wings flutter back. He hoped it'd hang together until he could get it down.

George Stuart and his men were still in the hangar when Hell's Stepsons reached the ground. They hadn't been able to get started at the house at first, and during the dogfight they had lost all interest in their mission. They were watching their first air battle and it was too much of an event to be lightly taken. Criminals could be captured almost at a given moment; dogfights came, for them, once in a lifetime.

Stuart said he had started over to the wreckage of the ships twice and had been fired on from the house.

"Wouldn't do to get nobody killed down here," he said.

"Right," said Jerry. He looked out at the thin smoke that was rising from the crash of the ships half a mile away.

"Reckon any of them are still living?" Stuart asked.

"Nope," Jerry laughed shortly. "They had quite a tumble. Now we got to get inside the dump. Rig up a gun."

It was old stuff to him. He was no longer Captain Jerry Frost of the Air Rangers. He moved to the door and squinted along the barrel of a machinegun. He had done that before. This was *El Beneficio,* once of Latin-America. He swung it on its pivot and trained it on an upper window. A steady tattoo beat against the wall, the glass tinkled before it. It stopped abruptly.

"Come outta there!" he shouted.

A head popped up in the window and a white shirt waved a lugubrious greeting.

"Come outta there!" Frost yelled.

A heavy-set man finally emerged through the big gate. He was disheveled, but he looked as if he might be something of a leader. Other heads bobbed in the window.

"We're Rangers," Frost said succinctly. "We want you."

The man addressed him in flawless English. "Isn't that irregular?"

"Yep," Frost retorted promptly; "irregular as hell. But you got a lot of guts to talk about irregularities. Go back in there and tell those guys to shake a leg out here. By the way," he added, "how come that black ship over there wasn't in on the dogfight?" He jerked his thumb.

"The pilot is sick. It might have been different if he hadn't been!"

"Yeah—who was it? Ricthtofen?"

"No—his name's Hoppy Douglas."

Frost grinned at that, "Well, well, well!" he said to the squadron. "This party ain't such a washout after all. I thought maybe Skip knocked Hoppy down—that guy was pretty good."

"You said it," Skip agreed. "He was tough as a boot."

"All right, you—beat it in there and herd 'em out here! If we have to follow you in there it ain't going to be so pleasant!"

The man took a look at Hell's Stepsons and the Rangers and promptly arrived at the same conclusion. He went into the house. In a minute or so, the inhabitants marched out. They marched as if they were eager to surrender. They paraded into the hangar in single file, before machine-guns and ugly, squat automatics.

"Which one of you is Douglas?" Frost asked.

There was no answer. The man who had emerged first said that Douglas was inside. He was too ill to walk.

Jerry shot him a quick glance. "All right," he said. "We're going after him. George—if there's any trouble inside, let these guys have it right in the neck." He turned back to the swarthy man. "Ain't nothing funny about this, is there?"

The man assured him there wasn't.

"All right. You lead the way."

They went through the gate into a large courtyard, and then into a large and spacious house. Hell's Stepsons moved alertly along the corridor. The man indicated a room and they stopped.

"Douglas?"

There was a feeble response, a throaty noise that seemed to float from nowhere.

"We're coming in," said Frost. "Anything out o' line and we'll blow you to hell." He barked the words savagely and went into the room. The others followed.

The room was poorly lighted, and for a moment they stood there to adjust their eyes to the interior. Finally Jerry made out a bed in the corner and moved to it, gazing down at the motionless figures.

"I'm Captain Frost, Texas Rangers," he said. "Come on!"

Hoppy Douglas cracked a laugh. "That's the funniest thing I ever heard," he said. "I'm too sick to move."

"Get a leg, Skip," Frost said. He was businesslike. He lost no motion when he was in action.

They picked him up and carried him out. Douglas said he was almost blinded by the sun. Frost curtly remarked that was too bad. They deposited him in the hangar.

"George, herd those eggs in the cabin plane. Split your men up and put 'em with the boys. I'll take Douglas in mine."

"Okey," said Stuart. "There's ten of 'em."

"That," Frost declared, "will just make a nice party. Skip, how's your bus? Ready to ride?"

"Hell, yes," said Skip. "I've flown crates in worse shape than that one."

"Fine," said Jerry. "We'll go back inside and see what sort of an outfit the boys have got. Come on, you!"

The swarthy man took them back into the house. They had a look at all the rooms, but there was only one which interested them. It was a biggish place, surrounding a patio and filled with vats and packing cases. On a table was a small printing press, much after the fashion of those machines with which itinerant tradesmen once used to turn out calling cards for high-powered young swains. There also was a large jar of acid.

Eddie Giles picked up a half dozen plates off the bench and handed them to Jerry. "Have a look," he said. "I think these are the things they used."

Frost looked carelessly and slipped them in his pocket. Meantime Perry had been prodding about the packing cases. He whistled softly and held up a handful of counterfeit money. "Can you imagine!" he said, awed. "More than a million, I guess."

"What's in those other cases?" Frost asked, nodding toward some boxes.

"Oh, everything," was the reply. "Opium… morphine—"

"Say," Jerry cut in in mock admiration, "you babies had quite a business, didn't you?"

Frost told Rowdy and Skip to carry some of the money out to the field. He picked up a short rod and went to work on the vats. He hammered the little printing press out of shape, then directed the piling of the crates that were left in the middle of the room.

"Might as well do it right," he said.

He struck a match, shielded the flame, and then saw it take hold. "Let's beat it," he said.

They went back to the field and learned that Traub had taken the magnetos off the black ship for a souvenir. "It won't do them any good now," he said.

"Right!" said Jerry.

"How about those pilots?" asked Giles. "Wanna go down there?"

"Nope," said Jerry.

Smoke curled from the window of the room, and with that thin signal rising, they loaded in their ships. Jerry personally attended to Douglas. The man complained that such a ride would kill him. Frost said he hoped not.

"Straight for Austin," said Frost. "We'll march these babies right into the Old Man's office!"

TWO HOURS LATER the wheels of their planes touched the flying field at Austin. But Jerry learned he had not been able to surprise the Adjutant-General. Not with the Border stuff such red-hot news. When the squadron came back across the river, the flash got to Austin. The Adjutant-General didn't cogitate at length on what it meant. He knew.

"Where've you been?" he asked Frost.

"A party, sir," said Jerry. "Here are some things." He handed him the plates. "We also got some money—bogus money—those hundreds, you know."

George Stuart was out of the cabin plane by now, and the Adjutant-General's eyes bulged when he saw the plane disgorge the prisoners.

"Who're they?" he demanded.

"Some guests, sir," said Jerry.

The Adjutant-General bit his lip and looked away. "What have you been doing?"

"Nothing, sir," said Jerry innocently. "We were attacked by four enemy planes and merely defended ourselves. Later, we had a party. In some strange way, the house caught fire—and we had to leave. We brought all the guests with us."

"Is this the truth?"

"Oh, yes, sir!" said Jerry. "And one of the guests is named Douglas—quite a pilot. He was sick, but we understand he knows something about the gang." He lowered his voice. "It's the best lead we ever had."

Stuart walked over with Douglas on his shoulder like a sack of meal. "Where d'ya want this guy?" he asked.

Douglas raised his head weakly. "Lissen, Frost," he said, with a tremendous effort. "You think you're pretty damn smart don't you? But you're not—you'll never know. They'll get you for this—" his voice trailed, and he suddenly became limp.

Jerry moved quickly to Stuart's side and lifted Douglas' head. It fell back as if on a spring. He turned to the Adjutant-General, his face a barometer of emotion.

"Jeez!" he swore softly. "After all this, the one guy that could have told us something kicks off!"

"It looks like we've just begun," said the Adjutant-General in a sort of a weary voice.

"Yes, sir," said Captain Frost.

He looked at Hell's Stepsons. They didn't see him. Their faces were turned to the south, where the muddy Rio Grande flowed through a land that bred mischief.

Renegades of the Rio

Jerry Frost and Hell's Stepsons step on the gas

THE BODY OF an unidentified white man, who had been shot through the head, was found four miles north of Espinard near the Rio Grande River on the morning of a crisp November day, which, in itself, was an item to attract only passing importance and routine investigation. For fifty years or more, similar discoveries had been made.

But in the afternoon of that same day an undertaker at Espinard accidentally discovered that one of the dead man's shoes had a false heel, and the undertaker, exercising that prerogative peculiarly his, investigated. He found the false heel contained a small sheet of paper on which a diagram had been inscribed; and what had been a case of only ordinary significance immediately became a case of great importance.

The undertaker consulted the sheriff, the sheriff mentioned it to an underling, and, having been solemnly sworn to secrecy, the underling mentioned it to a friend. By the following morning the entire citizenry of Espinard knew that reposing on a slab in their most modern mortuary was a dead man of mysterious past and death.

The little town seethed, speculated and then made its own deductions. For no reason really, because there was nothing sufficiently definite about the case to determine any one thing. But, so far as Espinard was concerned, it was open and shut. That diagram indubitably linked the dead man with the Black Ship Gang, a vast syndicate of illicit traffic which had kept all the state constabulary hopping.

Thus the day after the body was found, the telephone jangled in the headquarters room of the Texas Air Rangers at Gentry, ninety miles west, and Hans Traub, phlegmatic ex-Bavarian flight commander and now one of Hell's Stepsons, moved across the floor. He lifted the receiver in a manner quite indifferent.

"Hello!" he said. "… Not here… I say Captain Frost isn't here…Yes… He's on patrol… What?… Oh, any time now." He placed his hand over the mouthpiece and shook his head impatiently at Eddie Giles, former R.A.F. ace, who sat on the porch desperately trying to imprison a *siesta*. Young Mr. Giles paid not the slightest attention. Then Traub's voice took on a flash of animation. "What?" he shouted. Giles stirred petulantly and cocked a baleful eye. "Who is this?" Traub said. "… Oh!… Know who he is?… All right, Stuart… the minute Jerry gets in I'll tell him…"

He hung up the receiver and stood for a moment eying Giles, obviously about to explode with the information. He plainly wanted the young pilot to evince a little interest. But Giles didn't look up.

"The telephone just rang," Traub said finally.

"Yeh—I heard it." Giles shifted his chair. "Hottest damn' country I ever saw."

"There was somebody on the line," Traub went on.

"Yeh?" Giles swabbed a handkerchief across his face.

"Well, he told me plenty."

"Yeh?" He swabbed again.

"Yeh. George Stuart. Found a dead man over at Espinard last night."

"Well, what does that make me?"

Traub's mild manner was not disturbed. He knew Eddie Giles. And then he had big news. "Had a false heel in his shoe," he recited evenly. "And there was a map of some kind in it."

"Map?" Giles stirred in his seat and crammed his handkerchief in his pocket. Hans Traub beamed. In a country so temperamental, so devoid of news, even the most stolid person takes great pride in being able to make an announcement.

"Sure—map. Had a lot of funny stuff on it. Stuart wanted Jerry to come right over."

"Map, eh?" Giles repeated half to himself. He bit his lip. That seemed to him rather significant. The Rio Grande Valley was a hotbed of mischief and intrigue. A map might mean something.

"Sounds like something might be doing, eh?"

"I can stand it," Giles declared pointedly. "If maps mean action, I'm for bigger and better maps. I wonder—"

The drone of a motor slashed into the conversation and the men looked up. A silver plane glinted in the sunlight, from its lower wings gleamed the huge orange Longhorn's head that was the insignia of the Air Rangers—cockade of the courageous. The pilot blipped his motor and slipped down.

Eddie Giles grinned. He recognized the style. After a while in the flying service you can tell who is at the controls from the way the ship rides.

"There's Jerry now," he said. "Pretty tough on him—after a long stretch of duty."

Captain Jerry Frost, squadron commander, known ten years ago from San Francisco to Warsaw as one of the finest air fighters who ever stood on a rudder bar, eased his ship down, bounded along and brought it in to the starting line. He crawled out and hustled along to headquarters. He was tired; he was in a hurry to get on his bunk.

He took a look at the face of Hans Traub and stopped, swinging his helmet around his finger. "All right, out with it," he said. "I don't have to be a mind reader to know something's happened."

"Stuart at Espinard," Traub said. "He wants you to come right over."

"What's wrong at Espinard?"

"Dead man. Had a map in his shoe."

"Map of what?"

"Stuart didn't get that far. Found out you weren't here and didn't tell me much. Said it was important."

Captain Frost uttered an exclamation that might have been a deep sigh. "Maybe it is," he said slowly. "This may be the thousandth time." He smiled a little. "Nine hundred and ninety-nine times you investigate routine cases and nothing happens. Then the thousandth time you get repaid for all your trouble."

"Hans and I'll go with you, Jerry," said Giles. He mopped his face again. What he meant to convey was that anything was better than sitting on a porch where the temperature was nearly 100 degrees with nothing more diverting than a muddy river. Jerry shook his head.

"You and Hans better take a look down the river this after-noon—way down. Some stuff's been coming through the coast guard down there."

"Okey," said Giles. "Come on, Dutchy—shake the lead out."

"I'll go see Stuart alone," Frost said.

"Well," Traub put in, "if I were you, I'd get some rest first."

Frost gave way to a faint grimace. "After this I'll rest," he said. Always it was "after this." That was the way of the service. "Good luck," he said to them. "I'm changing clothes. Pretty stuffy upstairs today."

Hell was eternally popping up and down that river. For a long time the Black Ship Gang had kept them on the alert, and that had swung into concerted action since three of the earlier Air Rangers had been murdered. The triple murder virtually had wrecked that first squadron.

In desperation Frost turned to wartime friends who were, a few months previous, in the movies making air stuff, and enlisted them—three Allied aces and an ex-Bavarian flight commander, a combination called Hell's Stepsons; later as an official detachment of the Ranger service, led by Jerry Frost, they had shot down four planes of the Black Ship Gang and destroyed a counterfeiting plant at Lamaraz, Mexico.

From that blow the Black Ship Gang, naturally, recoiled slightly. But Frost knew full well it was only momentary, That syndicate was too big, too far-reaching, to be wrecked by a single episode. Even though it had remained apparently inactive, Frost knew, and the Adjutant-General's department knew, it merely was realigning forces.

And now Frost mused, shedding his boots, a dead man had been found. Perhaps that was a good sign. Perhaps they had begun to fight among themselves. What was the map the dead man had concealed in his shoe? It manifestly was important.

"Well," he said softly, "anything that happens will be an improvement."

LOAFING SOUTH OVER the Rio went the two silver ships that were Traub's and Giles', now only mildly curious about the message in the dead man's shoe. They were more immediately concerned with the country below them. At five thousand was Giles—twice as high, like a mother hawk, was Traub.

The ex-Bavarian worked best at high altitude, and until they came close to their objective he always kept his ship at close to ten thousand. There are two definite classes of war-time pilots—those who work best at low levels and those who work best at high levels. Traub was of the latter class. He floundered when he had to get down to fight. He preferred to have his enemies below rather than above him.

Now, however, there was little thought of that. Before leaving the home field Captain Frost had said to have a sharp look down the river, that some stuff had been coming through the coast guard. Well, that meant close to the Gulf. There was little chance of any excitement on this patrol. They'd merely have a look.

Upward of an hour later a village came into view and beyond it Traub discerned the pale body of water that was the Gulf of

Mexico. It was running whitecaps and from his altitude they took on the appearance of echeloned stripes. He located the town on his map, Rio Honda.

Eddie Giles was dropping lower. The sun seemed unusually bright and blinding. Traub jerked his head around and put his thumb close to his eyes to diffuse the rays momentarily. He had a funny feeling. Nothing there. He closed his eyes to cut out the dancing sparks; and then opened them suddenly. A faint bark reached his ears.

He knew that sound. Machine-guns.

He looked over and down. A cloud bank had dropped its covey. Three tiny, yellowish ships, reflecting the brilliance of the sun in an ominous glint, were swarming over Eddie Giles.

Their guns were spitting puffs of smoke. Giles had gone into a desperate climb to get out of the pocket. Quite plainly he was in rather a bad way.

Traub cursed himself for his stupidity and ruddered over. It was purely a subconscious move. Veteran pilots do things under the stress of battle which are entirely involuntary.

The tight little bus whipped over in a singing turn and shot its nose downward as the wind whistled through the wires.

Hans Traub was riding to the rescue in a grandstand seat.

The lightning-like movements and happenings of a dog fight are difficult to follow in ordinary circumstances. Pilots have little recollection of what goes on about them. But Traub was fully conscious of that sight below.

Those three planes were over Eddie like enraged hornets. He was unable to get out in a climb. Traub saw one of the ships let go a burst that caught Giles at the moment of a maneuver, and for a moment Traub thought he was going down.

Splinters flew from his cowling and the wind avidly seized at two long gashes in his linen on the left side. Giles managed to roll from the path of the bullets, and once out zoomed upward in an effort to let go a burst. Thus far he hadn't fired a gun.

But as he hung there in his zoom, just before he straightened out, the guns began to eat at him again. They hammered against his instrument board, through his cockpit, and Eddie Giles went cold all over at the nearness of death. He was trapped like a great bird that is held while the leaden hail gradually closes in.

Traub swore again in guttural German and heeled his throttle wide open. If Eddie could hold on for just a second more!

But Eddie couldn't. That was no discredit to him. They had him pocketed: he never had a chance. He slipped off his zoom, went into a spin and lazily dropped down. He was out of control—perhaps…

Traub groaned and watched, fascinated. He tried to pry his eyes off the spectacle—and couldn't.

He saw Giles' ship strike the ground, a tiny puff of dust arise; then all was still.

The scene played itself out in the tick of a clock. The three ships which attacked the Ranger were leveled out now in a broad dash. They had seen the silver hawk preen his wings and dive to the rescue and they were taking no chances. Their work was done.

Traub swore again and got on the tail of the one nearest him. He knew his distance was bad, but the madly fleeing ship was squarely in his ring sights. His guns jumped with delight as he thumbed the releases. But the range was too long.

Traub came out of his dive in a steady level that even then

rocked his wings, and took in behind. His motor was booming under the strain. It was getting the greatest speed its pilot had ever demanded.

As the racing ships pulled away from him Traub got a sort of nightmarish impression. It didn't seem real. Too much had happened in too short a space of time. His A3 was fast, supposedly the fastest pursuit plane equipped for battle. And yet those three enemy ships were becoming mere specks against the sky. They were far out of his range now. He was too far behind even to get in a burst.

"*Gott!*" He swore above the roar of his motor. "Are they phantoms?"

Still he held on. Then he realized his fury was making the chase rather absurd. He hadn't a chance. The specks were disappearing. And Giles was down.

He rolled over and came back to the scene of the disaster.

CAPTAIN GEORGE STUART, veteran Ranger, in charge of the detachment at Espinard, paced up and down in the shade of the hangar as a silver ship winged its way over the field, dipped low and came down to a landing. Then he moved out as it taxied in and greeted its pilot.

Captain Stuart was rough, rugged and indulged in no formalities. "Well," he said when the propeller stopped whistling, "we've got a hot one!"

"So Traub told me," Frost replied. He got to the ground. "What is it?"

Stuart spread out a crumpled sheet of paper on the wing of the plane. "Have a squint at that."

Frost did. He shook his head.

"I'll bite," he said. "What is it?"

"That's the thing that guy had in a false heel. It's a map."

"Sure—but what about it?"

"Well, it's the lower end of the Gulf Coast, isn't it? That ought to spell something."

Frost said, "Um-m-m-m," and fingered the paper again.

"Who was the fellow who carried this dope?" he asked.

"I dunno," Stuart said. "But he had *something*. Those guys—whoever they are—are running stuff up in that cove. Looks like they got a house in Mexico and a place in Jamestown."

"And Rio Honda is the center of the trouble."

"Exactly. But you ain't heard nothing yet. Last night the body of the dead man was stolen."

"What?"

"Uh-huh," Stuart nodded. "Stolen! Somebody got into the shop where the body was—and took it away. However, I didn't know anything about that until a little while ago. They're trying to keep us just as far out of this case as possible."

"You figure the men who got the body were after that?" He pointed to the map.

"Without a doubt. They probably killed him at night, searched for it, probably went back to report—and were sent back to get the body. That's my theory."

"Sounds plausible," Frost nodded. "But who was he—and where did they take the body?"

Stuart laughed shortly. "I never was good at riddles," he said. "I'm pretty lucky to know this much. You know how these country constables are—jealous as hell."

"Yes," said Frost. He knew. More than once that petty jealousy almost had defeated justice. There are those historians who cry that jealousy does not exist between peace officers—but they do not know this border. Frost knew that such a thing did exist, and in a big way too.

"What's the rest of your guess, George? You figure this bird was mixed up with a gang of rivals?"

"Looks like it. He had a map and somebody knew it. He got killed. There's something behind it."

Stuart told him to keep the map. "No good to me, and besides, I thought maybe you'd want to have a fling at dear old Rio Honda."

"You bet I do," said Frost sincerely. "And I know four others who'll be tickled pink."

"I guess they will. You know, Jerry, if I wasn't so old, I'd take a shot at that airplane business myself. I can't yet figure how you happened to get those four guys for your squadron."

"Tricks of the trade," Frost retorted. "I'm not worried about how I got 'em, I'm worried about keeping them. As long as I can find a little action now and then—"

"Reckon the Old Man is gonna rear up again?"

The "Old Man" was the affectionate designation of the Adjutant-General.

"Not if it's on this side of the river. Officially, he won't like it. Can't afford to. Personally, he'll be glad as hell. I happen to know that other gang had him pretty worried."

They milled around town for an hour or more and then drove out to the flying field. The moment the car came through the gate an attaché ran out.

"Captain Frost," he said, "they've been trying to get you on the telephone for half an hour!"

"Who's been trying?"

"Gentry."

Frost got out of the car. There was an alarming note in the voice. He went in to the telephone and got his connection at once.

"Hello!" he barked into the instrument. "Hello!... Skipper? This is Jerry..." There was a long pause during which Frost's eyes narrowed and he gripped the receiver so tightly perspiration formed in the palm of his hand. "Righto," he yelled. "I'm on my way!"

He strode back to the door. George Stuart was waiting, a querulous expression in his face.

"Eddie Giles just got knocked down by a strange plane on the South Patrol," Frost said succinctly.

"Serious?"

"I don't know." He inhaled deeply. "Well, George it looks like it's broken sooner than we expected." He gripped the hand of the weather-beaten veteran. "So long."

Their eyes met and held each other for a moment. Words meant little. George Stuart understood.

"Luck to you, Jerry," he said warmly.

Captain Frost squared his shoulders and went to his trim plane. He climbed into the cockpit and yelled at a mechanic. His motor caught in a roar; he revved it briefly, waved a hand at Stuart and bumped out. In a moment he was off, slid above the Rio Grande and roared northwest.

Stuart, a product of the old school, the hard school, watched the tiny speck in the sky that represented the new school, the scientific school.

"Attababy!" he gritted. "Up and at 'em!"

And as he turned away there was a look in his eye that seemed to express his belief that the glorious traditions of the Texas Rangers were not yet due to fade into history and oblivion.

CLIPPING ALONG AT a hundred and ten, Captain Frost's mind was filled with misgivings. What had happened to Eddie Giles? Young, to be sure, yet there were few pilots anywhere in the world who were more air secure, more reliable than he. Eddie Giles was the sort of a war-time flyer who never funked a patrol, who had a positive genius for doing the proper thing at the proper time. His record in the R.A.F. was splendid. How had this happened?

And, what was infinitely more important, had he been seriously hurt? That was the disturbing question. If Giles were out for a long time, the morale of the illicit traffickers would be tremendously improved, and morale ever is a precious thing even though it cannot be measured with a yardstick.

On the South Patrol. Um-m-m-m. In the neighborhood shown by that map he had in his pocket. Was there a connection? Maybe. That end of the river was too peaceful. Anybody with half a brain ought to know something was brewing. Maybe that map did mean something.

He swooped over the field at Gentry and circled for a landing. He blipped his motor, rammed his tail skid into the ground so hard he would have been grounded had he been a cadet, took off again, came down and rolled in. Johnny Rosenfield, dumpy mechanic, trotted out. He'd been with Captain Frost a long time, and he was no sap. He knew what that gesture meant.

"Take 'er in, Johnny," Frost called. He started for headquarters room on a dog trot.

Skipper Hinsdell and Rowdy Perry, home from patrol, met

him on the porch. They shook their heads nervously. Frost saw, even in his eagerness, his bewilderment, that their faces were grim. They were red-hot.

"Where's Eddie?"

"Hans took him over to San Antone," Skipper said. "Old Doc Quack or whatever his name is treating him. We told Hans to go ahead and take him to the hospital. Didn't know when you'd get back."

"That's okey," Frost said. "How bad's he hurt?"

"Got a busted collar bone and a broken wrist. Pretty lucky. Doc said he'll be in shape in a month."

"A hell of a lot *he* knows about it," Frost said. "When did Hans say he'd be back?"

"Pretty soon," said Hinsdell.

"Well," Frost said heavily, "I guess we've got to wait."

Neither Hinsdell nor Perry knew the particulars of the crash. Hans had merely said they were attacked. That was all. They spent two hours speculating on the new menace which suddenly had arisen. It had struck home. One of their own men had felt the sting.

Traub finally lumbered in. He came into headquarters like a tardy schoolboy who anticipated his teacher's wrath for negligence. He sat down.

"Not a bullet touched him," he said slowly. "Collar bone's smashed, wrist broken and he's bruised pretty bad. They said it wouldn't be long."

Frost sighed, relieved. "How'd it happen, Hans?"

"I'll tell you," Traub said after a pause. "We decided to go way down the river and have a good look. I was about ten thousand when we got to a little place called Rio Honda and—"

"Rio Honda?" Frost cut in swiftly.

"Yes," Traub said. "Know it?"

"Go ahead with your story."

"Well, Eddie was down a little lower. I guess we got separated a little too far. Pretty soon I heard a popping and I looked around. There was Eddie all gummed up with three little ships that looked like hornets.

"They had him in a pocket and were blasting right and left, so I came around and started for them. Before I came out of the bank, he fell and the three ships started across the river. I took in after them." He sniffed contemptuously. "You won't believe me but the way they got going was pathetic. I was kicking along at a hundred and forty and didn't even get close enough to get in a burst. I came back, picked up Eddie and beat it home. That's all there is to it."

"That's enough," Frost said tersely. "I can't figure what kind of ships they had to outrun an A3 like that."

"Neither could I," said Traub solemnly. "But they didn't miss doing it."

They were silent for a while. Then Frost said, "It looks like another damned gang."

They nodded affirmation.

"I got something to show you." Frost went to the desk and got a map of North America. He took a sheet of paper from his pocket. "Know that dead guy over at Espinard? Well, they swiped his body some time last night. But George Stuart glommed this map he had in that false heel—and look!" He laid it beside the same section on the larger chart.

Skipper Hinsdell whistled. "Say—that's right where Eddie got shot? Right, Hans?"

The ex-Bavarian said it was.

"So," Frost declared. "That's that! That's where the fun is—in Rio Honda. We can't go down there and get tough—not this time. Maybe I got a way to have some fun."

"Well, just remember," Rowdy put in, "we go four ways on any fun."

"Not this time, Rowdy," Frost said. "I got an idea. I need a vacation, so I'll run down there and see what it's all about."

"That's suicide," Traub said. "You can't fly down there alone!"

"Not flying," he grinned. "Not this time."

They protested stoutly against such a move, but to no avail. Frost had decided, and when he decided he was adamant. The more they argued against it the more he thought of his idea. He filed his report for the Adjutant-General, told Rowdy Perry to look out for things until he heard from him, Frost, and walked out of headquarters room.

"Say, we ought to make him take a nap before he goes," said Traub. "He needs some sleep."

"Don't—make—me—laugh!" retorted Perry. "I'll lay my dough on anything that baby tries, sleep or no sleep!"

A WEEK LATER a ramshackle automobile, that gave the appearance that it had been used by Brother Noah as a staff car, chugged down the main street of Rio Honda and there was labor in every chug. The day was blazing hot, which apparently further added to the discomfort of the man at the wheel. He looked eagerly up the street at a sign that indicated a garage—a welcome thing to look upon. He was patently afraid that the dilapidated automobile would buckle up before it made the haven of rest and repair.

Now, accustomed as it was to all manner of freaks, Rio Honda still was not sufficiently sophisticated to pass by this scene without interest. It was easily obvious that Rio Honda was enjoying the spectacle, that is, all of Rio Honda who were out. It was a small town on the southernmost border, at the head of a great cove where the Gulf of Mexico greeted the Rio Grande; its population was mixed—and a great many were inside. Those on the street laughed.

The lunging automobile got within perhaps a hundred yards of the garage, gave a spasmodic twitch much more violent than its immediate predecessors, and stopped. The driver turned to the tonneau as if he knew exactly what was wrong, ducked his head: and straightened up in a flash.

He had straightened before a sheet of flame, and he piled out of the seat. Helplessly he looked about; there was no relief or aid and the flames mounted higher and higher. Shrill cries of warning and excitement disturbed the placid little village; shutters popped open and sleepy eyes tried to convey the impression to inactive minds.

Nothing, of course, could be done about it. Everybody stood there and watched it burn.

That was exactly what Captain Jerry Frost had figured.

He felt a touch on his shoulder and turned to face a grimy man who was dressed in the garb of a mechanic.

"Your bus?"

"Yep."

"Ain't much good now?"

"Nope."

"How'd it happen?"

"You know as much about it as I do," Frost confessed. "She just went blooey."

There was a brief silence during which a Mexican mother happened to remember a movie she had once seen where a gas tank exploded, and chattered in a shrill voice as her urchin got too close.

"Well," the mechanic observed, "it's a circus for these Mexes. Where'd you started for?"

"California," Frost said. "I was going in the movies."

"Yeh," the mechanic said good-naturedly. "What was you gonna do—play janitor?"

Frost thought of his personal appearance and fully agreed with the classification.

"Nope—I was gonna do a little stunt flying. Now I'm stuck. Hell," he said with a burst of bravado, "there ain't no use crying over spilt gin."

"Nope—sure ain't."

"When does the next rattler leave?"

The mechanic looked puzzled. He finally grinned. "Oh—you mean train. Well, brother, I hate to tell you—but the trains don't come no closer than McFarlane—twenty miles over there." He gestured in a sort of circle. Frost thought that was a lot of help.

"That's tough. When does the next one go through?"

"Tomorrow. Stranger to this part of the country?"

Frost admitted he was. He was, he said, from New Orleans. "Was there a hotel in town?"

"Reckon you could call if that." He pointed to a two-story frame building which conveyed the thought, in two languages, that such was the case. One sign read, "LODGINGS," and the other read, "CASA Y RENTAS."

"Much obliged," said Frost. "You the garage fellow?" The

mechanic nodded. "Make me an offer on what's left of my auto?"

"Nope—she ain't much good." He paused shortly. "Tell you what I'll do," he went on, with the air of a man who is about to bestow a fortune on a worthy unfortunate. "I'll haul her off the street for the iron that's in 'er."

Frost's eyes twinkled. "Okey, she's yours."

The mechanic got sociable. "When you get through at the hotel, drop around the shop. It'll help you kill time."

"Sure," said Frost.

He found Rio Honda's lone hostelry quite in harmony with the country and the exterior view it presented. It was a typical Border rooming-house, one of those places which shrink and shrivel in the sun's rays and swell and become community centers at night. It was presided over by a bulking figure who said the room would cost two dollars.

Frost said that was all right, and followed him down a short corridor entirely devoid of all decorations, almost devoid of paint.

The man glared at him as he went out.

"Whew!" Frost said to himself. "Lovely dump, this!"

Still, he was not downcast. Things thus far had broken perfectly and as he washed his face and hands he hummed a little, and finally sat down in the window which overlooked the street. It seemed a little odd to him that such a locality, a locality as full of atmosphere as this, could be a part and parcel of the civilized United States. Rio Honda, he thought, should have been framed against a foreign background.

As a matter of fact, such was very nearly the truth. Rio Honda's citizens were, for the most part, peons: there were very few stores, a number of adobe dwelling-houses, a few frame shacks, and the town as such apparently merely existed.

Frost looked at it through the eyes of an artist. A motion picture director knows when a location is satisfactory, an author knows when good material is at hand, a painter knows a perfect scene. Frost realized that Rio Honda, could it have been laid out by a master criminal, could have afforded no greater possibilities for contraband commerce.

Quarter of a mile south stretched the Gulf, sloshing into tiny little coves along the coast; the Rio flowed on the edge of the village; below it was a barren fastness that was Mexico, above it the United States—and nowhere was there an over-abundance of population.

Rio Honda was made to order for smugglers.

Frost had every reason to feel pardonably proud of his entrance into this section, but for the life of him he couldn't. He wasn't exactly ill at ease, but he sensed a definite premonition of misfortune. He had begun to wonder.

The sun had slid down its arc rapidly and now he found his eye attracted by a steady glare that was only a few degrees less than had a mirror been turned into his face. At first that is what he thought it was. But closer scrutiny revealed his mistake. It was a slight thing for all its glare, and seemed to hang close to the garage and partly behind it, where rough boards, warped and weathered, formed some sort of screen from the street.

He presently reached the conclusion that it *might* be the tip end of an airplane wing, and with that realization came a sudden tightening of his muscles.

Well, he'd go see. The garage man had told him to drop in. So he would.

Of course there might be nothing in it. That pin-point gleam between two warped boards could be almost anything. The boarded-off space might have nothing to do with the garage. At least, the mechanic was the only socially inclined being he had yet seen. Such hopes as he might have entertained from that ordinary dispenser of town gossip, the hotel-keeper, had been promptly squelched at his first sight of the man.

A level glare was in the street as Frost poked his way along and turned into the open garage door. The immediate contrast with the interior gave an impression of utter darkness in the windowless garage. Frost shuffled slowly along toward the sound of tinkering that came from some place outside his immediate vision, possibly from behind a partition that loomed vaguely before him.

Simultaneously there came the soft scrape of a footfall at one side, the creak of hinges and the sudden blotting out of the sun's diffused glow as the door banged to.

Frost swung and ducked swiftly, his hand darting toward the automatic slung inside his belt. Therefore, the blow, from some unseen but heavy weapon, aimed at the crown of his head, merely grazed his temple and thudded sickeningly on his right shoulder. Frost was staggered by the impact and for an instant shoulder and arm were numb. The swiftly drawn pistol slipped from nerveless fingers and clattered noisily on the floor.

Trapped, huh? Grabbed the bait and walked right in, like a mouse nibbling the cheese and allowing the thing to close up behind it.

But that realization—and the blow—only made Frost the fighting man he could be.

As he staggered, two men catapulted into him, one from

either side. Arms encircled him—to catch the falling body, maybe. Hands grasped his throat and arms.

Then the little group exploded from within itself, disintegrated, shot apart.

Jerry's solid left smacked in the direction where a panting garlic-laden breath and the position of the encircling arms told him a face should be, collided with flesh and bone and went onward for another foot, pushing the face before it.

By sheer strength of will he forced feeling into that numbed right arm and swung viciously in the opposite direction, scoring again dead center.

In the momentary respite, he sank to his knees and groped for his pistol.

A searing light stabbed into his eyes from the darkness. It showed him his pistol a yard away. It showed also a black muzzle, shoved forward in the beam of the flashlight.

Then, from behind him, a cold voice: "Hands up, Captain!"

Frost turned to look into the muzzle of a pistol held by a man who remained in the background. He was tall and slender, with a grim face and tight lips. Instinctively Frost knew he was looking upon the leader. Probably the fourth man, the one who held the flashlight, was the friendly mechanic. The sounds of tinkering had ceased.

"What," Frost said, panting from his exertions, "does this mean?"

He was watching for a chance to resume the battle. But a false move now meant a slug of lead—or several of them—of that there was not the slightest doubt.

"That you're a prisoner," said the tall man. "Now be sensible and don't get smart."

Frost had difficulty restraining himself. He didn't know whether to have it out here or later.

"Yes, Captain," said the man, "this is quite a pleasure to see you. We thought maybe you weren't coming. You see, we expected you. Thompson—tie the gentleman up. We can talk better. But first pick up his gun."

Frost submitted to the tying process with all the grace he could muster. He felt a little disgusted with himself; for any manhunter to be trapped by his intended victim is a bit of irony they never appreciate. But it had happened. Frost couldn't dispute that. So he bowed to a potent fate.

His hands were bound securely. Thompson took the gun and had started to bind his feet when the tall man stopped him.

"Never mind the legs," he said. "Captain Frost won't try any of that funny business. He's too smart. Permit me to introduce myself and my friends. I am Robert DeWitt, those two gentlemen with the guns are Messrs. Bennett and Marvin and this gentleman"—indicating the mechanic—"is Goat Thompson. We are, as you see, partners."

"Interesting," Frost commented without tone. "But would you mind telling me exactly what this is all about? What are you going to do with me—and how do you know I'm the fellow you want?"

There was a general laugh. "You thought of that a little late, Frost," the tall man said. "As to what we intend doing with you, I cannot say. Kill you, I suppose. But we do know who you are, because we have been expecting you. Burning the car was an inspiration and might have worked—any other time. I must say, though, you've a lot of guts to come down here. It never was a question of *would* you come—but *when*. Do I make myself clear?"

"Perfectly," Frost said.

"And since the odds are a million to one you'll ever see your outfit again," the man went on. "I'll tell you something. The gentleman found dead in Espinard was a detective from Chicago—who had a map he never should have drawn. Until we caught you, I thought stealing his body was my masterpiece."

A detective. Well, that was one mystery solved. So DeWitt had the body stolen. Two mysteries solved. Frost told himself, ironically, he was getting right along with the case.

"Some day," Frost said unwisely, "you'll make a mistake. They all do."

"Don't be trite, Captain, or you'll disappoint me. A mistake is possible—but not probable."

The fight, vicious as it had been, had passed without unusual noise. No guns had been fired. No yells—except one explosive Spanish oath smothered by Jerry's fist. And he doubted if an outcry would have brought interference from outside.

"All set," announced DeWitt, after the mechanic had barred the door. "Let's go. The car's out the back way, Captain. Follow Thompson."

"Wait a minute!" Frost exclaimed. "You can't run away with me like this—you'll have the whole state down on you."

DeWitt merely laughed.

"Well, where are we going?"

"For a nice long ride, Captain. Across the Border. Take a farewell look at the old U.S.A., for the next time you see it, you'll be playing a harp."

"My squadron 'll be down here after you like a pack of eagles," Frost said.

"That's exactly what I'm hoping," DeWitt replied quickly. "In fact, I'm going to invite them. But, now—get on!"

A long touring car was standing in the enclosure behind the garage; beside it, a slip of a plane under canvas stretched loosely overhead. Frost would have liked to look at it more carefully, but they bundled him into the rear seat between two of the men, one of whom held a gun pressed meaningly against his ribs.

By devious ways a secluded spot on the river was reached in the gathering darkness—a boat ferried all of them across where another machine was waiting, concealed in the bottom growth.

FOR UPWARD OF two hours they drove through the rugged country that skirted the foot of the modest mountain peaks, through defiles and canyons and over roads which were more or less poor apologies for highways. Several times Frost asked for a cigarette. That was all. He puffed thoughtfully. He was rather inclined to believe DeWitt intended to do away with him—but not now. DeWitt had one of those complexes that impelled him to play with his prey before the slaughter.

Some sixty miles south they emerged on to a flat plain, and a village reared out of nowhere to greet them. It was one of those small communities which are sprawled on the plains and in the hills of Mexico for no good reason, probably a backwash of the fates. They not only exist but seem to thrive.

Goat Thompson shafted the automobile through the village and turned at its outskirts. DeWitt grunted, relieved, and shifted his position.

"We're almost there, Captain," he said. "I'm sorry if you're tired."

"You needn't be," said Frost. "I'm not."

They swung up a slight hill and came to a crest or a rise and stopped before a house on which was plastered, in ill-formed letters: "leon morales."

Beside the house was a field that extended several hundred yards, and Frost saw, in the starlight, there were three airplanes standing on the strip.

"How do you like my Air Service?" DeWitt inquired.

"Hot stuff!" Frost answered flippantly. He nodded toward the house. "This where I'm going to stay?"

"You guessed it. I hope you'll like it."

"Well, don't worry. I *got* to like it."

"You know, I rather like you. It's a shame you're a copper. I'd like to have you join us."

"Nope," Frost said. "You babies are going straight to the chair. I don't want to go that way."

"Lissen, you," DeWitt flashed. "Don't get me sore! You're below the river now—and anything goes!"

Frost clambered out of the car before the pertinent suggestion of the guns, and marched up to the house. They steered him through the patio into a small room. Several men were sitting around the table in the patio.

"Look," one said, "Bob's got a playmate."

"Looks like a tramp," another added.

There were four of them, and they formed a not unimpressive group. Three of them were accoutred in the garb of pilots. A fat Mexican came panting into the garden and eyed them curiously.

"Lock that guy up, Leon," DeWitt said. "Then we'll figure out what to do with him."

The Mexican locked the door on Frost, threw the key on the table, and went back whence he had come.

"Well," one of the pilots asked, "who is he?"

DeWitt sat down and lighted a cigarette. He inhaled deeply, at length, and blew the smoke high in a satisfied sigh.

"Get a grip on your chairs," he said, "so's I won't have to pick you off the ground. That guy is the famous Jerry Frost!"

The four men stared, incredulous.

"Frost! You mean the Ranger?"

DeWitt nodded. "Yep—Frost, the Ranger."

"Well, I'll be a dirty name!" somebody said. "How'd you bag him?"

"Never mind how—we got him. And I'm figuring on him helping me in that next deal, too."

"How?"

"A week from today Kelly brings in that cargo from the islands, and it's the biggest we ever got. I've been pretty careful and I don't think anything will gum up our plans. But those Air Rangers know Frost is or was in Rio Honda. Wouldn't a message to them, signed by him, bring 'em on in a hurry? And couldn't we wipe 'em out at one sitting?"

They regarded him impassively; and DeWitt was annoyed at their lack of enthusiasm.

"What's the matter?" he said sarcastically. "Afraid?"

"No," one of them said. "We ain't afraid. Just the same you can't go around bumping off Rangers like they were ordinary coppers. You've already put in a requisition for a carload of hell by knocking down one and getting Frost—and if you go getting much tougher, you'll have a fine little storm on your hands."

"Aw—lissen—"

"Shorty's right," another one cut in swiftly. "Understand I ain't saying I won't go through with it, but the point we're trying to get across is we got to be careful. You can't up and pull a stunt like that in a minute. It takes time. Them Rangers is plenty tough—they'd fight hell off the mountain. I know one of them, that Perry bird—and I'm telling you there ain't nobody gonna get him out of the air unless they get him when he ain't looking."

DeWitt agreed the men were correct, still he insisted this was their big chance.

One of the flyers named Barrett said go ahead. "But you got to be careful. Maybe you don't know 'em as well as you ought to."

"Sure, I know 'em! Maybe I just ain't yellow!"

At that the little fellow called Shorty fairly bristled. "Look here, Bob," he said hotly. "You watch your tongue! We ain't yellow! We knocked down one of them a week ago, didn't we?"

"That's just the point!" DeWitt snapped. "We're in just as much hell about that as we'll ever be. We'll use Frost as a decoy and then ease him off."

"You mean," asked Barrett, "you're gonna kill him?"

DeWitt bared his teeth in a smile and threw his cigarette away. "Sure—why not? He ain't a god or anything is he? Bullets 'll kill him, too, won't they? Besides, he knows too damn much."

"What's the plan? We wanna know."

"Simple," said DeWitt. He felt considerably relieved. "We'll draw 'em down here with a message signed by Frost and nobody'll ever see 'em again."

But his relief was premature. The pilots still were dissatisfied with the arrangements.

"Say, DeWitt," said Shorty, "I got brains enough to know you've got us nailed any way we go, but I'm kicking loud and long about this. I ain't going to take no fall for you or nobody else!"

"That so!" exclaimed DeWitt. "Well, get funny and beat it back to the States. Go on! I'd have every flat in the country on your tail. Maybe you could laugh that off!"

"Sure," grinned Shorty. "I said you had us nailed. I ain't ducking the job or nothing—I'm just telling you, that's all."

"And in the meantime," interposed Barrett calmly, "your buddy from the Rangers is getting an earful of all this." He nodded to the room where Frost was held prisoner.

"Yeah?" DeWitt's exclamation was more of a snarl than anything else, and he got to his feet with his gun in his hand. The old light flared in his eyes.

Shorty got up and intercepted him. "Don't be a damn fool, DeWitt!" he barked. "Sit down!"

DeWitt did, after a moment. Shorty regarded him with light contempt. "You'd been a big man, Bob, if it hadn't been for that rotten temper of yours. You're always popping off about how clever and smart you are—and then you get into a tailspin and crumb yourself. How you're gonna decoy those guys if you kill Frost now?"

It was a pertinent question. DeWitt realized the truth of it and straightened up. "Leon!" He raised his voice and the fat Mexican appeared. "Get me some paper and an envelope. We're going to have Frost write us a letter."

JERRY FROST WAS as philosophical as possible under the circumstances. He had heard the conversation, all of it, without straining his ears, and he knew that trouble was brewing and he knew that he was marked for the victim.

But he had been in jams before—and escaped. That was great consolation.

Heretofore his contact with Border runners had been more or less impersonal. He had looked at their activities from afar. Now he was getting a closeup of a violent, reckless gang in action. They were, he was convinced, little different from any other, perhaps a little better equipped. They specialized in liquor, but there was no contraband of any other type too dangerous for them to handle.

He had heard them say he was to be a decoy, which, he hoped, he would not be: but at the same time he knew his value to the sovereign State of Texas ended when he died. That is to say he intended to hang on to his life as long as possible.

He was not surprised when the door opened and DeWitt and two other men entered. He recognized one of them as Goat Thompson, the mechanic, whose part in this organization seemed to be holding his tongue and waving a gun.

"Captain," said DeWitt, and he again was the oily individual, "I want you to write a letter."

"To whom?"

"To your squadron."

"Why?"

"I want you to tell them you are all right, and that in case they get a wire from you, they are to follow instructions fully."

"Which," said Frost, "I shall not do."

"No? In that case I'll send it myself and do away with you."

Frost cogitated briefly. He did not feel the situation was finally settled. He thought there might be some way…

"I'll write it," he said suddenly.

DeWitt grinned and handed him the paper and a green fountain pen. An unusual fountain pen. Heavily embossed in a gold scroll effect. Just the sort of pen a vainglorious man would possess. But Frost was struck by something else. It was not the first time he had ever seen it. Where, when—he couldn't remember. But he did know he had seen it.

"Well, take it!" DeWitt barked. He shoved the pen at him. Frost took it. "Sit down!" Frost sat down. He looked at the pen curiously, felt its weight. It might throw some light on the mystery—if he could remember. He was striving diligently to connect it. But too much had gone through his mind since then. The image was almost washed away.

"Write what I tell you," DeWitt ordered. *"Rio Honda, Texas, November 12. Dear—"* he looked at Shorty *"*—what's his name?"

"Rowdy Perry."

"Dear Rowdy," DeWitt went on. *"Everything is fine. Think I'll have something pretty soon. Looks pretty good. If I wire you to come; go to Rio Honda and follow road south sixty miles into Mexico. There is a house on the left outside the village and near it is a water tank. Ought to be easy. That's where they are. Don't come until I wire or I'll be in trouble."*

"Fine," DeWitt approved. "Now sign it and address the envelope to Rowdy Perry, Texas Air Rangers, Gentry, Texas."

"You know all about us, don't you?" Frost asked.

"It's my business to know," DeWitt said. He took the letter, folded it and handed it to Shorty.

"Go mail this from Rio Honda," DeWitt said. "Take Thompson with you and don't come back until you get that message from Kelly."

A moment later Shorty and Thompson were on their way, the room was deserted. Captain Frost was alone.

He was glad of that. He wanted to think. He wanted to think about that pen. Where had he seen it? He wrestled with the memory that constantly eluded him. But he was in a hurry. The thing was moving to a climax—and he wanted to know where he had seen that green fountain pen. Somewhere, and DeWitt had not been the owner.

His predicament was serious. He knew that now. He had written a letter. He had to get out of there and stop the Air Rangers. He had to. Yet—where had he seen that pen?

BUT THERE WAS no escape for Jerry Frost. It struck him as grimly humorous that he could be penned in such a hastily improvised cell and still be so secure. He wasn't particularly frightened, because danger had been a constant companion for years; it merely was that he wanted a chance to fight.

For days he had been caged in that tiny room. His food had been shoved at him through an aperture in the door. He had not been permitted to wash. He had grown bearded and disheveled.

It seemed a foregone conclusion that he was to be executed. But even though there was slight hope, Frost clung to the idea that this was not his way to go—fatalistic philosophy so characteristic of adventurers. He felt there was a break somewhere, it merely was a question of being patient and not rushing the issue.

Leon Morales was a cigar maker. It was his duty to put in each cigar an allotment of morphine. Frost thought that was terribly crude. But its very success might have been founded on that reason. At best though, Morales was a tool.

Seven days dragged by. The house of Leon Morales had been strangely quiet of late. There was no confusion, no raucous voices, no drunken brawls. Silence had succeeded the absence of DeWitt and his men. Frost could feel, in a vague way, that the forces were gathering and the action was crystallizing.

On the seventh day Morales pushed back the slot in the door and handed in a plate of food. The plate was filled with a wider variety than ever before. Variety in Mexico means the same food prepared in half a dozen fashions.

That struck Frost as odd. "Why"?" he demanded, motioning to the plate.

"DeWitt come back tomorrow," Morales said ominously. "Mebbe he come back today. He come soon."

Frost grinned. So that was it. DeWitt was coming back. That meant he was being given extra attention before the execution.

For a brief instant he stood there, his mind whirling. All the hours he had spent trying to devise a means of escape flashed before him in a sort of hopeless parade; the veins in his forehead bulged as he realized the nearness of the climax which would find him so desperately helpless.

And in that instant his inspiration came. It was now or never. Morales had his hand through the slot holding the plate of food with only his wrist exposed. But that was enough.

Frost struck swiftly. He fastened both hands around that wrist and yanked suddenly. Morales' surprise caught him relaxed, and his entire arm was through the narrow panel. Frost bent down against the elbow savagely.

"Open that door!" he hissed. "Open it—or I'll break your arm in two!"

Morales swore rapidly and fluently, and struggled; and the more he struggled the tighter his arm was pinioned. All the time Frost was applying the pressure.

"*Carajo!*" he cried. "*Maldito!*" They were curses too terrible to translate. "Leggo, leggo!"

"Open that door!"

Frost applied more pressure. He firmly intended to break the arm unless the door was opened.

Morales made a final effort to free himself. He pulled with all his strength, and the effort cost him considerable pain. He groaned, and with his free hand thumped the latch on the door. He fell against it, and it popped open to precipitate him against its oak boards, his arm dangling uselessly.

Frost leaped on his back and fixed his fingers around the fat neck.

Morales grunted inarticulately and fought with his uninjured arm, but he could do nothing. He finally moaned and sank to the floor, Frost falling with him and never relinquishing his grip. For a long time they lay there, the spatulate fingers of the Ranger cutting into the Mexican's neck like a garrote.

When Frost got up Morales was definitely dead. And it never occurred to him that the killing was anything but justifiable.

He crept along the side of the patio to the outside, and once in the brilliant sunshine again he ran, crouching, to the undergrowth behind the house to get his bearings and begin the journey back to the Border. That would have been, he later came to know, certain death. From where he stood, the Border was a good sixty miles through a strip of land on which not even wild animals could exist. But he didn't know that. All he knew was that he must get miles between him and the house of Leon Morales. Capture now meant instant death.

Those were natural impressions. He was free for the first time in what seemed ages, flight was the sole thing in his mind. His brain was not in condition to make logical deductions. And then out of all that welter of cross thoughts and wild imaginings there came a hunch.

They are funny things, hunches. Strange things. Men who are at eternal loggerheads with the world soon learn to respect them. Hunches come and the adventurer acts. Hesitation means disaster.

Frost had a hunch to wait for DeWitt to return with his ships and his cargo of contraband. Why not, he asked himself. The undergrowth where he was hidden was but a scant hundred yards from the flying field. They had to land there.

His idea was to steal a plane. And it had to work. It was a gamble with his life as the stake. But that was nothing new.

So he sat down to await, with characteristic poise, the coming of those ships, He didn't know when it would be, he didn't particularly care. All he knew was that he would wait. The jaws of the trap had come so close to him before that this now seemed a double-riveted cinch.

There is little pleasure in being cooked under a tropical sun awaiting the moment to gamble with your life. Frost regarded it as stoically as possible. He moved around for hours, seeking the shade of the mesquite bushes—pitiful apologies for trees.

Heat waves rose in giddy undulations, there was not a breath of air. For such an ordeal Frost was not prepared. Years ago he could have withstood this with no discomfort, but he had been a veteran of several Latin-American campaigns then.

The sun was high before a disturbing noise reached his ears. It was unmistakably the drone of a motor. Presently there were other drones that rose and fell, and then he saw them come out of the sun. There were three tiny specks and a lumbering craft that he knew was a heavier cargo plane.

He flattened himself against the ground and waited. They dropped low over the field and landed.

He had but one chance—a desperate chance. He had to take it; he had no other alternative.

He crawled slowly toward the field, wriggling like a dough-boy on listening post detail. He stopped a scant fifty yards from one of the little planes which stood there, its motor idling and popping an invitation.

Frost recognized DeWitt beside the cabin plane and he could tell from the gestures and movements of the men that they were excited. They were moving crates out of the fuse-lage. Presently the motors of the big monoplane wheezed and came to a stop.

Frost could hear snatches of their conversation now.

"... they'll be here soon...." He knew that meant the Air Rangers and he went sick all over. DeWitt had baited the trap with their own captain—himself... "Get the guns..."

The men started toward the house, as one of the others who had gone ahead came dashing out and shouting at the top of his voice:

"He's gone! He's gone!"

Frost had a split-second in which to act. All trace of nervous-ness was gone. He was as calm and deliberate as if he had been sitting on his own bunk. His co-ordination was perfected.

He rose slightly and dashed for the little plane. He didn't look to either side—only ahead. He momentarily expected to hear the sping of bullets. He crawled on the wing and piled into the cockpit, knocking the throttle open before he had taken his seat.

The little bus fairly jumped out from under him. In direct defiance of all flying laws, he shot across the ground. This was no time for technique. His life was at stake.

Then the storm broke. A hail of lead ripped through the camber.

He yanked back on the stick and zoomed until he reached a near stall, then ruddered over. He felt safe now in looking below.

The two sister ships were rolling across the ground.

He laughed into the teeth of his motor. Back in the air! The little part of him that had died in confinement glowed and came back to life again.

He headed toward the Border. Somewhere in the air were the Rangers, rushing to what might have been a rendezvous with death. Traub and Perry and Hinsdell. He had got them into it—and he had to get them out. He had to stop them. Nothing else mattered—nothing.

HE THUNDERED ALONG at a hundred and fifty, amazed at the performance of his captured machine. It was so far in advance of the A3 type he had been using that there was no comparison. He touched the trigger to warm his guns and sucked in his breath deeply as they chattered through the propeller in tiny red and orange spurts.

He looked behind him. Two dots, the sun glinting on their blades. The pursuers! Frost laughed gladly. The wind was in his hair at last! He eased his throttle forward and scanned the heavens ahead.

He patted the cowling of the little ship. "I don't know where you came from or what you've been used for," he said admiringly, "but you're one sweetheart of a bus and I don't mean maybe." Irrelevantly he thought what fun it would have been to hook up with some Fokkers in this baby.

Then the ground suddenly parted and Rio Honda sprawled into view—an ugly community from the air. Ahead he saw three specks. His heart swelled; he wanted to shout.

The Rangers were riding!

As they drew close Frost raised one hand high in the air. His answer was a burst from the forward's guns.

They hadn't understood. He waved again. Another burst.

And then he knew. They thought he was the enemy.

In desperation and something that amounted to fright, he banked over, trying to escape the fire, but he still waved and signaled in the manner they should recognize. But the forward plane thought the pilot of this ship a little goofy for not wheeling into position and fighting. The Ranger's plane rolled over to get in another shot.

Out of the corner of his eye he saw the two little planes had come up to the scrap and had been caught by the Rangers. There was a neat little dogfight going on over to the left. But he had his hands full trying to save his own life. He thought he recognized the pilot.

"Rowdy!" he shouted. "Rowdy!"

The motor bit off his words, hurled them back. God, Jerry thought, it'd be hell to go like this!

He had to get away. He rolled over and turned tail.

And then he noticed, and his throat got tight, that there was but one Ranger left in that dogfight. Where had the other gone? He looked down. There it was. It was down. Standing in good shape—but down.

He turned to the plane following him.

"Rowdy!" he screamed again. "For God's sake, let me alone! This is Jerry!" He waved frantically, trying to signal him that there was one plane left alone to fight it out with two enemy. "Go help him!" he screamed, maneuvering in an effort to keep those guns off him.

But the pilot gave no heed. He was busy fencing for an opening.

Then something clicked in his brain above the roar of the motor, above the mad barking of the guns, above the screaming wires. Duty! Regardless of what happened, a comrade was in distress. Nobody could cut the patrol now.

He came up in a sharp zoom that astonished the Ranger pilot, and rolled over. He straightened out and nearly tore the throttle off the fuselage as he slapped it open.

"—— —— 'em!" he said through his teeth. He was a wild man. Helmetless, without goggles, he shoved his head into the slip stream to locate his prey and then sank back to look through the shield. The Ranger behind didn't matter now.

His eyes were narrow slits, the wind was tearing at his lids, trying to pry them open. He glued them to the sights. A yellowish object loomed.

"Lady Luck," he hissed, "ride my guns now!"

Rat-t-t-t-t-t-t! Rat-t-t-t-t-t-t-t!
Rat-t-t-t-t-t-t! Rat-t-t-t-t-t-t-t!

He thought the guns would rip themselves off the cowl, so vengefully did they belch.

He whistled on at close to two hundred.

Rat-t-t-t-t-t-t-t-t-t-t-t-t-t-t!

He held them open—wide open. To hell with stoppages—to hell with everything.

Before the terrific onslaught, the yellowish ship seemed to split in half, jumped upward under the last long burst, and then slipped off in a crazy, aimless spin.

At that moment his camber splintered and his dash popped full of holes. He thought it was the end. Watching those holes pop in the dash, he was reminded of a vaudeville act he had seen when a kid. A marksman high in the gallery cut initials in a soft board on the stage. He shot from behind, you couldn't see him—only the holes. This was like that.

Then he realized he was near the ground. In a last supreme effort he literally stood on his rudder bar and his stick. A dozen lights popped before him, hot needles rammed themselves in his shoulder. There was a queer, ripping sound—then a loud crash.

He knew all that. He knew he had smashed. The curtains were almost drawn. In a vague way he thought this was the end. Then he felt the cockpit double up. He distinctly remembered being snatched out by a giant, unseen hand. Then he floated away into the dark.

HE WAS LYING there on a flat strip of land, twenty feet from his plane, when they found him. There must have been a dozen or more khaki-clad figures around him when he finally recovered.

He tried to grin, but he felt the effort: was rather silly. Still, one had to do something when one was flat on the ground. He tried to get up but his fingers closed on thin air. His back hurt him. Then he remembered he had been stung. It still stung. It throbbed in every muscle.

He only knew, in a nebulous way, that he had been hurt. He tried his voice. "Hello," he said. They were strange words. It seemed as if he were shouting, yet was barely able to hear. But he was glad his voice worked.

"You're under arrest," was the merciless retort.

They were trying to pick him up, when a well-known form came across his vision. Distorted as that vision was, Frost recognized him.

"Hello, Rowdy," he said with an absurd attempt to be nonchalant.

Rowdy Perry's mouth popped open, his shoulders dropped. He stared at the bearded face. Then he recognized it. Still he stared; he was trying to find his tongue.

"Jerry!" he half whispered. He dropped on his knees. "Jeez!" he swore softly. "It was you!"

Jerry nodded weakly. "It's okey," he said. He reached for the shoulder to pat it. He was trying hard to be brave. But it hurt. And he was in a hurry to get in his words before his voice stopped. "Who're the soldiers?"

Rowdy Perry got a grip on himself.

"National Guard," he said. "I had them sent in. And they got plenty of liquor. The Old Man put the town under martial law."

"How—"

"Don't struggle" said Rowdy. "I'll tell you in time."

"Tell me now," Jerry insisted.

"Well, I knew something was wrong from that letter. So I called in the Old Man and this morning we raided the town. Now, listen, Jerry—you're hurt. Hey, soldiers, gimme a hand!"

They picked him up and carried him to an automobile. Every move was painful. But Frost stood it. Rowdy was holding his hand. That helped.

"I'm okey, Rowdy," Frost said. "Can't kill an old trouper. My shoulder is bunged up a little—"

"I'll say so," Rowdy declared. "I'm sorry, Jerry. Now we're going down to grab those other eggs."

"They've got guns."

"So've we!"

"But, Rowdy—"

His voice beat into the air. Rowdy Perry had gone back across the field. He shouted across: "Hurry him, now!"

With Rowdy gone, Frost felt oblivion coming on again. And he fought grimly against it. Only to lose. He felt a slight bump and that was all. He had drifted away.

IT WAS A matter of hours. He felt much better. His shoulder felt tight but he soon learned this was from the bandages. He was in a bedroom in the hotel. There was a blur of figures. He moved his head. It didn't hurt; he felt like shouting. Instead he laughed.

Rowdy Perry, Skipper Hinsdell and Hans Traub laughed too. They were considerably relieved.

"Greetings," said Frost. "The old motor's been cutting out again."

"Yeah," said Hinsdell. "Here's a friend of yours."

He stepped back and Bob DeWitt moved forward. He was handcuffed.

Frost nodded. "Great stuff, Skip. The Old Man 'll be tickled."

"Yeah," Traub put in, "and when he sees the stuff we've

bagged, he'll be more tickled. And there's a half dozen more coming over with the militia. This is what I'd call some haul!"

"Didn't," Frost managed, "somebody get knocked down?"

"Nope," said Traub. "They shot my prop off, but I got down all right."

Skipper Hinsdell laid a hand on Jerry's head. "Rowdy told me it was you who ducked into that dogfight just in time, Jerry," he said. "I owe you a lot. I thought it was kind of funny one of their own guys would be helping me—Rowdy told me." He pressed his hand against Frost's forehead again, a gesture more eloquent than he could make in any other way.

"Forget it," said Frost. "Say, DeWitt—" he broke off sharply. He had caught sight of the tip of that green fountain pen again. For a week he had cudgeled his brain trying to remember where he had seen that pen—for a week. Now it came to him in a flash. Out of a clear sky. Frost sucked in his breath in a swift intake. His jaw dropped. The knowledge was almost overpowering.

"How long am I down for?" he asked abruptly.

"Not long," said Rowdy. "You got some in the shoulder—by the way, Eddie's up. Raised hell because he didn't get in on this party."

"He wouldn't worry if he knew what I know, eh, DeWitt?" Frost laughed.

"I ought to have bumped you off that first day," DeWitt growled.

"You sure ought!" Frost agreed heartily. "You've let me in on some big stuff—bigger than anybody imagines. If I told them they wouldn't believe me, would they, DeWitt?"

"What do you mean?" he asked quickly.

"That." Frost pointed to the green fountain pen.

"What about it?"

"Nothing—only I remember where I saw that before."

DeWitt fell back a step. In the darkened interior of the room his face suddenly went white.

"Smart, careful guy, aren't you, DeWitt? Never make a mistake. But you let that pen gum you and your whole gang. I know now."

Frost did know. It came to him like a bas relief. He had seen that pen in the fingers of the chief of police of Jamestown. There could be no mistake. *In the fingers of the chief of police at Jamestown!*

A new avenue had opened. How far would it go? Who would be involved? Frost didn't know, nobody knew. But he told himself he was going to find out.

DeWitt recovered from his shock. "I swiped that pen—"

"Too late, careful—too late," Frost cut in. He laughed and turned to Hell's Stepsons: "So Eddie was griping, was he? Well, tell him he needn't worry about missing this party. There'll be another one—and a humdinger too."

He was pretty tired. And the war seemed to have just begun. But he was in bed—and he never muffed an opportunity to take advantage of a situation, so he rolled over and closed his eyes.

The Little Black Book

Hell's Stepsons do a little cloud busting

BIG JOHN DAWSON, one of the hardest coppers who ever stood behind a police shield in the Texan city of Jamestown, closed the door of his office and clicked the night latch against possible intrusion. He moved to the windows to make sure the shades were down to their fullest, clumping about the floor with annoyance in every clump. Then he squared off, grunted and shifted the stub of a black cigar to a corner of his mouth.

"Sit down, Flash."

A look of tolerance on his slender, wan face, Flash Singleton sat down. You knew from the flamboyance of his dress he would have a nickname like that. He seemed slightly youngish, and altogether his appearance suggested his sole career had been riotous living. His eyes alone belied that. They were narrowed and cold.

Big John Dawson swung around on his left heel, braced himself as if his office was a ship and he expected it to list, and stared at his unwelcome visitor. He was definitely, thoroughly and completely displeased.

Twenty long years had passed before he reached this office whose door bore the imprint, "Chief of Police." Twenty long years of service from the residential beats through the plainclothes squad, the detective squad, the central bureau—finally to come to a swivelchair and a glass-enclosed office. It was a tedious climb few coppers could survive. But Big John was hard.

"I thought," he said, measuring every word, "I asked you not to come here again."

"You did." Jamestown's prize racketeer nodded in slow rhythm and rearranged the folds of an expensive and gaudy greatcoat which lay across his lap. That was a gesture characteristic of Flash Singleton. "But I got news."

"No news," declared Big John, biting off the words, "is important enough to bring you here. It ain't safe for neither one of us. People might misunderstand."

"Let 'em," said Singleton succinctly. "Did you know Jerry Frost was in town?"

Big John's eyes lighted and he stepped back a pace or two. For a moment he was motionless. Then he removed the stub of the black cigar from his mouth and hurled it against the wall. It struck with a soft, liquid squish and left a brown smudge. There were innumerable smudges of the same color.

"Frost?"

"Yeh." Singleton laid his greatcoat on the desk and thumped his soft felt hat back on his head. "And you don't need but one guess. DeWitt fell apart in that Rio Honda mess and loud-mouthed."

Dawson shook his massive head. "Nope—he was a four-flusher and he was cocky, but he wouldn't squeal."

"Then what's Frost doing here? This ain't a health resort!" He sat back and released the venom. "That guy has messed with me for the last time. Get that? The *last* time! Them lousy Rangers—"

He was biting off the words through the side of his mouth. Big John Dawson knew the signs. "Now, lissen," he said. "There ain't gonna be no chopping, Flash. Not with this fellow. You may as well understand that right now—no chopping! Your gorillas get Frost and we may as well pack up."

Singleton cut him off with a thump. His hand banged the top of the desk. His eyes narrowed. As from habit his right hand snaked to the specially tailored pocket in his coat. Flash Singleton never took a chance.

"Get a load of this, Dawson—and get it in a hurry. I'll run my business like I double damn please and no flat-foot is gonna tell me where to get off. You're on *my* payroll, not his. You gotta nerve!"

"Oh, hell, Flash, you get yourself worked up—" His tone was conciliatory.

"All right, all *right*. I'm worked up then! I gotta license to be worked up, ain't I? Frost staggers in, Petrone's mob spots me, and you barge around all over the place like you don't give a damn. That's worry, ain't it?"

"Sure," Big John Dawson, still conciliatory, agreed. "Sure." The reckless aggressiveness of his visitor had reduced his height and the strength of his voice. "But look at this thing sensibly. If you chop Frost the whole pack of 'em 'll be down on us. There ain't no use you getting in a sweat because a Ranger comes to town. I'm the one who ought to worry."

"Oh, yeah?" Singleton was contemptuous. "Say, do I look like I just drove in with a load of turnips? What the hell's happened to your thinking machine? This guy ain't hardly out of the hospital yet—and he comes here. To recuperate, I guess!" He stood up. "Well, I got other ideas. I got Britsu on his tail right now. Frost got a lead in that Rio Honda mess. I ain't dumb!"

"Maybe he did," said Dawson. "But we got to figure—"

"Figuring's out," snapped Singleton. "You keep your eyes open and your hands off!" The racketeer felt pretty much the same about Frost as Dawson did. But he didn't want Dawson to know that he agreed with him. He took his hand out of that specially tailored pocket. "If there's any handling to be done," he said. "I'll do it."

"Okey," said Dawson heavily. He always felt weary after a meeting with Singleton. Singleton was violent. Big John Dawson kept telling himself how much he disliked the racketeer. Singleton domineered him, bulldozed him. Him—Big John Dawson, the hardest copper… Big John kept singing a hymn of hate to himself. Some day his courage would lift. He was trying to get out of Singleton's grip. Well, there was one good way. Some day…

"Take a look outside and see if Al and Capello are there."

One of the hardest coppers who ever stood behind a police shield in Jamestown heeded the command and inserted his huge bulk in the door. He turned back almost at once. "They're there," he announced. He interposed a final warning. "Flash, you'd better take it easy. Frost ain't got a nerve in his body. He's just one long gut."

Singleton paused, his hand on the door and looked back over his shoulder. He was so close to Big John Dawson that his hot breath fanned Dawson's cheek. "I got medicine to cure them guys who think they're brave because the papers say so. If Frost's in for a visit everything's jake. But if he meddles—well, it's just too bad. Nobody's gonna gum up my racket—nobody! Not even Jerry Frost." He glared, and slammed the door.

Outside in the corridor he slipped quickly into his greatcoat, turned up its broad collar, and pulled his soft felt hat down over his eyes. Two hawk-eyed men who had been waiting stepped to either side of him and closed in until they were abreast.

They marched hurriedly out of the corridor, went down the long granite steps to the pave, and stepped into a sleek underslung automobile. The automobile, parked in a restricted zone—Flash Singleton's gesture to the majesty of the traffic ordinances—fluttered its gears and rolled away.

It looked like an ordinary car. But the police of Jamestown long ago discovered it wasn't. It was steel throughout. Its glass was bulletproof, and it weighed enough. It was specially designed and was no less formidable than a tank.

Flash Singleton took no chances.

THE CAR ROLLED down Mulberry Street to Twenty-fifth Avenue, the fringe of the business district, and came to a stop before the yellow marquee of an ornate and garish facade. A resplendent sign proclaimed it *El Algeria.*

It was a cavernous supper-club of modern design which bordered on the cubistic and was Flash Singleton's contribution to the culture of Jamestown. It also was headquarters for him and his handpicked guerrillas.

The door of the automobile swung quickly open and Single-ton with his two guards stepped out, passed under the marquee and disappeared through an enormous, filigreed door. The long sleek car started down the street and soon was lost in the traffic. Flash Singleton had dismissed his mobile arsenal.

He again was behind steel walls.

Down the multicolored interior of *El Algeria* he marched, his men a step behind. His bearing was regal. This was his empire; here came the best (and the worst) of Jamestown, dazzled by its profligate splendor, fascinated by the air of mystery, and pleased by the food and the entertainment. *El Algeria* was safe. Jamestown knew it.

Flash Singleton had gunned his way to the top. He too, was hard and he had not become hard in one day. He was born that way and every day he lived he got harder. He had spent his youth in apprenticeship to the Five Points' gang, four of whom had burned to death in Sing Sing. That was a fitting alma mater—and Flash Singleton was a successful alumnus. He had learned his trade from the masters and improved on their technique.

He had a motto: "Cops like dough and law is just tricks." *El Algeria* proved it.

He marched to the orchestra pit, oblivious of the morbid glances he attracted. He stepped down, nodded to his band boys, turned a corner and disappeared behind a broad mural that flanked the pit. That mural depicted a Conestoga wagon halted on a prairie, with fiercely arrayed Indians in the back-ground. In the foreground lithe pioneers were shouldering their rifles. It was indigenous art—the sort Texas fairly ate up. Singleton liked it too. It concealed a strongroom.

That room was honeycombed with exits and was a well-stocked arsenal.

Singleton never took a chance.

The door clicked behind him and he nodded for his men to sit down. They were his lieutenants.

One of them was slender and wiry. He was a Sicilian. His name was Capello and he was hot-blooded and impetuous. But he was a polished killer. The other lieutenant was square-faced, broad-shouldered. His name was Al Thomas and he looked like a politician out of the mauve decade. He was no politician. He was a former newsboy.

From newsboy he graduated to manager of a domino parlor because he could swing his fists and wasn't afraid of hell or high water. Then he got a job cooking alcohol in a North Side basement for fifteen dollars a day. His ambition soared. He took over a strip of territory to which Vito Petrone believed he had a prior claim. Petrone was Singleton's worst enemy. Petrone sent an emissary to remonstrate with Thomas and Thomas sent him right back—feet first and with four bullets in his skull.

Flash Singleton heard about it, a scout substantiated it and right there and then Al Thomas was drafted for bigger and better things.

They sat there as Singleton explained the new menace in low tones. He finished his speech, lighted a cigarette and leaned back.

"So," he said. "That's all of that. He's the guy that bottled up DeWitt at Rio Honda and confiscated that prize stuff from the islands."

Al Thomas Spat. "Hell," he said, "let's chop him." There was nothing subtle about Thomas.

"Not now," said Singleton. "Maybe Dawson was right. We'd better not get in a hurry."

Capello looked up. His face was sardonic. "Don't wait too long."

"Don't worry. Dawson said any rough stuff would cause hell. Dawson knows more about them than we do."

"Dawson," put in Thomas quietly, "is yellow!"

"That ain't neither here nor there. Sometimes he's a horse and buggy and then sometimes he's pretty smart."

Capello looked up again. "I could get Frost so's nobody would ever know it." Capello spoke lovingly of his art.

"Jeeze!" Singleton exploded. "Don't you bums ever use your conks? No matter who gets him the result'll be the same. Every damn soldier in the state would be down on us. He's—"

"A copper," purred Capello. "And a copper will always be a copper."

"Right!" Thomas agreed heartily. "And this one picks a great time to make his bow. Petrone cut in this side of Twentieth Avenue again. Everything happens at once."

"Yeh?"

"Dumped off a cargo on Nettleton for three-fifty. That's our five-buck line."

"Did you see Nettleton?"

"I'll say." Thomas grinned. "I told him my old man was in the tombstone business and that business was bad. I told him we didn't want any more trouble."

"There won't be." Singleton said pointedly. "The next time you can give Nettleton the works."

From somewhere within the room came the muffled tones of an electric bell. The three men started involuntarily. Al Thomas got up slowly to have a look. Singleton rose, his hand in his pocket. Capello moved to the head of the table and reached for his automatic. Thomas peered through a narrow slot in the door and reached for a button.

A dapper individual swaggered in. His name was Britsu and he handled a sub-machine gun as nonchalantly as a garden hose. He had the somewhat dubious distinction of being the best chopper in the business and it was his boast that when he chopped 'em they stayed chopped.

Singleton asked. "Where's Frost?"

Britsu's olive face broke into a wide grin. "You'd never guess in a million years."

"Ixnay on the funny stuff, comedian. Where is he?"

"You told me to follow him, didn't you. Well, I did."

"Then what the hell are you doing here?" Singleton was getting sore.

"Didn't I say I followed him?"

It took Singleton thirty seconds to figure it out. "You mean," he asked incredulously, "he's here?"

"Right here in old *El Algeria* sitting over in a corner."

"Well, I'm damned!" Singleton said.

"He came straight here. And he never looked anywhere but straight ahead. I had a hundred chances to bump him off," he added a little regretfully.

Singleton bit his lip and looked at Thomas and Capello. He got no inspiration from them. They were dumfounded. That Frost would invade their headquarters never, in their wildest flights, occurred to them. They had never heard that a good offense is the best defense.

"And maybe you'd like to know that a couple of the Petrone

rats were tailing him too." Britsu broke the silence. "They're out to kill somebody."

"A sweet monkey wrench in this machinery," said Thomas.

"I don't see why you guys should get gray trying to figure it," said Britsu. "It looks damn simple to me." His meaning was unmistakable.

Singleton's face flushed and his lips tightened. "Unpin your ears, Britsu, and lissen to this." His voice was strained. "Nobody's gonna fool with Frost—nobody. Not even if we have to shoot those Petrone pimps off his tail."

"But—"

"No buts and no ifs!" Singleton was throwing his slender body between Frost and the storm. Not for altruistic reasons. Not at all. There was something more vital to him at stake than the life of one Texas Ranger. Far more vital. It was his own life. "That guy ain't no common flat and you can't slug him like you would an everyday copper. He's got the whole State behind him and if anything happens to him we'll all get wrapped up in some electric wires. Personally, I don't care a damn about smelling myself cooking!"

But even that vivid picture had no effect on Britsu. He was a supreme egotist. He held all constabularies in utter contempt. "We can't let Frost muscle into this," he said, "not even if he's got the British Navy behind him. We got too much in this game—and I'll gamble with the chair to protect my end. And I don't mean maybe! Frost or no other lousy dick is gonna tear down my playhouse."

The others seemed to take heart from his words.

"Britsu's right," said Thomas. "We can't let this guy—"

"I said—*lay off!*" Singleton fairly shouted the words. He'd seen these incipient mutinies before. He knew how to quell them. His hand went into that coat pocket again. "I'm telling you for the last time—lay off. This is my racket, too. And as long as I'm giving orders they'll be respected." His body trembled and looked weak, but his eyes were clear and his lips firm. And his gun hand was steady. The cheapest thing in the world to Singleton was a human life. Those lieutenants knew it.

Bz-zz-z-z-z! B-z-z-z-z! The warning bell. Singleton himself went to the slot. He was a little excited. He was too emotional, he told himself and cursed. He looked out. It was a waiter.

"What the hell do you want?" he snapped.

"A gentleman—"

"Don't you know I'm busy?"

"Yes, sir, but he insisted. He said you'd know. His name is Frost."

Singleton let the panel back and faced the steel door. That was a wild moment. When he turned around he had himself under control again.

"Well," he observed, "he wants to see us. He thinks maybe we won't come—but he's dead wrong. We'll all go. But get this—there'll be no rough stuff no matter what happens. I don't want nothing to happen to him any time—least of all in this place. Remember—no rough stuff! Come on."

Flash Singleton and his lieutenants passed out through the pit and on to the floor where Jamestown, unaware of the drama that was being unfolded, danced loop-legged. Most everybody was bleary-eyed.

Singleton and his men walked to a table in a corner. A young appearing man sat there. His features were smooth, but his look was hard. In his eyes was the restless light of a man who had known the far places and the dangers that lie therein. He had. He was a former adjutant in the Lafayette Escadrille, a lieutenant in the old 47th, had done a hitch with the Kosciusko in Poland and was known throughout the Latin-American countries as *El Beneficio*—a wild Americano who fought for the love of fighting.

His name was Jerry Frost and he was the commander of the air wing of the Texas Rangers.

Singleton stood before him. His lieutenants moved around in a fan-wise deployment.

"Frost?"

"*Captain* Frost," he emphasized. "Sit down."

"I'm Singleton." Frost's curt answer and his light command had roughened the steel in Singleton's voice. It went all over him. His eyes popped. He instinctively hated him. Frost was self-possessed, and fearless. Other coppers had cringed.

But they sat down. Singleton sat directly opposite Frost. Capello, Thomas and Britsu sat on the edge of their chairs. Their right hands were below the table. Frost grinned. Singleton tried to look as if he was injured. It was a poor effort.

"I don't suppose," Frost said. "I have to tell you why I'm here?"

"Maybe yes, maybe no." Singleton drawled.

"In that case," retorted Frost, his voice just as colorless. "I'll get right down to the point. The Adjutant-General of the State of Texas wants to know how long it will take you to close up and get out of town."

Flash Singleton sat back as if a heavy hand had struck him in the mouth. He tried to speak but could only gurgle. His face went from light purple to white. His gaudy bow tie twitched over his Adam's apple.

"Yeh?" he finally managed. "Strong-arm stuff, eh?"

"Nope," said Frost. "Just a friendly little tip. They've passed the buck to me—and I want to get along as soon as possible. Now how long before you can fold up and breeze? Tomorrow?"

"Lissen," Singleton flamed. "We ain't moving nowhere! But if you're smart *you'll* beat it—the sooner the better. I'll give you a friendly little tip: it ain't healthy for coppers around here."

"So I've heard," Frost returned calmly. He was still at ease. "But I'm bringing you orders from the commander—close up or get closed up. I thought maybe you'd like to know exactly where we stood."

"That's white of you," Singleton sneered, "but we ain't moving today or tomorrow or next week. We're here—and we stay!" He would have given a lot then to lift his gun. His lieutenants were straining at the leash. Under the table their knuckles went white.

"Why," said Frost, "be a damned fool?"

"You ain't got nothing on us. You couldn't get anything on us in a thousand years."

That was a confession that Jamestown's chief and its commissioner were exactly where Singleton wanted them. Singleton couldn't help bragging.

Frost nodded. "Maybe not. I'm just telling you." Frost didn't need any confessions. He had iron clad proof. He also had a fountain pen he had got off the leader of a Border escapade—and that pen had once belonged to Big John Dawson. "Singleton, this is your last night. You're closing tomorrow."

"All right!" Singleton said leaning over the table. "Now I'll give you something. Beat it! Get outta here as fast as you can! There ain't nothing gonna happen while you're in my place—

but the minute you cross that door I ain't responsible. There's been a mob tailing you all day. But that ain't my worry. Now get the hell outta here!"

Frost arose slowly. "Thanks," he said sarcastically. And as he turned away, "Maybe we'll meet again."

"Nope," shot Singleton. "I ain't going where you are!"

The Ranger turned his back. Capello's hand came up with lightning speed and an automatic gleamed.

Singleton threw his arm against the Sicilian's wrist. The gun rattled on the table and was quickly swept out of sight. "You filthy wop!" he grunted. "Have you lost your mind? Britsu!" Britsu looked and Singleton nodded.

Britsu got up and walked away. Thomas sauntered off. Then Capello. Singleton sat still. He sat where everybody could see him. He was framing his alibi.

CAPTAIN FROST WALKED out into the star-studded night still unaware of the enormous effrontery of his visit to *El Algeria*. He saw nothing particularly courageous in it; it merely was the easiest way out. He knew his assignment should have been handled by the metropolitan police and would have been had not Singleton's money flowed into the city hall in an undiminishing stream. Singleton long ago had learned that some men who pound a beat for a hundred and fifty a month can be induced to look the other way five minutes a night for a century note; that some officers come a little higher and that some chiefs and commissioners come even-higher yet. It was his business to find who they were and to charge the expense to overhead.

So Jamestown was wide open. And the Rangers had been given the job....

Nights always were impressive to Jerry Frost. He remembered them best of all. Particularly the soft nights in the tropics... Oblivious to the traffic rumbles he walked on and on. Nights... there was that time in Belize when an outraged father found him holding a warm-lipped daughter close... and Rima... that was in San Salvador... in the shadows of the old mission north of Santa Tecla... Rima was exquisite... but her old man was supporting Cabuya and Frost was fighting for Diaz... Right after that he went over to help Maranga in Rio Rita... old fat Maranga...

Frost walked on and on. He had no way of knowing that an automobile was slowly following him; that two pairs of eyes were focused on him.

Captain Frost was on the spot.

He became aware suddenly that danger was near. Intuition broke through his reveries with a crash. He was crossing an alley between two buildings. He felt a rush of damp air, and his hair stood on end. Danger. He sensed it then, completely awake.

He cleared the alley in a single leap. He had a picture of an assassin hidden there. He never knew how to account for that hunch, just as he never knew how to account for any of the others that had stood him in such stead at some time or other. But this hunch dwarfed all the others. The hesitation of a fraction of a second would have been fatal.

The tinny echoes of a machine-gun broke through the traffic roars. A jet of orange spurted from an automobile tonneau. Lead slugs thudded into the side of the building like raindrops on a slate roof. The automobile whirled around a corner and was lost.

In a purely mechanical move Frost darted into a protecting doorway. He tried to think but couldn't. His thoughts were colliding with each other. He stood there until he felt foolish. The automobile was gone. The attack was ended. He went back to the alley and picked up a handful of twisted lead slugs. He grinned like an abashed school boy and dropped them in his pocket.

So they were spotting him. Well, he reflected, he was glad they were talking with machine-guns. That was a language he understood.

He carefully made his way to the hotel. Fifteen minutes later he had the Adjutant-General of the State of Texas on the wire.

IT WAS SHORTLY after dawn the following morning that the old-fashioned wall telephone jangled in the little frame building at Gentry that was headquarters of the Texas Air Rangers on the Mexican Border. An individual who had, until that moment, lain like a log, rolled over and blinked his eyes in the glare of a young sun. Young but powerful for all its youth.

The telephone jangled again. He sat up. He was Hans Traub and he loved his sleep. But he was wide awake now. The big ex-Bavarian always came awake fast. He smothered a perfect yawn and got up.

"Hello!" he shouted in the instrument. He listened for a moment and cleared his throat "Yes, sir," he said respectfully. He glued his ear to the receiver and repeated the "yes, sirs," for two minutes. Then he hung the receiver up and faced the bunks.

"Hey!"

Three forms did not stir.

"Hey!"

Hans Traub muttered and yanked the cover off each bed. He popped each man loudly with his open hand.

"Hey there!" he shouted, "Jerry's in a bad way!"

The three forms roused themselves.

"Jerry—" said Traub. "Let's go!" Sullenly they began dressing. "Who the hell moved my cigarettes?" demanded Eddie Giles. He was the baby member of this outfit—Hell's Stepsons. Nobody paid him any attention.

"Jerry's got himself in a jam," Traub remarked, pulling on his shirt.

"Where?" asked Skipper Hinsdell.

"Jamestown. They took some shots at him last night. The old man said it looked bad."

"Gimme a cigarette," said Giles, stamping into his boots.

"Pipe down, infant," said Hinsdell.

"We got business to tend to."

Rowdy Perry merely grunted. He was inclined to be something of a dilettante. Rowdy had a peculiar aversion to any sort of early reveille. It was a hangover from the old days at Issoudun and Colombey les Belles.

They dressed and went to the hangar.

Little Johnny Rosenfield, stubby mechanic who was the best rough and tumble fighter who ever bunked in Romorantin, met them with a question in his mild blue eyes.

"We're shoving off," said Traub. "We're joining Captain Frost at Jamestown."

Rosenfield cupped his hands and barked into an adjoining room: "The dawn patrol!"

A couple of less important mechanics sauntered out fully

dressed. A lot of them sleep full pack in the Border country.

They wheeled four ships to the starting line and twisted the propellers. The blades caught with a roar and a rush of air, rose and fell as the pilots goosed the throttles.

Rosenfield came out of the hangar with an armful of belts and dumped one in each plane. It was ammunition.

"Set?" he shouted.

They nodded. He lifted his hands and the blocks came out. There was a whirl as the backwash rose and one by one the planes lifted. From their wings and fuselages gleamed the orange longhorn's heads, insignia of the Air Rangers.

The planes circled and headed northeast.

THERE IS AN old saw in Texas that it takes but one Ranger to quell one riot. Jamestown sat open-mouthed when four more of them moved up, making the five that comprised Jerry Frost's crack air squadron.

Their names were plastered in the papers often. Those names had news value. Captain Jerry Frost, Hans Traub, Skipper Hinsdell, Rowdy Perry and Eddie Giles—either of those would have been good for a double column head in the *Times*. The five together meant a spread.

The four arrived shortly after noon and when they got to the hotel they found their commander lying full length in a sample room that had been converted into temporary headquarters.

"Greetings," he said.

Traub snorted disdainfully. "We expected a corpse," he said. "Where did you get hit?"

"I didn't," said Frost. "But it wasn't my fault."

"Mightn't it have been a bad dream?" asked Hinsdell.

"*Might* have been," said Frost. He pointed to the bed.

They saw a score or more grisly souvenirs. They were twisted lead slugs.

Frost grinned. "Was I dreaming?"

Perry slowly shook his head and stared at the bullets. "They must be tough eggs."

"Not now," said Frost "They had to be tough to get the way they are now. I've heard a lot of bullets in my time, but never any that sounded like those. They were dirty."

"Part of that Rio Honda gang?" asked Traub. Traub was thorough. He was incisive. He was Teutonic.

"Undoubtedly," replied Frost. "Singleton's got a graft here that's a knockout. The chief and some higher-ups are either hog-tied or scared. These babies around here murder merely for the exercise."

"Well," said Perry, "I'm no prize beauty in a ground fight, but the old man said we were going to clean up this town and his orders got to be filled I 'spose."

"Maybe," said Giles, "we'll get to do a little cloud-bustin', too."

They regarded him curiously. It was not so much what he said as the way he said it. Eddie Giles was a youngster but that sounded old. Come to think of it, he was both young and old. Those lads who lived through the fiery baptism at Arras usually were.

"Meaning what?" asked Frost. Ordinarily he wouldn't have paid any attention.

"I saw something coming in."

"What was it?"

"Seaplanes."

"Seaplanes?"

"Sure—seaplanes. It looked kinder odd." He reached into Hinsdell's pocket and got a cigarette, took Frost's butt and lighted it. He inhaled deeply. "They were haulin' 'em in a hangar on that lake just north of town. I sort of got the idea—"

"Yeah?"

"—that maybe we weren't supposed to see 'em. And then I got to thinking that was a perfect set-up for running stuff in from the Gulf."

The phlegmatic Traub said: "That's an idea."

Captain Frost flipped his cigarette butt into the gobboon, smiled at his marksmanship, and blinked his eyes at Giles. It made Eddie a little sore. Frost always did that when he didn't believe the story he heard.

"Look here," he flared, "are you trying to insinuate I didn't see what I saw?"

"Not at all," said Frost quietly. "But I'm damned if I see anything odd in a couple of seaplanes on some lake. That's where they're supposed to be. Anyway, we've got enough trouble right in this man's town." He looked out of the window for a moment and his eyes saw an office wherein people worked. He regarded them enviously and then went on. "I'm sort of glad we finally got together in this thing. It won't be any cinch—you can lay to that. This business might cause some of us—I mean—if—oh, hell—" his voice trailed off and he looked out the window again. He couldn't say what he wanted to.

But there was no need. They understood.

"Righto!" said Giles.

"Sure," said Hinsdell.

Hans Traub grunted, "*Ja!*" and let it go at that.

Rowdy Perry didn't say anything. He just stared. They were pretty close together then. Giles wondered if he hadn't better say something. Somebody ought to.

"Jerry," he said, "I got a dame in this burg who is dying to meet me. How about me running out there for a little while?"

"Dear, dear," remarked Traub. "Don't you know all the mamas heard you were on the way and locked up their daughters?"

Eddie was unruffled. "On the level," he said. "That dame would never live over it."

"I'd rather not have you splitting around, Eddie," Frost protested mildly. "I got a lot of lead dumped at me last night—"

"But," laughed Giles irrepressibly, "*I'm* not a famous airry-plane pilot, *Mister* Frost." He laughed again infectiously. Frost laughed, too. Giles went in to slick up a bit. It was bluff, of course—this dame business. He wanted another look back at that lake, but he didn't want the boys to know it if he found nothing.

ALONE IN HIS office sat Big John Dawson, elbow on his desk and his chin in his hand. He was worried. He stared at a wall that was yellow plaster, on which hung portraits of a few old-time predecessors, and on which were many brown smudges. He swayed back and forth in his chair, and came back upright to hold his head again. He was worried—and the thought nettled him. He was either getting old or weak, he didn't know which. He was a hard copper, and hard coppers never worried about anything. If they did, something was wrong. And here he was worrying.

Headlines blazed from the afternoon papers. Hell's Stepsons were in town. Something big was doing. The papers hinted at it. Big John snorted. Hell! Of course something big was doing. And he was in the middle of it. Hell's Stepsons. He rolled the words off his tongue in an undertone.

Why hadn't he let Singleton chop Frost?

For the life of him he couldn't tell. Nor did he know that, in spite of him, Singleton had made an effort. Frost was alive at that moment by the grace of Providence. Big John told himself he should have let Singleton have his way. The more he thought about it the sorer he got. What in hell had he been thinking of anyway?

He'd never been opposed to chopping before—a vicious term that means exactly what it implies, turning the muzzle of a machine-gun at somebody and letting go. Big John was not opposed to that. His finer sensibilities might have revolted if he'd stopped to think about it, but he didn't stop to think about anything. He was in too deep. Big John wasn't scrupulous about how his victims shuffled off.

He was an old-timer. Twenty years he'd spent in crime, and he knew it outside and inside and down through the middle. He knew it too well. Long acquaintance with crime in all its phases had developed a sort of false security. That had got him mixed up with Singleton. In the crafty hands of the gangster, Big John was so much putty.

He'd never earned more than $4500 a year in his life, and when Singleton handed him five one-thousand-dollar bills one night it took his breath. That was more money than he'd ever seen in one bunch before. He fell and didn't even look back. And it had kept coming.

For nothing at all. Really, just some trifle that didn't matter, some little violation that nobody would have thought anything about. Nothing big, you understand. Singleton was too subtle for that. But Big John was nailed. Singleton finally put the pressure on him—and made him like it.

Flash Singleton was bad medicine. Dawson knew that. It's a wonder everybody didn't. He'd come to Texas in a trail of blood and settled in Jamestown. The metropolis of the most expansive state in the Union was the strategic point for contraband trade from Mexico. Jamestown had had crime before Singleton got there, but it was bushleague stuff. Singleton was a high-powered executive. He took the bush leaguers and made them into big leaguers. In the process of this education it was necessary to buy police. And Singleton was no piker. He bought the big boys.

Jamestown was virgin territory, and no sooner had Singleton settled it than hard after him came Vito Petrone, a tough from Chicago, who set himself up in direct competition. Big league stuff was Petrone's forte, too, and he found he couldn't buy the cops. They were already bought. So he imported visitors from other parts.

They came with hardware in their baggage and murder in their eyes. Singleton's guerillas massacred them as fast as they came in, and a few of the wise ones beat it out again. For the first two years there was a lot of murders. Singleton was a messy killer. He had no more technique than a bull elephant. He used to leave them lying about the streets with their heads half blown away. The results were effective on others.

Jamestown was, by degrees, shocked, appalled, indignant. One courageous newspaper could have checked it. But Singleton was in big business. He would tolerate no sort of interference. He was allied with heavy advertisers. A big advertiser can stop anything he wants to in most provincial newspapers. Advertisers in Jamestown ruled the press. They had their choice—minimize crime or lose contracts. They minimized crime.

In the day of free speech it was unbelievable. Free speech in Jamestown was a lot of hokum. Singleton....

Big John Dawson sat and stared at the wall and thought about it.

His telephone rang, and he swore roundly.

"Hello," he grunted. Then he said, "Right away."

He stood up. That call was from his commissioner. The commissioner's ire was prodded. Every time that happened the blow fell on Big John Dawson. He swore again and went out into the hall.

In the hall he passed detectives, plainclothes men, uniformed patrolmen, hangers-on, and said nothing. He didn't so much as nod. Behind their hands they whispered. "My God, the lion's loose again." Then they looked the other way and embarked on considerable speculation as to what had happened. There was a lot of intrigue in the Jamestown police department. Somebody was always being reduced or promoted. Big John Dawson's moods were infallible barometers of headquarters atmosphere.

He got into the elevator, mumbled, "Fourth," and refused to look at the asinine Commissioner of Public Works who was trying to get a wedge in so he could make a crack about Hell's Stepsons. He got off at the fourth floor and walked by the luxurious city offices where weak-jawed men sprawled and let ward-heelers tell them what to do. He passed into the office of his immediate superior, nodded abstractedly at the secretary, and moved across the threshold of the inner sanctum. He thumbed the night latch on the door from force of habit and looked up. A man sat at the central desk.

"Hello, John," he said.

He was a cadaverous individual of fifty years or more who had lived in Jamestown a decade. Before that nobody knew anything about him. Nobody cared. All you had to do to get elected was get on the right side. For ten years he had been what is called an upstanding citizen, which means little. He looked as if he was stupid and dull and that he needed a guardian to handle his business and a guide to help him get through the traffic without losing a leg.

But he was nothing of the sort.

He was stupid and dull like a fox and might have been another Singleton if his early environment had been the same. The first lesson he learned in public office was that the newspaper men in his town were lazy and traveled in packs, were underpaid and would sell their memory for a suit of clothes, a fifty-dollar bill and a quart of gin. Most any of them would forget plenty for that. His next lesson was to learn that every newspaper was afraid of the stringent libel laws, and that he could get away with murder as long as he covered it with a coating of patriotism.

Yes. Big John Dawson's commissioner was stupid and dull.

He looked up at the massive form before him, his eyes glinting along the brass buttons. His fingers touched an afternoon paper.

"I suppose you've seen the papers?" he asked testily.

"Hell, I can't forget 'em," replied Big John. He sat down and lighted a cigar from the humidor in an open drawer.

The commissioner clucked, slapped the drawer shut with a bang, and said: "What does it mean?"

"How should I know?" demanded the chief. "Maybe the Adjutant-General is getting ready to run for governor. It looks like one of them lousy election gags."

"Not to me, it doesn't," said the commissioner bluntly. "It looks like they marched a little hell right in our own backyard. What'd Singleton say?"

"Plenty. Was all for chopping Frost and I had a weak moment and talked him out of it. I wish to God I'd let him alone now."

"Yeah?" The word crackled. "Dawson, you're losing your guts. They're wrapping you around the head with a rubber hose and you're cavin' in just like a hophead after his shot wears off. If you'd touched Frost we'd been nailed to the cross. Now, I want you to pass the word along to let those guys have a free hand. Let 'em do anything they want to. Cooperate with 'em—and don't be jealous. Send your men out to round up some gang-sters. I don't give a damn whose they are. We've got to fill the jails. And we don't want any gunplay. The last time one of your cops got excited and killed a guy I had to make a personal visit down to the newspapers to keep it out. You gotta be careful. I can't keep murders out of the papers forever.

"As you go out tell Miss Fanning to send in the reporters. You might break up that dice game in the downstairs press room and have all the weak-minded police reporters come up too. Tell 'em I've got on my whiskers and red clothes and something for their stockings. That'll get 'em!"

"All right," said Big John. He was at the door.

"And Dawson," went on the commissioner in that same hurried tone, "don't lose your guts!"

Dawson nodded and went out.

Ten minutes later the commissioner was surrounded by

newspaper men. He was issuing orders of the day. It was a patriotic message to the Jamestown citizenry and felicitations to the Rangers. The newspaper men were diligently at work. There were two reasons and both lay before the commissioner.

One was a bundle of bills.

The other was a bottle with the cork out.

FIVE HOURS LATER Eddie Giles opened the door of the room occupied by Hell's Stepsons, stepped inside and said, "Guess what?"

Captain Frost stopped shuffling a deck of cards and said: "Where the hell have you been?"

"Out at the lake. I found out something."

"Yeah, we know," said Traub. "You found out the water was wet."

"No, something about the seaplanes."

Hans Traub squared around in his chair. He saw Giles was serious. And he became serious. They were flying buddies. "How does it happen you go running around without me?" he demanded. "Suppose you'd got your head knocked off, eh?"

"Lay off, Hans," said Frost. "Give him a chance."

"Well, it was like this. I went out there to see if I really saw those boats. And I did. I got into the hangar, too. They've got pontoon-buses and they've got guns behind on tourelles. They're running stuff in from the Gulf and I'll bet my life on it. It looked to me like they're ready for action any time."

"So am I," grumbled Hinsdell. "I've been in this damn room so long I'm nervous as a bad lady in church."

Frost smiled and said, "Keep your shirt on, Skip. You'll be having plenty of fun soon. Things are starting now."

Things were. Realizing the exigency of the situation, the police raided eight places and arrested a score of men, but Frost knew those places were maintained only to be raided when the emergency arose.

"We're going down to Singleton's tonight, Eddie," Frost said.

"Closing time's come for 'em. I told them and they didn't even say maybe. In fact, said they wouldn't. So we're doing it for them."

At 10:30 o'clock that night the five men strapped on their gun belts, five men whose master was the law—above the earth, under the earth and on the earth.

"There'll be no kidding," said Frost. "If it gets rough aim at their noses. And stay together. *Andale!*"

Their destination was *El Algeria.*

MULTICOLORED LIGHTS BLINKING in an otherwise drab night. Long lines of parked automobiles. Faint strains of music. Fainter laughter. A little hilarity.

Five men moving slowly up the pave.

The footman cocked a suspecting head. They looked odd to him. Grim. And stags seldom travel in fives. He thought they'd pass by. But they didn't. His dander rose and, just as quickly, fell. They compelled respect. He nodded. The doorman nodded. He was got up like an emperor's lackey. He grinned as if he paid for the privilege of wearing that Christophe outfit.

The five men stepped through the portals. The faint music was now coarse and cacaphonous; it hammered about their ears. *El Algeria's* band was getting hot. The lights were diffused... festoonings swayed idly and tiny lights flickered in a dome some sign-painter tried to make look like heaven... perfumes... exclusive...

Captain Frost led the way down the room beside the wall. Hell's Stepsons had no compunction. They shoved half-tight dancers out of their path. Everybody seemed plastered. Ahead of Captain Frost loomed an individual whose expression would stamp him even if his garb didn't. He was the head waiter. The Ranger stopped.

The head waiter recognized him. He started, his lips framed a sentence that was never uttered. The expression on Frost's face froze it. The head waiter hesitated and in that moment was overcome by a rush of obeisance.

"Yes, sir?"

"Get Singleton," was the quiet order.

The head waiter glided into the crowd. Captain Frost stepped backward to the wall. It was a lesson—ay, a bitter lesson—he had learned in the tropics. The reasons were clear. Hell's Stepsons did likewise.

By now they were being regarded curiously. A newspaper man who had initiative and imagination and had anticipated trouble was there and he whispered to his companion. "That's them—Hell's Stepsons." In a moment the warning had gone the length and breadth of the room.

"Hell's Stepsons!"

Dancers slowed up, idled and finally stopped and stared. They were, to be sure, in the cups, but not too far to be insensible of the sudden tension which had been raised. They congested, formed a sort of semi-circle. They were familiar, collectively and individually, with this group of men. They were fighters who had marched up and down the world seeking adventure. They were Hell's Stepsons—a name plastered on by a movie press agent and now quite permanent. Not a woman of those who looked failed to admire; not a man failed to envy… Hell's Stepsons against the wall, their faces set.

The crowd parted and Flash Singleton was disgorged. Behind him came his bodyguard. They resembled nothing so much as rattlers.

"Well?" said Singleton, his face in a cast of hate. His hand was inside his pocket. His every nerve was on edge.

Captain Frost's expression was unchanged. "I told you," he said. "Last night you tried to get me. Tell those people to get out. You're closing up!"

The flame in Singleton's eyes leaped.

"Like hell, I will," he blustered. "I got an injunction which orders you to let me and my business alone!"

He was falling back on the law—the law he had always maintained was "just tricks."

"That won't work this time, Singleton," said Frost quietly but forcefully. "That injunction is no good—not even if the Supreme Court issued it. You're closing up, and by God, you're closing right now!"

Frost's teeth were in the words. Hell's Stepsons shifted their positions slightly. They took a little more room. Singleton's lieutenants widened their base. Both sides were ready to shoot it out. The crowd, as if impelled by a great magnet, moved closer.

Singleton's rage mounted. He was being made to look absurd. Nothing is more maddening to a gang chief. Their pride is deeply etched. Singleton's eyes were narrowing.

Frost knew what was going on behind those slits.

"Any rough stuff," he said tersely, "and you babies burn in the big chair. This is your finish, Singleton. Tell 'em to get out."

Meantime the head waiter had got word to the band that

gun play was imminent. The tempo of the music straightway increased. The band had been rehearsed for just such moments. It blared forth *fortissimo*. The snare drum popped in staccato explosions that sounded like pistol shots. The snare drummer knew what it was all about.

Flash Singleton's heart came back with the music. His courage rose. "I told you," he said, "that I wasn't moving. That still goes!"

Frost nodded and spoke to the crowd in trenchant words. "You people will please leave quietly and at once. This place is being closed by the orders of the Adjutant-General of the State of Texas."

Those who couldn't hear what he said divined his message, and the crowd slowly moved out. Some of them were reluctant to leave.

Singleton moved his arms in the faintest sort of gesture.

"Stay where you are, Singleton," Frost said.

The music reached new heights of loudness. Hell's Stepsons stood resolutely. After a while the hall cleared. Only the racketeers and the Rangers remained, facing each other across a ten-foot gap of highly polished floor.

"Singleton," Frost said, "I want you for attempt to murder and a few other little things. If you're smart you'll come along quietly."

Frost took a step forward. Singleton took a step backward. The lights unexpectedly went off. The hall was in the blackest sort of darkness.

Crack!

A ruddy glow lit the interior. A bullet pinged into the wall behind Hans Traub.

"Ugh!" the Ex-Bavarian grunted. He dropped to the floor and leveled down on a silhouette. He fired and rolled over.

Bang! Bang! Bang!

Crack! Crack!

There was a symphony of explosions. The powder smoke was acrid. It stung their nostrils.

Flat on his belly in front of his men was Jerry Frost. Every time there was a roar and a flash before him he fired in that direction. When the roars and flashes ceased, he stopped. Hell's Stepsons warily waited. There was no more firing. There was the sound of rapid footbeats instead. They ceased. Hell's Stepsons waited a little longer. The only sound was the rise and fall of their breaths. Even those sounded loud.

Frost wriggled forward, his hand touched something and he shuddered and snatched it back. He lay quietly and waited. He reached out again. The something did not move. He felt further. It was a body.

He rolled over and spoke in a whisper.

"Skipper?"

"Okey."

"Hans?"

"Ziemlich wohl!"

"Eddie?"

"Stinko, old thing, stinko—" Traub cut him off with a muttered oath.

"Rowdy?"

Perry grunted. "Turn on those damned lights."

Frost crawled to the inert form and dragged it back to where they lay. "I got a surprise package here and it's just about blotto," he said. "Now let's get out before those yeggs bring back a load of *minniewerfers*."

They got up, flexed their arms and breathed a bit easier. All of a sudden there was a pounding on the door. Hell's Stepsons dropped back on their bellies.

The door burst open and there was a scuffling of feet that sounded like a frightened army. Flashes of light darted about the place.

Frost said dryly: "The cops."

Perry said: "Yep, the cops. Right on time as usual."

The cops pulled up at the five figures on the floor and concentrated their lights on them. Hell's Stepsons made no move to rise. It didn't occur to them that they presented an inelegant spectacle.

It was more than inelegant to Inspector Bill Turnax. It was downright funny. So he guffawed loudly. Metropolitan police and Texas Rangers are never very compatible.

"Well, well, well!" Turnax laughed. "If it ain't Captain Jerry Frost. He faw down and go boom!" He laughed again. The cops joined in.

"I'd like to sock him in the nose," said Hinsdell.

"What the hell?" said Frost.

Turnax stopped laughing and his flashlight stopped dancing. "Yeh—what the hell? We get a report of a gun fight and break our necks getting over here to find the joint dark and boy scouts all over the floor."

Hinsdell said: "Another crack and I'm gonna bust him!"

"The boy scouts darkened the joint," Frost said derisively. "And the boy scouts closed it up too. How you like them apples?" Frost sprang to his feet.

Inspector Turnax muttered something that was inaudible. Then, plainly: "You closed *this* place."

"Tight as a drum! And for good measure we shot some of the boys in their pants."

Turnax fumed. "You're getting highhanded." A light fell on the lifeless form. It lay in a pool of blood.

"My God! You've killed somebody! Take the body, men!"

That made Frost sore. He got the inspector's arm and whirled him around.

"Lissen, copper—lay off! You're not riding to glory on my shirttails tonight. This is mine—and I keep him. You bust in here an hour late and then want to take charge. Well, you can't do it! Pick him up, fellows, and let's go!"

And go they did. They carried the body as if it were a slender sack of meal.

They took it to the morgue. It was Britsu. You could have driven a truck through the hole in his chest. A forty-five automatic at close quarters is bad stuff.

They searched him, found four-hundred odd dollars, some change, a thirty-eight revolver that had not been fired and a little black book that was about three inches long, two inches wide and an inch thick.

Captain Frost opened it, gasped, shut hurriedly and saw the undertaker had noted it. He stuck it in his pocket. They stood around a while and went out to the street.

The blackness was beginning to fade from the sky before a full moon and the clouds were slowly lifting. The cool air beat on Frost's cheek. Out ahead the traffic was still rolling and nobody seemed to realize what had been done. It always struck Frost as odd that after a big scrap the world moved just the same.

"Jerry," said Giles, "those guys have beat it for those seaplanes. We've got 'em nailed and they know it, let's have a look."

Ordinarily Frost would have been amused at that. He would have argued. He was the arguing kind. But occasionally something clicked with him. There was no speculating then, no dispute, no loss of motion. It clicked and that was all. It did now.

"Maybe," he said, "you're right. The air'll do us good. What do you think?"

"I think," said Eddie, "they're beating it for the Gulf. Singleton's smart. He made arrangements for it."

They got one of the mortuary sedans and started for Withers Field. Captain Frost pulled at the visor of his cap and buttoned the flap of the pocket that held the little black book.

BIG JOHN DAWSON personally dragged in Vito Petrone, personally docketed a charge, and went into his office. He was tired. He was all fagged out. His nerves were raw and he was desperate. Otherwise he never would have arrested Vito Petrone. Under normal conditions he wouldn't have touched him with a twenty-foot pole. Petrone knew too much. The wop would welcome the chance to talk.

Big John Dawson was in a hard way. He knew crime and all its ramifications. But nothing else. He felt rather vaguely that things were happening. He was fighting against a maelstrom... and it was sucking at him...

He wasn't particularly surprised when he learned *El Algeria* had been raided and that Britsu had been rubbed out. It only served to loosen more of his grip. His world was slipping fast.

Inspector Turnax came in. Big John was in no mood to talk to anybody, "Beat it, Bill," he said. "I'm busy."

One look at his chief told Turnax a lot of things. He hardly knew the figure before him. No longer was it square-shouldered. It's chin high. It was round and flabby. Dawson's face was lined, the flatness in his eyes conspicuous. Turnax had been in the business a long time too, and he was no sap. He knew.

Something akin to sympathy welled within. Turnax was on the square and he was hard—but in that moment he knew his chief had been crooked. And Big John knew he knew it. But they had stood side by side and shot it out in too many dark alleys not to feel deeply for each other. Dawson had been Turnax's pal. And Turnax was loyal.

"Take it easy," he said. "You've got to hear this some time—and I'd rather tell you myself."

Big John looked up. "Tell me what?" he demanded harshly. He tried to bluster. But the effort was lame.

"Well," the inspector began, fumbling over his words. Conversation wasn't easy. "Well, after it was all over we came back by the morgue to take a look. They'd got Britsu. Later on we picked up Capello. He asked us about the book."

"Book? What book?"

"Frost got a book off Britsu—a little black book. Capello had come back looking for it. He said Singleton gave it to Britsu so's if he was picked up, he wouldn't have it. Britsu got bumped off—and Frost got the book that had all the names in it."

"Yeh," said Dawson weakly.

"It was Singleton's payroll."

Big John slumped down in his chair. His head drooped. The bottom had fallen out. He made no pretense of hiding it from his inspector. Twenty years it had taken him... long years. And now...

"Well, so long, Bill," he managed. His voice was queer. It sounded like that of an utter stranger. "You'd better grab some sleep, Bill. It's been a tough night. And it'll be just as tough tomorrow."

He got up enough courage to look at Turnax. He was a fine figure of a man, slender and narrow like a tent-pole and a good head on top of it. A fine figure. Once upon a time...

"Bill," he half whispered, "don't ever let 'em get you. Don't ever take a tie, Bill—or anything. It's easy to start."

He looked again. So did Turnax. Turnax had no illusions about the game. It was a tough master. You worked all your life for something and when you were just about to get it—pouf! And it was gone. Bill Turnax knew. In that instant he renewed his oath of the service... faithful... honest...

He clamped his jaw. "Well, so long, John. The wife 'll be sitting up." It takes a moment of tragedy like that to make a man think of his wife.

"So long, Bill. And—oh, Bill—phone the missus for me, will you? Tell her I've got to stick around and not to get upset. Mind?"

"Sure not, John. So long."

"So long," he said.

The door closed softly.

For a long time Big John sat there without moving. Just sat and stared. Then he pushed the cap back on his head and wiped off the stream of perspiration that had been dammed by the tight rim. He reached for the telephone.

"Hello," he said. "Hello... Commissioner? Dawson... Heard

about the raid?… Oh, Singleton's place, of course… Say, Frost's men bumped off Britsu and got a book off him… yeah… you know what that means… yeah… s'long."

He replaced the receiver and grinned. He got up and took his gun out of its holster and laid it on the desk. He looked at it as if it was a fetish. Well, in a way it was. He'd lived by it for twenty years… a hard copper. And now… he'd always said when he went he wanted to go with his boots on…

He picked up the gun. Then he moved to the wall and snapped off the lights.

THE HANGARS AT Withers Field lay in the night like elephants plopped down in the middle of a safari. Red lights shone from the windcone towers, an enormous spotlight revolved from the top of a transport office.

Hell's Stepsons rolled up to Hangar Four and stirred the mechanics. Captain Frost tersely barked orders. The mechanics looked goofy and said: "Huh?"

"Damn it!" said Frost. "The flood lights! We're going up!"

Inside Hangar Four it suddenly became day. In a moment the field lights went on. The battle planes of the Rangers were rolled to the tarmac.

"Eddie," yelled Frost, "you're in front this time."

One motor coughed and caught. Another. And another. Dull red flames poured from their exhausts. Hell's Stepsons buckled on their helmets.

Frost yelled, "Keep those lights on until we get back!"

"Okey, sir!"

"Ready, Eddie?"

"All set!"

"Let's go!"

Eddie Giles was up and in his pit in almost a single motion. He snapped his goggles in place, checked the wind, and fluttered his hand. The others signaled ready and Giles bounced out, the first off. He was to point the course. He bumped across the field and turned. Behind him lumbered four things made monstrosities by the night and the bright floodlights. They turned too.

Giles shot into the air. They skyrocketed after him.

A few passing motorists slowed down, shook their heads and went on. All flyers were crazy anyway.

Hell's Stepsons roared over the broad expanse of water that was the lake. It lay like a bubble lacquered in moonlight. Around the fringe were glows from the resorts and bathhouses. A few automobiles crawled along, their feeble lights heightening the weird effect. In the distance was the recrudescence that was the metropolis.

Eddie Giles swooped low in front of the hangar where he had seen the seaplanes. He had marked it well. He hedgehopped, widened his bank and saw it was empty. Of course, it would be. The seaplanes were headed for the Gulf and freedom.

He zoomed back into formation, stood in his cockpit and motioned forward. He slipped into his pet position in the seat, stuck the nose of his A3 on the course and loaded his guns. He looked at his board. Air speed 150. Altitude 2500. R.P.M. 1750. Bank indicator neutral. His motor was humming like a mad metronome. Eddie Giles grinned. God, but it was great to be back home!

Behind him rode the Rangers.

Straightaway for two hours he held the air lane that was the shortest route to the Gulf. That left him an hour to gamble. The A3's carried fuel for six hours but the margin was never pressed.

As they roared over the city that was Houston, Hell's Stepsons cast anxiously about in the clear night for some sign of their quarry. They should have been overtaken by now. The seaplanes could not do more than an even hundred. The A3's could do around a hundred and eighty if pressed.

The thought that they might return empty-handed stung them like a hot wire.

Then ahead and to the right two moth-like shapes were seen. Giles first thought it was a mirage. The night plays queer tricks on a flyer's imagination. He leaned forward and closed his throttle a little.

Those moth-like forms were the seaplanes.

Before he could signal Hell's Stepsons there was a jagged crimson burst from ahead that cut through his wings. He felt his plane stagger under the impact.

"Whoosh!" he ejaculated.

He climbed, the lead still eating at his plane. The flexible guns were shooting at him—the guns on the tourelle. They could be fired from any angle. He flattened out and leaped ahead.

Hell's Stepsons, he saw, were climbing behind him. They were taking no chances on those enemy guns.

In the hands of a cool man those tourelle guns are infinitely more to be feared than the guns on the cowl. They can be maneuvered before the best pilot can move his ship. The only solution in that case is to run for it or have a comrade draw their fire.

Frost was trying to do that. He was jockeying. He nosed over, thinking he was out of range, and a double burst raked his fins as a sort of warning that his judgment was bad. He went into a drop and fell a thousand feet.

Hans Traub was high above, but he was nosing over. He sent his ship into a dive and opened both his guns. Coming down through the night at almost two hundred miles an hour the silver plane looked like some monster from the Inferno with long, drooping, red probosces.

Hinsdell, Perry and Giles were in a bunch. They had adopted a hands off policy and kept an eye on the other ship. It seemed content to drift along but had shown no signs of belligerency.

Observation planes were crude and clumsy like hippopotami and you could run rings around them, but at close quarters they were hard fighters with a sting.

Traub was trying to draw the fire so Frost could make the thrust.

The gunner in the seaplane fell into the trap. He looked above and saw Traub's flashing plane and immediately lost his head. He wheeled his gun and let go at the ex-Bavarian.

The moment the flame burst Frost zoomed. It was like the starter's pistol when the runner gets away perfectly. Frost's timing was superb. The black belly of the seaplane dropped before his ring sights and he touched his trigger.

One long burst. The seaplane quivered and Frost rammed his stick forward just in time. His center section missed the pontoon by a fraction. He got out in front and looked back. He was greatly surprised to see the ship still hung in the air.

Traub had slowed up, and Frost went back close. There was no fire. Both knew what had happened.

The gunner had been knocked off.

Frost grunted and got on the seaplane's nose. He motioned to the northwest several times, and the pilot slowly turned. The pilot was in no bellicose frame of mind. He seemed glad to turn back to Jamestown.

But the other pilot was recalcitrant. He headed for the Gulf in a defiant climb.

Giles mused. "He wants to play," so he went after him and let him have a burst through the fuselage by way of warning. That sobered the pilot. He turned and got in line.

It was a strange caravan that returned to Withers Field. It was a stranger crowd that gathered. Funny how things like that get bruited about.

Hell's Stepsons knew the seaplanes were certain to crack up, and the seaplane pilots knew it. But they never wavered. It was admirable the way they drifted down. They were sweet pilots and no mistake.

The first seaplane floated down and went into the dirt. There was a sharp crack and a cloud of dust. Its undercarriage had gone off cleanly; it rose on its nose, wavered and then went down.

The other plane met an identical fate. But the pilot of this one tried to profit by the mistake of the other. Twenty feet off the ground he left his ship—a dark figure plunging downward.

Hell's Stepsons landed in a rush, kicked off their switches and dashed to the wreckage. The crowd followed.

"Get back!" shouted Frost. "Damn it, get back!"

From the debris of the first plane they dragged Flash Singleton and a pilot so badly smashed he hardly was breathing. Singleton was covered with blood and they knew he was done for. It had been he at the gun—and Frost's burst of lead had got him all over.

The other plane contained Al Thomas. Thomas was smashed badly too. The pilot who jumped was smart after all. All he got was a broken leg. Altogether it was not a pleasant scene.

The wail of an ambulance siren rang out. Somebody had waked the driver. They always stay at the big flying fields. They are necessities. The siren scattered the crowd, and the ambulance roared up dramatically and stopped. The driver got out and ran around to get the stretchers.

The wounded were loaded in.

"We ride, too," said Frost.

He and Traub got in the front seat with the driver and Perry. Hinsdell and Giles got in the rear. Giles was, as always the case in big shows, facetious. He crawled in the vacant stretcher and said to Hinsdell: "Call me at eight, please." Flash Singleton groaned and muttered an oath and Giles said, "Pipe down, you cheap thug, and let a kiwi sleep."

They rattled to town at top speed. Ambulance drivers dearly love that, anyway. They slithered into the driveway of the Charity Hospital and jerked to a stop before the side door.

The operating room was ready for three patients. That was one too many. Al Thomas was dead. He died with Skipper Hinsdell close to his head, trying to understand inarticulate jumbles of words.

Flash Singleton was dying. They gave him a hypodermic and waited for the end. The surgeon said they hadn't long to wait. He said it was a miracle he was living now—the thread was slender. His torso was riddled and his skull was fractured.

Singleton was wiry and stubborn. He held on to that slender thread with a fortitude that was remarkable. At intervals he was conscious. Frost spoke to him in one of those moments.

"You're checking in, Singleton," he said. "Where are those places on the Border?"

"Britsu," he whispered, "what—"

"Dead," said Frost bluntly.

"You found a book—"

"Yeh, a book."

Something of the old spirit flamed in the eyes of the gang chief for a moment. "Burn it," he said. He repeated, "Burn it."

"What about the Border?" Frost persisted. "Who is the Black Ship gang. What is it?"

Singleton opened his eyes.

"You're going, Flash," Frost urged. "Hurry."

The gangster winced from a throb of pain. "They—wanted—me—" his voice faded and he stopped. In a moment he began again, "Something big—that gang…"

His eyes widened and he gasped. Frost dropped from his haunches to his knees.

"The gang," he repeated, "the gang—"

Singleton's head dropped forward. Then he was still.

For a moment they stood there. Frost slowly arose. The surgeon fiddled with the needle. The ambulance driver vainly tried to solve it. He thought they were cuckoo.

Frost said slowly: "There's a great big bad break. He almost said something."

"Something big," Hinsdell mused. "Something big. All we've got to do is sit and wait."

"Come on, lad," said Frost to the ambulance driver. "Give us a lift."

They came back in the ambulance. They got out at the entrance and walked up the steps. The lobby was nearly deserted. Two porters were rolling up the carpets and a big vacuum cleaner was whirring. The two porters looked at the five men curiously, then exchanged knowing looks. Some fellows who had been out tending to monkey business. Monkey business was right.

Hell's Stepsons got off the elevator at their floor and walked to their room? Frost inserted the key, opened the door and switched on the lights. He said:

"Some good breaks and a bad one. I wonder what Singleton was trying to say?"

Nobody knew. Nobody even hazarded a guess.

Traub said, "Those ships cracked up like plate glass. I won't forget that soon." He laughed. "I guess I'm a little crazy."

"*Guess* you are?" said Giles. "You know damned well you are."

Traub glared and retorted: "You're a great big pain to me, you little wisecracker."

"Go to hell, you squarehead," Giles flared back.

Skipper Hinsdell grimaced and kicked off his boots. "Oh, for God's sake! You ten-year olds are always snapping at each other. You oughta be in a kindergarten somewhere!"

Giles' undershirt popped him in the mouth. He got up in a rage.

"Who threw that? I can lick the guy—"

Socko! A pillow smothered his words. Big Hans Traub was standing on the bed in a Jem Mace pose. "Lay off my buddy," he said. "I can razz him—but nobody else can."

There was no talk of what they had done. They had played a game and won. They had a right to let off steam.

They hustled for the shower like schoolboys.

Captain Frost was the last one to bed. He telephoned the

operator that he was, under no circumstances, to be disturbed. He made sure by plugging the bell. He got in bed and rammed an object deep in his pillow slip. It was a little black book.

Then he took a look at his men, felt a warm glow that rose to his shoulders, and went to sleep.

THERE WAS A disrespectfully loud hammering at the door. Eddie Giles had one eye open as always, and sat up. The knocking continued. Hell's Stepsons stirred uncomfortably.

"Who's there?" Giles called gruffly.

"Buck Winn, of *The Courier*," came the voice from the other side. "How about opening up?"

Giles looked at Captain Frost. Jerry was up on his elbow. He shook his head.

"Come back tomorrow," Giles said.

"All right, I'll wait. I got a stool and my lunch and the only way you can dodge me is to go down the fire escape."

Giles and Frost looked at each other. From the tones there was no doubt the reporter meant exactly what he said. "He's a go-getter," said Frost. "That's damned remarkable in a newspaper man in this town. Let him in, Eddie." Eddie got up and opened the door.

In walked a disheveled young man, his face oval in horn-rim glasses. You could spot him for a reporter a block away.

"I've been fighting those other bums for two hours," he said. "I even had to crown a smart-Aleck off the morning paper. So here I am." He looked around at the reclining forms. His *savoir-faire* was priceless. "Quite a night, eh?" he grinned.

"Oh, dear, no," said Giles. "Only a lovely little lawn party."

Buck Winn widened his grin. "You're kidding me."

Giles looked deeply injured. "Me? I couldn't."

"Well," Winn went on, "you birds sure kept us up all night. Hell was popping all over town. Look!" He held up an extra edition of his paper. The headlines were three-line, ninety-six point bold gothic, eight columns wide.

RANGERS RAID NIGHT CLUB

Four Dead: Chief Suicide In His City Hall Office

Famed Hell's Stepsons Fight Thrilling Night Air Battle

OFFICIAL GONE

Racketeer Leader Dies From Wounds;

Order Session of Grand Jury

"Looks like a lot has happened," commented Traub. He felt that was enough to contribute to the interview and rolled over and pulled the cover over his head.

Captain Frost stared at the paper, "That on the level?"

The veracity of his great paper questioned, young Mr. Winn didn't know whether to be offended or tickled. He took a look at Frost's jaw and decided he was tickled.

"Sure! Dawson blew half his head off. Vito Petrone's in jail. Flash Singleton is dead and that Ichabod Crane of a police commissioner is A.W.O.L. There's hints," he sniffed, "of corruption. The Grand Jury is due to bust loose this morning."

He stopped and waited for somebody to say something. But no one did.

"Look here," he went on, "there was something said around headquarters about a little book that caused all the trouble. Said it had a lot of names in it. How about a squint at it?" He leered at Frost through his spectacles.

Frost reached into his pillow, concealing the movement with his body, and palmed the book. He got up and stepped into the bathroom.

"What about the book?" the reporter insisted.

"There wasn't anything in that book," said Frost, poking his head out. "Nothing your paper would print."

The reporter's jaw sagged. "Aw, hell, captain," he said. "That won't work. Dawson bumps himself off, the commissioner skips—why? That little book! See?"

"No," said Frost. "I don't. Enough damage has been done already. Even—get that—*even* if there were any names in there, it wouldn't count. If you've got to write something tell 'em we're shoving off for the border pronto."

"Aw, hell, captain—"

"Eddie, kiss your boy friend goodbye and show him out."

"Aw, captain—"

"Come on, fellow," said Giles. "You heard the cap'n."

"Aw, lissen—"

But the rest of his words were lost. Giles had closed the door behind him.

Frost came out and sat on the edge of the bed. "Something big," he mused.

Giles looked at him.

"I wonder what Singleton was trying to say?"

"Forget it," Giles said. "He wasn't in no condition to say anything. He was raving."

"I'm not so sure," said Frost. "I've got reasons—"

Giles wrinkled his brow.

"You mean," he said quickly, "you know something we don't?"

Frost didn't say anything.

"I know," said Giles. "It's that book—"

"No," said the commander. He was a poor liar. His face gave him away. The black book contained valuable information.

"What is it?" Giles asked.

"Nothing—maybe," said Frost. "And maybe a lot." He lighted a cigarette. He puffed slowly.

"Only this," said Frost, "we aren't through with them yet. Not by a long shot. Eddie," he went on soberly, "what would be your limit in stopping that gang.

"My limit would be the sky," said Giles. "Why?"

"It may have to be," murmured Frost, as he looked out the window.

Frost Flies Alone

A trap for Jerry Frost of the Flying Rangers

FROST FELT THAT he and the woman were being followed, had been followed since they crossed the Border. As they emerged from the Plaza Madero and turned down the crooked street towards the Café Estrellita he became acutely aware that footsteps were proceeding in the same direction as himself and that the owner was trying to attract as little attention as possible.

To satisfy himself that he was not the victim of his own imagination, so often the case when he invaded old Mexico after nightfall, he halted briefly before a shop window, wherein baubles were exhibited, and whispered a caution to his companion. The moment they stopped the footfalls ceased. No one passed. Quite evidently someone was following.

Fully alive now, his nerves on edge, Frost spoke to his companion, and they walked on. In the distance he could see the lights of the Café Estrellita and outside the shadowy forms of customers at the sidewalk tables. Frost walked slowly, his ears strained, but did not look around. He was still being followed. Moreover, the number of steps behind him had increased. There were now two or three men. The street was narrow and the footsteps loud; overhead the stars blinked and from a hidden patio nearby there floated the dim tinkle of a guitar.

As the woman passed the dark, dank interiors she gave way to a swift rush of apprehension and took Frost's arm nervously. He leaned over and whispered: "Don't get excited, but I'd like to know if you can use a gun."

She moved her head closer. "I'm sort of jumpy," she apologized lamely, "but really, I can use a gun. Fact is—" her confidence returned "—I've got one." She patted her voluminous handbag. She went on lightly. "I haven't been a newspaper woman ten years without learning a few things."

Frost said, "Oh!" rather contritely, and steered her into the café without looking back at his pursuers.

La Estrellita was a little square room overcrowded with tables at which, outside and inside, sat perhaps half a hundred persons. The ceiling was almost obscured by cigarette smoke, and there was all the variety of noises commonly associated with Border joints. It was the hour when Algadon blazed with the specific intent of luring tourists, although the patronage here was now, as far as Frost determined in a hurried glance, mostly native.

At one end of the room was a bar at which two Mexicans were mixing drinks; behind them was the traditional frosted mirror and long rows of bottles. A square-shouldered, semibald man was busy plying a rag with what amounted to violence and one look at him left no doubt concerning his origin. He was one of those old-time American bartenders driven into Mexico by prohibition.

Glasses and spoons littered one end of the bar and near this end, on a raised platform, sat a quintet of native musicians languidly strumming their guitars. They simulated indifference, ennui, hoping to chisel a round of drinks from a sympathetic tourist. The house was bare of sympathy.

Frost led his companion inside and half way to the table he had mentally selected he recognized the unmistakable form of Ranger Captain George Stuart. Frost slowly passed Stuart's table and said under his breath:

"Don't look up, George. Just get set. Hell's fixing to pop."

The only indication Stuart heard was an almost imperceptible movement of his fingers as he knocked the ashes off his cigarette. Twenty years on the Border had given him perfect control of all his faculties, had deadened his emotions.

Frost went to a table near the end of the bar and helped his companion into a chair. Then he sat down, facing the room and glanced at George Stuart.

There passed a look of understanding. Stuart crossed his legs and as he did so slid his six-gun inside his thigh by means of his elbow. At that moment three men came through the doorway, looked hurriedly about the room and walked to a table near Frost. As they sat down their chairs scraped and the sounds were audible above the maudlin talk and the soporific music.

The three of them were young, Mexican in cast of countenance, with sharp faces and narrow eyes—of a general type with which the Border, from end to end, teems: shrewd, crafty wastrels who will turn any sort of a trick for any sort of a price.

Frost ordered two bottles of beer from a waiter, and looked at his companion.

"I'm afraid," he said, striving to be unconcerned, "I've got you into a mess—and the only way out is straight ahead."

"You think," she asked, inclining her head slightly, "those men—"

"I don't know," Frost said. "But I've got a sweet hunch you're liable to get a good story before this party ends. There's a window directly behind you. If—*if* anything happens, get out and keep going."

"You talk," she said, "as if you regretted bringing me."

Frost eyed her. "I never have regrets," he said, "they're cowardly. Just the same it didn't look this foggy when we started. If we tried to get out now we'd never live to reach the street."

"As bad as that?" She was smiling and the smile annoyed Frost. He didn't answer. He thought her question was stupid. Hell, of course it was bad. She had no business here. But that was the way with the newspaper tribe—all of them. Especially women. They thought that their profession was protection. Helen Stevens, however, seemed more officious than any other Frost had known. Probably, he presumed, because she was to author a series about Hell's Stepsons for an indubitably important organization, the Manhattan Syndicate, Inc. But, even then, Frost told himself again, this time bitterly, she had no business here.

Few spots on the Border are safe for a woman after dark; Algadon was no spot for a woman at any time. But Helen Stevens had insisted and as the final persuasive force she had even brought a letter from the Adjutant-General. And here she was.

It looked bad.

The waiter returned with the bottles and two glasses. He poured the drinks, placed the bottles on a tray, and started away.

"*Psst!*" said Frost. "*Deja los botella.*"

The waiter turned, surprised. "*Como?*"

"*Deja los botella!*" Frost repeated, more sharply.

The waiter lifted his eyes as if invoking divine compassion on the fool before him; and put the empty bottles back on the table. He moved away, slightly puzzled; but no more so than the newspaper woman.

"How odd!" she observed.

"Not at all," Frost said. "I've got a lot of funny little habits like that." He didn't feel it necessary to tell her experience had taught him there was nothing comparable to the efficiency of a beer bottle at close quarters; or that he had a deep-seated hunch it would be at close quarters soon.

He took a sip from his glass and looked at his companion. Her face was unworried, lovely. He thought of that moment on route to La Estrellita when she had, momentarily frightened, touched his arm. Her face betrayed no fear now—nor anything that remotely approached fear. From the tranquility of her demeanor she might have been sitting in the refinement of an opera loge instead of a Mexican dive where the air was charged with expectancy. Frost felt, irreverently, that if he, accustomed to tension, was slightly ill at ease, she, unaccustomed to anything of the sort, should at least have shared a portion of that discomfort. It mildly annoyed him that she didn't.

She reached for the glass with her long fingers and as she lifted it she drummed her fingers lightly against the stem. Out of the corner of his eye Frost saw one of the three men who had followed him lean over and whisper to his comrades. He also saw George Stuart move forward in his chair, ready to get into action in a split second.

Helen Stevens was speaking in a dulcet voice. "Is this," she was saying, "typical of Border towns?"

"Is it possible," Frost countered, "that you are a stranger to Border towns?"

She laughed and her eyes beamed spiritedly. "Of course."

"In that case it's typical. Just the same," Frost went on, "I wish we hadn't come."

"Why?" she demanded. She seemed positively to be enjoying it. "I'm glad," she went on, rippling, "that I can see you against your proper background." She inclined her head. "Captain, I'm afraid you dramatize yourself fearfully."

For the second time in the past few minutes Frost was the victim of mixed emotions. She alternately stirred him and irritated him. Now he was in no mood for tea-room repartee.

"Please," he said, "let's not get personal." He contemplated that remark and decided it wasn't exactly what he wanted to say. It sounded flat. So he hurried on, "Miss Stevens, you mustn't get me wrong. Our men have been having a tough time along this river with an important gang. We are constantly expecting things to happen—anything. To you that may seem dramatic. But I am only cautious—" he lifted his eyes "—and thinking of you."

"You needn't," she said suddenly. "I'm all right."

Somehow he didn't quite think so. He was alarmed—rather definitely alarmed. Notwithstanding his attitude of indifference he felt that something was going to happen before they got out of La Estrellita. He knew the signs. It was the sort of a prelude that always traveled along in the same slot. Never any change. Had he been alone he could have forced the issue. But he was not alone. There was a woman with him—a personal charge. That sort of cramped his style. Jerry Frost had been in the habit of meeting trouble half-way.

Three men had followed him. Why? Footpads intent on robbing a tourist? He dismissed that thought. They knew very well who he was— should have known—and even if they didn't, George Stuart was there. Every man, woman and child in Algadon knew the rock-ribbed Stuart. He was part and parcel of the Border country. Men who stalk American game along the Rio with a Ranger within the same walls are bent on a mission more sinister than robbery.

Did they think Frost had on his person the valuable black book he got from Flash Singleton in the little episode at James-town—the little black book the gangster had carried, giving names and information? He didn't know. But there was a voice within him—a small, still voice that roused him to the alert. It bred expectancy. Helen Stevens had thought, and said so, that this was theatricality. Frost smiled reflectively. She could think what she damn well pleased. He had no fault to find with his intuition. It had saved him too often.

"Do you think," she whispered, "any of the gang is here now?"

"*No se,*" he shrugged. "They're everywhere."

"But I thought I'd read that Hell's Stepsons had broken it up."

He cast her what was intended to be a rueful grimace, but it hardly was that. "No," he admitted, "we've made only a small dent in it. We've caught only the little fish."

She moved again, this time her body. She placed her hand on Frost's wrist and swayed her head a little. "I hope," she said suddenly and, he thought, softly, "you get the big ones!"

Frost felt she was animated by deep sincerity, and as quickly as his suspicions had mounted they disappeared. They might have been dissipated by the touch of her hand, by the proximity of her lovely face, by the faint smile on her lips; but dissipated they most assuredly were. Helen Stevens was a good-looking woman of the type which has been vaguely classified as a man's woman. It had been a long time since such a creature had been as close to him. He became poignantly and swiftly aware that he had been missing something.

He patted her hand gratefully, sighed like a silly schoolboy and said: "I hope so, too."

There was a scuffling sound from the front of the house and a man got up unsteadily. After an hour he had become aware that the orchestra was not functioning well.

"*Una cancion!*" he cried. "*Canta!*"

"*Si, si,*" came the chorus.

The musicians on the platform be-stirred themselves and stroked the strings with a little more life than they had previously evidenced. They played a few bars as a vamp and then lifted their voices in a plaintive rendering of *La Cucaracha*, camp song of that immortal renegade—Villa.

They finished and were rewarded with loud applause. It was to be expected. *La Cucaracha* is a sort of provincial national air. It brought back flashing memories of the Chihuahua stable cleaner who later flung his defy in the teeth of the government: "*Que chico se me hace el mar para hacer un buche de agua…* I'll use the ocean to gargle!"

The lethargy in La Estrellita was falling away.

Frost looked at the table where the three men were sitting. They were, to him, plainly agitated. Their heads bobbed excitedly, and one of them exchanged wise looks with the bartender. After that the bartender moved slowly down the rail with affected nonchalance. Frost pretended to be thoroughly immersed in his drink and his companion. But he was not too immersed in either.

Something was about to occur.

"Remember," he said aside to the woman, "the window is directly behind you. It looks like trouble is coming. Understand?"

"Perfectly," she said quietly. She reached for her bag, and opened it in her lap. Her hand slipped inside and closed about the butt of a gun. "Don't worry."

"I won't," he said. He meant it. The calmness and sureness of her decision relieved him. Again he admired her, found himself wondering what sort of a companion she would be in more agreeable surroundings.

One of the three Mexicans got up. The impression he meant to convey was drunkenness. Frost got no such impression.

He caught the eye of George Stuart and nodded. Stuart nodded likewise.

The Mexican started off between the tables, ostensibly intent on reaching the bar. He never got that far. He purposely stepped out of the way to trip against Frost's foot, almost falling to the floor. He righted himself and poured out a volume of Spanish; swept the glasses from the table.

Here it was. The big blow-off. Here it was. Frost had been waiting, taut as a bow-string.

He leaped from his chair and put all his power into a short uppercut that landed flush on the Mexican's chin and sent him reeling ten feet away against a table.

"Beat it!" he said to the woman.

His right hand went to his hip after his gun and his left hand groped for the empty bottle. But he had lost a precious few seconds. He turned to find himself looking down the blue barrels of two pistols held in the hands of the remaining pursuers. It was too late to draw his own weapon.

The career of Jerry Frost might have ended on the spot had it not been for George Stuart. He had come from behind softly, but fast, and brought the butt of his gun down upon the head of one of the Mexicans. It was a terrific blow. The man groaned and fell to the floor. Stuart quickly threw his arms about the other's shoulders.

Frost availed himself of the lull to take a step backward and look for Helen Stevens. She was missing; and he had no time to speculate on where she was or how she got away. Through the door came five men, as tough looking as any Frost had ever seen. They were rushing forward recklessly, intent on but one purpose. Everybody in the room had risen by now, offering the quintet slight impediment.

Frost swung the beer bottle with all the force he could muster, and it crashed against the head of the man with whom Stuart was wrestling. The Mexican's cheek bone ripped through the skin as if by magic, and blood poured down his face. He instantly grew limp; and Stuart let him slide to the floor.

An unseen hand pressed the switch and La Estrellita was swept into darkness.

A pistol cracked, light blue and scarlet, and the bullet whistled by Frost's head. Pandemonium arose. Frost stepped to one side; not a moment too soon. The pistol barked again. From the flash Frost deduced he had been in direct line of fire. If—

There was a stampede towards the door. Frost lashed out in the dark, heard a grunt, and lashed out again. A third time he swung the beer bottle; this time it shattered. Spanish blasphemy ascended. La Estrellita was an inferno. Tables and chairs rattled, glasses crashed, and a loud voice shouted:

"Luz! Luz!"

Someone was calling for lights and it struck Frost that the sensible thing to do now was retreat before the lights went up. So he shouted for Stuart to follow him, ducked quickly, and moved towards the window. His escape was made difficult by the cursing, wedging mob. Everybody was fighting to get outside. Frost lunged with his fists, and a blow banged against his jaw. He reeled, almost fell but came up swinging. Outside he could hear the shrill whistles of the police. The Mexican constabulary was calling, like no other police in the world, for order.

Frost set his teeth and flailed his arms. And every time they went out they struck something. He dived forward and some of the mob went down before the force of his body. He got up and climbed over, carrying others in his mad march to the exit.

He wanted to shout at Stuart again to let him know where he was, but even in that chaos of mind and flesh, Frost realized to cry out now would be to betray himself by his voice. So he fought his way slowly to the window.

He could see it as a rectangle of outside light a few feet ahead and he pushed and struggled and continued to swing. He thrilled to the power in his long arms and his fists... a form loomed in front of him in clear silhouette and he started a blow from the floor. His fist crashed against the blurred vision that was a head; there was a smothered exclamation, and the man went down.

Frost shifted his arms and got his pistol, and as he came near the window he swung again and again; then of a sudden he became aware that his legs were not moving. They were imprisoned in a human vise.

He fell forward.

But he did not hit the floor. He fell on top of several squirming bodies; and realized he had been pulled down in the confusion. Fearful lest he be trampled, he yanked himself up again by means of somebody's coat and was thankful he still had his pistol. He came to his knees, then full up, and, finding he had sufficient space to move his legs, kicked lustily at the form on the floor. There was an oath.

He reached for the window, anchored his hand and pulled. He finally made it. He climbed up and literally fell into the night. With the first intake of air he thought of the woman and Stuart.

Where were they? Safe? There had been, he reflected, but two pistol shots. So far as he could determine neither had found a mark. Mexican marksmanship is, notoriously, bad; their first love is the blade. And the blade is, generally, silent. Had?… The thought sent Frost into a rage. Still, Stuart was a veteran. He had been in hundreds of brawls… and yet…

Regardless of everything now, Frost lifted his voice:

"George! George!"

As if in answer to his reckless cry, George Stuart tumbled through the window.

"Thank God!" Frost panted. "Hurt?"

"Nope!" Laconically. Then: "You?"

"Bruised." Then: "George, I've got to find the woman!"

They moved quickly across the street. The mêlée in the café continued. The police were puffing at their whistles and occasionally shouting in an official voice that did no good; there was general discord.

"In the meantime," George said, "we're in a fine shape to stop a slug or two. Let's step on it."

They walked rapidly towards the international bridge.

Stuart said, "Who the hell was that dame?"

"A newspaper woman the Old Man sent down—but I'd rather not talk about it."

"I don't blame you," Stuart said. "You had a swell idea—bringing her to this town. She damn near got us messed up."

"I know that now. But it could have been worse." He went on quietly, "You saved my life, George."

George Stuart rubbed his chin reflectively and pretended he didn't hear.

"Where do you suppose she went?" he asked.

"I tried to tell her what was coming," Frost said. "If she was smart she went across."

They had gone so far now the sounds in La Estrellita were but murmurs. Overhead the stars blinked on; once in a while the Rangers caught the music of guitars as an indolent part of Algadon, impervious to the excitement, sang on.

"Know those yeggs who started the fight?" Stuart asked, matching the strides of the long-legged flyer.

"Never saw 'em before," Frost said. "I guess they were hired by the gang. I wonder," he mused, "where it'll all end?"

Stuart had no answer for that one. They walked along silently.

"I hope," Frost went on, as if to himself, "she got back okey. I sort of had the idea she could look out for herself."

"Well," put in Stuart truculently, "she had a swell opportunity of doing that little thing tonight."

"And she wasn't bad looking," Frost went on in the same tone.

"Yeh—I saw that, too."

At the international boundary they exchanged pleasantries they did not feel with the customs officials. Frost asked for the woman. The officers said they were sorry, but no woman had passed into the States. Frost stoutly insisted they must be mistaken; they insisted just as stoutly they could not be.

George Stuart was familiar with their technique. He said, "Well?" to Frost in such a tone his meaning was clear.

"A mess," Frost exploded—"a first-class mess. God," he breathed, "if anything's happened... Well," resolutely, "I can't go back without her. That much is a cinch."

Stuart lighted a cigarette and said, "Anything you say, Jerry. Wanna take a look at La Estrellita?" thus leaving the plan of action to the flyer.

"It's not a question of wanting to, George. But the Old Man sent her—"

"Sure." Stuart turned to the officials and requested, with a trace of belligerence, that if the woman who had crossed with Frost returned she be detained. He then divested himself of certain pertinent remarks. "Jerry—you're the biggest damn fool I ever saw. You know how you stand around here," and, having unburdened himself, he again became the fighting man with a terse, "Hell, let's go!"

And with no more than that they swung back to La Estrellita, whence they had so recently and so narrowly escaped with their lives.

The café had quieted somewhat when they returned. Stuart and Frost made their way inside. A few patrons had come back (a great many had never left), but many of the tables were over-turned and everywhere there were unmistakable signs of the fight, notwithstanding the expeditious work of the café's ubiquitous emergency corps. The five-man Mexican orchestra was back on the platform playing in the same listless fashion which forever characterizes their music. This was a bland lot of musicians. A brawl, a pistol fight, a knife duel—nothing to them. Every night was just another night.

Their hands on their hips, the Rangers stood inside the door of the café and returned glare for glare. There were low murmurs of recognition as they entered.

They summoned the proprietor.

"I know this guy Rasaplo," Stuart said. "Lemme do all the talking."

Rasaplo waddled up solicitously, portly after the vogue of Mexican café owners, with long mustachios and sagging jowls that could be either fierce or cherubic. At this moment he chose for them to be cherubic. He rubbed his hands as if Frost and Stuart were patron saints who had stepped from their *nichos*, and smiled broadly.

"*Señors,*" he said, "I am sorry—vair sorry." He looked from one face to the other, seeking some indication of official forgiveness. There was none. The Rangers stared at him and through him. Rasaplo quailed somewhat.

"Now lissen," Stuart said, his voice steely. "The *capitan* here brought a woman with him—*la mujer Americana. Ella desvan-eca*—disappeared. *Sabe* what that means?"

Rasaplo's eyes widened in surprise. His whole person registered consternation. Great actors, those fellows. Rasaplo lifted his hands in horror.

"*Imposible!*" he managed. "Never in La Estrellita. Never! La Estrellita ees—"

"Yeh," Stuart cut in; "I know that speech backwards! La Estrellita is a little nursery where mommas leave their children." He clucked heatedly. "Nix on that patriotism stuff, Rasaplo! Your dump ain't no different from any of the others along this creek. Now get this—the woman disappeared in here tonight—and she's got to be found. Tell me something before I—"

"But," Rasaplo wheezed, "I am in the back room when a gun go boom! and the place get dark. I know no more."

Stuart looked at Frost and nodded. "Well, in that case," he began, his meaning clear, "I guess we'll—"

Rasaplo said quickly, "Mebbe Pete know. Pete always know." He went briskly to the bar and engaged a bartender in conversation. He was the one Frost had seen moving down the rail before the lights went out. From the way the patrons eyed the scene the Rangers could tell they still were annoyed at having their evening interrupted. They were content, however, merely to stare.

But the bartender was mystified, too. There was no misinterpreting his gestures. He didn't know how the fight started, and he didn't remember any woman. All he knew was that after the lights went on again several natives were carried out, semi-conscious.

Rasaplo darted a swift look around, leaned over the bar a little farther, and something changed hands. Stuart and Frost both saw it at the same time. They went forward.

"Gimme that!" Stuart commanded.

Rasaplo grinned abashed, and handed over a letter. "They give it to the boy to mail," he said. "I do not know anything."

The letter was addressed to Captain Jerry Frost, Gentry, Texas, and there was a two-cent U.S. stamp in the corner. Frost ripped it open. A note on the back of a menu. It said:

"Thanks, Captain, for the woman."

It was written in that peculiar, flamboyant foreign style. Frost fingered it blankly and held it up for Stuart to see. Stuart said to Rasaplo: "Where's the waiter who got this?"

Rasaplo summoned a sleek servitor, who eyed Stuart and Frost with an expression that can only be called baleful.

"Who gave you this?" Frost held up the letter.

The waiter shrugged his shoulders to say he couldn't remember all the patrons; but made no answer.

"Who gave you this?" Frost repeated.

"I no remember," he said. "A man—" as if that would help.

RASAPLO INSERTED HIS broad bulk into the scene to give his employee whatever protection he could muster. "He know nothing," he said. "He get the letter and boom! the place go dark. Mebbe we get miedo—and no mail letter. But—" His voice, colorless, trailed off.

Stuart gestured disgustedly to Frost. For the time being they knew they were against a blank wall. Trying to elicit criminal information from some Mexicans can be—in some instances, is—nothing short of impossible. Indeed, some of them are so

clumsy in trying to remain innocent they incriminate themselves.

The Rangers knew they could do no more; and, too, they
were chancing further trouble by remaining in La Estrellita.

"Come on, let's go see the cops." On the way out Stuart went
on: "But don't expect too much of the law here. It's quite probably the rottenest force in the world. Maybe, though—"

They went around the corner to the police station, and Frost
soon learned that Stuart had properly classified the Algadon
police. They said they hadn't the faintest idea what happened
to the woman; moreover, they gave the impression, and it
was true, that they weren't in the least interested. They were
without the slightest degree of enthusiasm, and raised their
brows superciliously to convey the thought that if the Rangers
couldn't look out for their own women they shouldn't expect
anyone else to.

Stuart said to Frost: "I'd like to sock this gang in the jaw."

Frost nodded abstractedly. He wasn't particularly concerned
with that. It was the woman. His last hope, for the present, had
fled. She had been his responsibility, his personal charge, and
to return to Gentry without her likely would cause compli-
cations. She could be one of a thousand places. He rephrased
Stuart's words: he had been a damn fool.

And the Old Man. He'd raise hell. Well, what the hell? He'd
just have to raise it, that was all. There wasn't anything they
could do about it now. Anyway, it was partly his fault. He'd
never brought her over if the Old Man hadn't written that
letter. "Let her have a look at Algadon by night," he had said.
The exact words. Let her have a look by night... Well, she'd
had one.

Frost damned his thoughts and turned to Stuart. "Should I have kept her there and taken a chance?" he asked. "Didn't I do the right thing when I told her to get out?"

"Sure," said Stuart broadly, consolingly. Under his breath he rasped: "I'd like to sock this gang in the nose!"

Back at the boundary the Customs officers said no woman had passed since Frost and Stuart were last there, and the Rangers swore roundly and stamped across the bridge. They were headed for the police department in Gentry.

Fifteen minutes later the telegraph wires of the Border country were humming a message, soon to be broadcast over the nation:

> Kidnaped in Algadon, Mexico, on the night of February Eleventh: woman answering to name of Helen Stevens, representative of Manhattan Newspaper Syndicate of New York City. About five feet five inches, hundred ten pounds, light brown hair, blue eyes, teeth unmarked, wearing brown coat and skirt, flat-heeled two-tone shoes. Notify Texas Air Rangers, Captain Jerry Frost Gentry, Texas.

Stuart and Frost then went to the barracks of Hell's Stepsons and dived into bed. George Stuart, again exhibiting remarkable mental control, went immediately to sleep.

Not so Frost. He rolled, pitched, tossed and fretted at his impotence.

WITHIN SEVENTY-TWO HOURS the Manhattan Syndicate, Inc., of New York City, had taken official cognizance of the disappearance of one of its representatives by bringing the matter to the attention of the ranking officer of the sovereign State of Texas. Powerfully allied, as are all important syndicates, it lost no time in applying all the pressure at its command.

Messages were exchanged and the austere Mexican government moved, as a gesture of courtesy, a detachment of *rurales* into Algadon. Nobody, of course, expected them to achieve results.

Helen Stevens had disappeared as completely as if the earth had swallowed her.

Yet the law, tank-like in its motion, rumbled on.

The spotlight was fixed on Hell's Stepsons, and its glare was not favorable. The spectacular work done in the past was forgotten.

On the fourth day after her disappearance there was a conference within the great, gilt-domed state capitol at Austin, in the inner office of the governor's suite. There were three men there: the Great Man himself, the Adjutant-General and Captain Frost.

"It is unfortunate," the Governor was saying; "most unfortunate." He was tapping his glasses against his chin: a dignified patriarch, product of the expansive state he represented— rugged, sincere and honest.

"Yes," the Adjutant-General agreed. He was commander of that crack constabulary, the Texas Rangers, the personification of the ideals of that brigade. Big and gaunt he was; you knew at a glance, the sort of an official who would, if needs be, climb into the saddle himself and take the trail.

"The woman," the Governor went on, "is well connected. We cannot, in any event, let up in the search."

"But, sir," mildly demurred the Adjutant-General, "we are trying. I feel," he went on, "somewhat responsible in a personal sense. I insisted Captain Frost take her across."

"No," Frost said quickly; "the fault was mine."

"Well," the Governor declared, "whose fault it was is beside the point. We have got to do something at once."

"They're a tough lot," Frost mused. He spread his hands on the desk. He was, for obvious reasons, highly uncomfortable. "Gentlemen," he said, "I agree that we are being made to look bad. But what else can we do?"

"It has been my experience," said the Adjutant-General, "that this gang never strikes blindly. There always is a motive back of every crime. What was it in this case? Why did they kidnap Helen Stevens? Revenge? Hardly. Ransom?" He shook his head. "No—something else. Some reason we don't know yet."

Frost nodded. "If I had the slightest idea where she was," he said, "I'd go get her—no matter where that happened to be."

Silence.

Then the Governor said, "Perhaps we ought to ask for a bigger appropriation for the Ranger force. Increase them. Move some of them south." He looked sagacious. "The only bad feature about movement like that is the publicity. Our opponents always construe that as inefficiency. It gives them something to talk about. I dislike having this case noised around."

"Well," Frost said bluntly, "the only way to keep it in the family is to let me have a crack at it alone."

Then the unbelievable happened. The immense, carved door swung open noiselessly, and the Governor's secretary entered.

"I'm sorry, sir," he addressed the Great Man, "but I've a message for Captain Frost."

"For me?" Frost asked.

"Yes, sir—forwarded from Gentry."

The Governor said: "Come in, Leavell, come in."

The secretary walked to Captain Frost and handed him the message. Frost made no move to open it until the secretary had departed.

"May I—"

"Certainly," said the Governor.

A deep silence fell. Frost read the message without even a blink of the eye and passed it over the desk to the Governor.

He put on his glasses and read aloud:

Coast Guard Cutter Forty-Nine sighted Rum-Runner Catherine B longitude ninety-seven east latitude twenty-seven near Brownsville with woman aboard answering description Stevens stop cutter outdistanced stop rum boat one of former Al Thomas fleet.

O'Neill.

The Governor removed his glasses and tapped them against his chin again. The Adjutant-General looked at Frost. Frost looked out the window.

"I sort of thought so," he soliloquized.

"Al Thomas," mused the Governor. "Who is that?"

"A gunman killed in a plane smash a couple of months ago after a dogfight with Hell's Stepsons," Frost replied. "His men seem to be carrying on."

" 'Cutter outdistanced,'" the Governor went on. "I wonder how—"

"Please, sir," Frost put in. He was on his feet now. Hours of inactivity, of recrimination, of criticism, rushed to a climax which crystallized his attitude. "Please, sir—I'd like to play this alone. Single-handed. It started mine and—" his voice was grim— "I'd like it to finish the same way. I don't want any help."

"But, Captain—" he began.

"Of course, Jerry," said the Adjutant-General in a placating voice. "You can't go streaking off like this!"

Frost raised his hand. His face was in a cast of resolve. "Please," he said again, firmly. He looked at the Adjutant-General and the Adjutant-General understood. "I've got to go it alone."

The Governor nodded; Frost saluted and went out.

As the door closed the Adjutant-General smiled and offered an observation to his chief. "I'd hate like hell to have him after me."

COAST GUARD CUTTER Forty-Nine's base was at Corpus Christi, and it was towards there that Frost turned when he hopped off from Austin. He was at Cuero in fifty minutes, stopping only long enough to wire Jimmy O'Neill that he was on his way and to notify Hans Traub he again was temporarily in command of the Air Rangers.

"I'm riding alone on the Stevens case," he telegraphed.

Two hours and fifty minutes after he had circled the dome of the state capitol, he dipped into the airport at Corpus Christi and taxied his battle plane into a hangar. He got O'Neill on the phone at the government docks.

"Coming right over, Jimmy."

"Great," said O'Neill. "Ox Clay is here. You'll like him."

Frost did like Ox Clay. That name ought to awaken memories of sporting page devotees because Ox Clay was pretty well known back in '21 and '22 when he was ripping football lines to shreds for the Middies: little, square-jawed, built like a bullet, and innumerable laugh wrinkles around his eyes. "Hello, Jerry," he greeted the flyer. "I've heard so damn much about you I feel as if we're old friends."

"You're no stranger yourself." Frost returned. He said to O'Neill: "Well, Jimmy, I've just left one of those high and mighty conferences. Believe you me, Missus Frost's young son has got to do something and do it pronto. What's it all about?"

"Ox can tell you more than I can, Jerry. He was riding Forty-Nine himself."

"I'll say I was," Clay retorted with a grimace. "And the way that baby slipped away from Forty-Nine was nobody's business. We took a couple of shots—it wasn't good target practice. We only scared her faster."

"What about the woman?"

"I was getting to that. It's that Stevens skirt—no two ways about it. They let us get pretty close—and then kidded us by pulling away. But nobody can tell me I didn't see her during those first few minutes—brown suit, brown hair—"

"Right!" said Frost. "Sounds like my little playmate. What about the boat?"

"Well, she used to belong to the Singleton outfit. Name's the *Catherine B.* Lately taken over by Thomas, and then his gang got it when you fellows rubbed him out. She's the prize of the Gulf, can store about three thousand cases and make close to forty knots. We've never got her because she's fast and then there are hundreds of little coves along the coast she ducks in when trouble appears. When we saw her she was heading to sea."

"We've got plenty of dope on that outfit," O'Neill said. "But so far it hasn't done us any good. We know they load on the stuff at Tampico, Vera Cruz and God knows where else—and about a hundred miles out they transfer it to the launches."

"I see," Frost said. "The launches don't dare get out farther than that?"

"Exactly," Clay put in. "They work close to the Mexican side. There must be five hundred coves between here and the Laguna de la Madre."

"If we could grab the *Catherine B*," O'Neill said; "we'd stop a lot of the smuggling. What's your idea about this, Jerry?"

"Well, I'm going to have a look for her," Frost said quietly.

They thought he was kidding.

"Bring your bathing suit?" Clay asked.

"I'm serious," Frost said.

"Really?" Incredulously.

"Hell, yes, Why not? I'll get pontoons and try to take her. She can't outrun my boat."

"It'd be suicide," said Clay, shaking his head.

Frost laughed. "Lissen, Ox—I admit it may seem funny to you, but it doesn't to me. Besides, I've *got* to do it. How am I going to know when I see her?"

"Easy," said Clay. "Brass taffrails. She's ebony black all over but for her taffrails. You can see 'em rain or shine. She carries one funnel, looks perfect alow and aloft, has a heavy stern and her cutwater and bow lines are as pretty as I ever saw."

Frost laughed. "I don't get that conversation," he said. "But I did understand about the brass. I don't guess I can miss her."

"You can't," O'Neill said.

"Definitely made up your mind to go it alone?" asked Clay.

"Yep. Would it be possible for me to requisition silencers?"

Ox Clay swung open a drawer and took out two pistols fitted with longish muzzles. "Presto!" he said. He handed them to Frost. "I'll let you use mine."

Frost stared at them curiously. "This," he said, "is the first time I ever saw a silencer. Are they apt to jam?"

Clay grinned. "The first shots will be all right. After that you gamble. Hope they'll do you, Jerry. They're my contribution to your success."

Frost took an automatic out of his hip-holster and one from under his chamois jacket. He said: "I'll trade for the time being. Now one thing more and I'll blow a bugle over your grave. Will you phone Roland at the field that I'm on my way and be sure and be in."

"I'll phone, but don't think that gang on the *Catherine B* will be a pushover. It's a tough mob."

"I know." Frost shook hands with each of them. "Well," he said, "so long."

"So long. Good luck."

"Thanks."

He sheathed his pistols and walked out. Ox Clay looked at Jimmy O'Neill.

"Lotsa guts," he observed.

"You said it!"

Major Oliver Roland, commander of the flying field at Corpus Christi was a stout admirer of Jerry Frost personally and professionally, being a veteran airman himself, but he thought Frost's plan to take the air in an effort to locate the kidnaped woman was a wild idea.

"It's all wet," as he put it.

Frost said no.

"Ridiculous—and dangerous."

"Neither," Frost retorted crisply. "I can't afford to think of either one."

"You ought to." Sternly: "Just because you've had a lot of success along the Border you think you're invulnerable. That makes you cocky and breeds overconfidence. You mustn't get that way."

Roland's tone was firm, but inoffensive, and Frost grinned. "I'm not overconfident. I've got good reasons not to be." He was thinking of that time not so long ago when he escaped in an enemy plane, to think he had the world by the tail on a down-hill pull, and was promptly shot down by his companions. "I'm not overconfident," he repeated. "But I am curious—curious as hell. It's up to me to get that woman—and with your help I intend to!"

Oliver Roland knew flyers. He looked into Frost's eyes—clear. He looked at his mouth—tight. He looked at his chin—square under pressure of the jaws. He decided the young man knew what he was doing.

"Very well," he surrendered. "Want a flying boat?"

"Nope, pontoons. Just pontoons. Will you fit me?"

Roland nodded. "On the condition that you forget where you got 'em."

"My memory's awful," Frost smiled.

It required little more than two hours to fit the pontoons and service the ship; and then the silver-winged bird cascaded through the Gulf of Mexico, left the water in a stream of fume, and turned its eager wings southward.

That bird was a fighting ship of the Texas Rangers, carried

two thousand rounds of ammunition, a veteran pilot who had a brace of silencer-equipped pistols, and, what was infinitely more important, a stout heart.

JERRY FROST WAS riding alone. He climbed to fifteen thousand feet better to deaden the roar of his motor, and swung down the jagged coast line. The Gulf lay beneath, a somber expanse as far as his eyes could see, its surface rippling with white-caps: long, thin, broken lines like the foreground of an etching. Far down the lanes he could see the funnels of a boat which seemed to hang on the edge of the world, so slowly did it move.

The coast line was dotted with innumerable coves and the waves rolled against them to be broken into effervescence. Frost reflected that Ox Clay had been entirely correct. There were so many of these serrated sanctuaries which afforded natural shelter for the lawless they could well defy the maps. No cartographer possibly could have marked them all.

Frost rocketed down the coast line for a hundred miles and then veered over the Gulf in a wider flight. Already he had come to realize that finding the *Catherine B* out here was no sinecure for a young man who wanted action. There was, however, one consoling thought: he, at least, was in the air with a definite objective.

The *Catherine B* had been seen in Longitude 97 east and Latitude 27. He consulted the map on his board. That would be, as near as he could roughly estimate, fifty miles out of the Laguna de la Madre in a line with Rockport and Vera Cruz. Of course, she wouldn't be there now. But she had started there— and there was a reason why. It was not, manifestly, chance. She was on her way to keep a rendezvous.

Frost kept cudgeling his brain seeking a motive for the kidnaping of Helen Stevens. It probably was the least remunerative thing the gang could have done. What could they hope to gain? Didn't they know they would only attract official attention? And that the less attention they attracted the more success would attend their missions?

It seemed, to Frost, inconsistent, imbecilic. But—they had her. He couldn't very well get away from that—they had her. And it was up to him.

It seemed simple. "Two and two," he said to his instrument board; "make four."

A long way out from the Mexican coast his eyes were caught by a tiny boat that was slipping through the water, leaving a long wake, and he deduced she must be running all of thirty knots. Even from his height he knew the speed was unusual. His heart jumped. He came as close as he dared and maneuvered to get the sun on her. He looked closely. No brass reflection. A rumrunner, but, now, inconsequential. Frost was not interested.

He rolled back closer to the coast and maintained his vigil for thirty more minutes. Then he looked down and was surprised to see another boat. Bang, like that. He had been looking away for only a moment and when he gazed below the boat was there.

He thought probably the lowering sun was playing tricks on him, so he stared intently. No mistake. A boat. Speeding southwest; occasionally outlined against wide swells. If the first launch he saw was speeding there was no adjective for this one. She was, comparatively, doing more than that. And she looked capacious and businesslike now that he could see well. Worth investigating.

He turned the nose of his ship up and climbed. Over to the left was a perfect cirro-cumulus formation which invited him with its natural protection, and he went for it. As he took a gap in the fleece his eyes caught a reflection.

Brass!

The *Catherine B!*

He offered a silent prayer for the cloud bank and took a hurried compass reading. The course the boat was holding was in a straight line with Galveston. The big traffic route! But it could dare. It could show its stern to ninety-nine out of a hundred…

Frost knew it would be fatal to attempt a landing now. Too much light yet. Something might happen. He thought about that rather sharply. An unknown grave in the Gulf was not appealing. That was the way Nungesser and Coli went. And Pedlar. And Erwin. Poor old Bill. There was a tug at Frost's throat. He had gone through many a dogfight with the Dallas ace…

No, Frost knew, he couldn't go down now. Must wait. Hang back and wait for the dark. A big gamble then. A big gamble. Now it would be death.

He guessed the dusk was less than an hour away, but it was a bad guess. It was eighty minutes away and they were the longest eighty minutes Frost ever spent. Occasionally he stole through a rift in the bank to check his quarry to make sure it was within range. The *Catherine B* had now reduced its speed and was drifting idly: quite plainly at its trysting place.

Frost was forcibly struck by the profundity of the situation. Below was a rum boat a hundred miles at sea; above was a formation of clouds which concealed an eagle of justice. Soon that mass of clouds would part to disgorge a winged courier of the law. Why did those clouds happen—just happen to be there? Providence? Frost went off into an endless speculation about the omnipotence of the Creator.

And he found time to breathe a cautious prayer. Cautious because he had never done so openly. It struck him as cowardly. So he prayed quietly and cautiously.

He had decided to go down now in a few minutes.

The sun reached the end of the world, slid off the rim, and reached with long, tenuous fingers for a final hold, missed and fell into the lap of night. Frost was constantly amazed at the swiftness of the sunset; had always been amazed. Yet it is a source of indefinable joy to airmen to see the sun sink from the sky, for at fifteen thousand feet you seem pretty close to the heart of things. Frost probably always would be stirred by such manifestations, no matter how exigent the conditions under which he viewed them. They mildly disquieted him; made him wish he had been an artist.

"Hell," he said to his instrument board, "you're only a lousy airman. Get your head back into this cockpit!"

Night slipped up and five minutes later it was dark. Frost dropped out of the cloud bank among, it seemed, the fledgling stars which were timidly trying their wings, and looked for the *Catherine B.* The Gulf had lost the blackness so apparent in the sunlight and now had become opaque to a faint luminosity. A wayward light flickered below on deck. The light revealed the boat Frost had come to take—and he had determined to take it. Bellerophon felt the same way about the Chimaera.

Frost took off his gauntlet and slipped the silencer-equipped .38 into the seat beside him. Its touch comforted him, reassured him. Of a sudden he picked it up and pulled the trigger. No other sound broke above the throttled humming of the motor.

"Hot stuff!" he said to the sky. To the instrument board he said: "Well, here we go!"

He fell into a glide and kicked his switch off. It was his farewell to the air. Dropping fifteen thousand feet his motor would get cold, too cold to start again in an emergency. But, he told himself, there must be no emergency.

A quarter of a mile back he nosed up into a sort of drift, timing the distance with that weird sense all good flyers possess. And his landing was a tribute to long years of feeling his air. The premium he collected was munificent—his life. To have failed meant death.

The *Catherine B*, on the spot of its meeting, drooled in a wide circle, and as the little battle plane slowly moved by the stern, Frost could plainly read her markings:

CATHERINE B

Galveston

Frost kicked his rudder bar around and turned in towards the boat. He flattened out against its sides when he saw a spurt of flame and heard the crash of the report. The man shot from the rail amidships. Frost leveled his gun and fired. Then he quickly threw his anchor rope over the rail. There had been no far-carrying report from his gun, but the man dropped. He was out on the wing in a moment, over the rail in another, and had tied his ship off with a loop knot.

Attracted by the explosion, a husky fellow shoved half his bulk through the wheelhouse door and Frost saw him level his gun. The Ranger shot from the hip; the man collapsed in the door and rolled on deck. He never knew what had hit him. Frost ran forward.

There was a scuffling sound aft and a man's head and shoulders appeared. He seemed to rise out of nowhere. But he was cautious, had come to investigate what he thought was a shot.

Frost tensed his muscles and gripped his pistol. He pressed himself close to the skylights as the man stepped out gingerly and came towards the wheel-house. He was roughly dressed. He had nearly reached Frost's side, when he stopped suddenly and sucked in his breath in a swift intake. He had seen the plane.

In a flash Frost was beside him. He rammed the gun into his ribs.

"One crack and off goes your head! Get down flat!"

Silently, the man obeyed. He stretched out an arm's length from the second man who had been shot.

Frost said tensely: "That guy is dead. You didn't hear my gun go off because it's got a silencer, see? Now answer my questions and answer 'em quick!"

"All right," the man grunted.

"How many on this tub?"

"Six."

"One of them a woman?"

"Two women."

"Two!"

Frost thought that over.

"What's this boat doing out here?"

"Meeting the *Mermaid* at midnight."

"Liquor?"

"Yep."

"Well, I'll have to give you the works to get you out of the way," Frost said grimly. He meant it. The man knew he meant it. The game had gone too far to take chances.

"I'm a Texas Ranger."

"I know," was the answer. "We been expecting you. But not like this. You're Frost."

"Expecting me?" Frost thought probably he hadn't heard aright.

"Sure. Catherine said you'd come."

"Who's Catherine?"

"Flash's girl."

Frost rolled his tongue against his cheek. "Singleton?"

"Yep."

"I didn't know he had a girl."

"I'll say he had."

Frost hesitated, his mind in a turmoil. The man misconstrued the silence.

"You ain't gonna kill me?" he pleaded. "I'll do anything—"

"Okey," Frost said offhand. "Go over there and call the crew up here. And remember that I've killed two of this crew—and you'll be number three if you make a false move. I'll slug you right through the back of your head. Get up!"

The man walked to the poop ladder, Frost a step behind.

"Hey—Hans!" he yelled through his cupped hands.

Shortly there was a mumble from below.

"Come above and bring Marcelle with you. Hurry!"

Two men climbed out on deck and stood beside the ladder. They hardly were up before Frost stepped out from behind the man and leveled his gun. "Get up in a hurry!" he barked.

They slowly complied.

"Now," Frost went on tensely, "unless you do exactly as I say I'll kill you!"

He looked at the man called Hans. "Throw your gun away!"

The light was feeble, but Frost could see the man scowl. He made no move to comply; he merely grunted.

"Get that gun overboard!"

Still the man said nothing. One of those hard-boiled seamen.

Put–t!

The flame leaped from Frost's gun; there was a muttered oath and the man grabbed his shoulder and moaned, "I'm hit! I'm hit!"

"Get that gun overboard! The next time you stop it with your head!"

There was no mistaking the command now. Frost disliked to shoot the man, but this was no time to quibble. They must be impressed with his determination.

The man groaned and threw his gun overboard with the arm that was still serviceable.

"Get that hand back in the air! And you—throw that gun over! Now yours!"

The men discarded their pistols. Frost lined them up and backed them towards the hatch. "Unbatten it!" he commanded.

They did.

"Pile in!"

"What?"

"Pile in!"

"But, we'll—"

"In there!"

The wounded man called Hans was the last one down. The others aided him. They disappeared below the top, and Frost wrestled the hatch and battened it down as if heading for the open sea. Then he retrieved his pistol and moved to the wheelhouse. The man who lay on deck had been shot through the mouth, and evidently was a first officer. Frost noticed the wheel was chained, so he dragged the body against the skylights and went to the foredeck where he had glimpsed the first sailor.

He had pitched forward on his face, his gun at his feet. Before Frost stooped to inspect him, he kicked the gun across the deck into the water. Then he tugged the man over, saw he, too, was dead, and came back to the after companion. The night now had come on full. The stars were gleaming and a pale moon glowed off the starboard.

Frost went down the steps slowly. He walked along the passage and heard sounds of music, struggling to free itself of the confinement and get into the air. He could sense the struggle. He paused at the cabin door and listened. An electric gramaphone. Someone evidently was unworried. He rapped on the door.

It opened and he thrust his foot inside. He pried it open with his leg and entered, his gun drawn.

He faced a woman—and gasped.

"You!"

"You!"

His companion of La Estrellita!

Here—in full panoply, arrayed like a queen; against a background of luxury. For a moment he was nonplussed. A lot had happened. This was the crowning blow. He gradually recovered, and thought about the awkward picture he presented there with his pistol drawn.

"Miss Stevens," he coughed, embarrassed. "Er—"

"How do you do, Captain?" she said. "Sit down." Frost did so. "Do you find it helps the effect when you visit a young lady with drawn revolver?"

Frost grinned. "Well, I hardly expected to find you like this. I thought—"

"Yes," she beamed; "they are good to me, aren't they?"

She nonchalantly moved across the cabin to a wall telephone. He thought that rather an odd thing for a prisoner to do—telephone. That simple act brought the pieces of the puzzle together with a click. Frost had just been told there were two women on board. One he expected to find a prisoner—Helen Stevens. But this woman was no prisoner—

Catherine!

With pent-up fury he leaped from his chair and was beside her before she could get an answer. He snatched the telephone out of her hand and replaced it. He faced her, flushing with anger.

"Get away!" he said. "And I hope it won't be necessary for me to kill you!"

She lifted her face in a half sneer. "Well," she said, moving in a swagger, "how long do you think you can get away with this high-handed stuff?"

"Don't make me laugh," Frost said.

There was the sound of a knock on a door in another wall than that by which he had entered.

"Who's in there?" he demanded.

"Find out for yourself," she snapped.

"I will," he said. He observed her with something not unlike admiration. "So you're Catherine, eh?" He was a little taken aback. Disappointed. Once he had had an adventure with her.

Men do not easily forget such things. Now it all came back in a rush… her indifference to the danger in La Estrellita… the tapping of her fingers on the glass was a signal….

He glared: "You tried to trap me, didn't you? Tried to get me killed?"

She laughed. "Why not? You bumped off the only man I ever loved, and for that I'm going to *get* you, Frost. What a pity those saps didn't kill you that night in Algadon!"

"Yes," he mused; "what a pity! You know—you're a damned attractive woman to be mixed up with a rotten gang like this."

"I'm going to stay mixed. You can't bluff me, Frost. I don't scare worth a damn."

"Maybe you don't. Oh, by the way; I neglected to tell you I locked three of your thugs in the hold. Also," this casually, "I had to bump off a couple of 'em. Now who's the woman in the other room?"

"Nobody. That is—"

"Get that door open, or I'll tear it down!"

She got up sullenly and unlocked the narrow door. Through it another woman stumbled, her hair disheveled, her clothes wrinkled, her face worried. She saw Frost and stopped short.

"It's all right," Frost said reassuringly, "I'm a policeman. Who are you?"

"I'm—"

"Don't you talk!" came the swift interruption. "This bum means no good." She tried to reach the woman's side, but Frost intervened.

"Never mind her," he said. "I'm Frost of the Rangers."

"Oh! Frost!" she murmured the words. "I'm Helen Stevens. I've been a prisoner for a week."

"Huh! Are you a newspaper woman?"

"Yes."

Frost grinned broadly, spread his legs and said: "Well, sit down, ladies, and get comfortable. This ought to be good."

Then it was that Frost observed both women were about the same height and build, and that the genuine Helen Stevens wore a brown ensemble similar to the one worn by his companion that night in La Estrellita. He began to see the light.

"A week ago," said Helen Stevens, "I was kidnaped in Jamestown, drugged and brought here. I don't know why. I never had an enemy in my life."

"There's no puzzle there," Frost said. "This jane here is the ex-sweetheart of an ex-racketeer who was allied with the Black Ship gang and bumped off by Hell's Stepsons. She wanted revenge on me; the way to get that was remove you and assume your identity." He smiled appreciatively. "That right, Mrs. Singleton?"

"You go to hell!"

"So," mused Helen Stevens, slightly more at ease, "you're Captain Frost. I was on my way to see you—had a letter from the Adjutant-General. It was stolen with my luggage!"

"I got it," Frost grinned. "You'll learn after a while that this is a high-powered gang you're dealing with."

Helen Stevens was surveying the broad figure of Jerry Frost, remembering tales of his prowess in the skies of France and in the jungles of Latin America—*El Beneficio* they called him then—surveying him in frank admiration.

"I think," Frost said, "it would be wise to get going. This boat has got a date I'd rather not keep. First, I'm afraid we'll have to tie up the hellcat."

The hellcat got to her feet, her eyes burning with passionate hatred, and leaped at Frost. She landed in his lap and they both went over backwards with the chair. His pistol rattled on the hardwood floor.

"Get that gun!" he yelled, a moment before she clawed at his face. She interposed a few choice oaths, and hammered Frost about the ears with her fists. They squirmed on the floor inelegantly until he managed to get a hammer-lock on her arm. She swore and cried out in pain.

"Pipe down and I'll let you go!" Frost said. "Otherwise I'll break it off." His eyes fell on the silk cord knotted around port hole draperies and he said to Helen Stevens, "Get that cord."

She untied it and brought it to him. Frost slipped it around the woman's wrists and tied her hands behind her. Then he took off his belt and strapped it tightly around her ankles. To complete the job he took out his handkerchief and crammed it in her mouth.

"Now," he said; "I need a bandage."

Helen Stevens did not hesitate. She lifted her dress, revealed a sheeny knee and a silk petticoat. She ripped it, jerked off a strip and handed it to Frost.

"Great stuff!" he said. "I'm beginning to think you'll do!"

"You're damned right I'll do!" she admitted.

Frost tied the gag and then stepped back to inspect his craftmanship. Apart from the woman's squirming, and nobody has ever invented a way to stop that, he had to confess it was very good.

"Not bad for a beginner," he observed.

The woman grunted and her eyes flashed. Frost picked her up and deposited her, none too carefully, on a lounge. He whispered in her ear: "Now we're going up to take the wheel." She grunted again, and in a fit of temper wriggled to the floor with a bang.

Frost looked at her loftily. "All right, baby—suit yourself."

Helen Stevens handed him his pistol and said: "Don't you think it would be wise to use the radio and let somebody know where we are?"

Frost slanted his head from side to side as if he had known her a century; decided she, too, was a fluffy bit of femininity. His light mood was sharpened by his success. "Another great idea," he said. "Let's have a look."

They came on deck together, he holding her hand. It was, like the night, warm and soft—he remembered snatches of books and stories he'd read about women... regal poise... generations of aristocrats to produce one like this... long lashes... and full red lips... He even tried to recall some poetry.

He looked at her suddenly as if he knew she had read his thoughts. He was blushing... She laughed. He laughed too— not knowing what else to do.

They entered the wheelhouse of the *Catherine B* as she rose on a long swell, poised herself, and settled into the valley of the Gulf. It was dark and quiet, only a light glowed from the compass box; Frost found the switch and pulled it. A light sprang into life at the top of the pilothouse.

On one side was the wireless and without further ado Frost seated himself and cut on the switch. The motor hummed, tiny sparks glowed, and he adjusted the head set. He tapped out a message hurriedly. Presently there was a light cracking sound in the headphone and he bent over his task. He finished and sat up.

"They're on their way," he said.

He took a look at the binnacle and moved to the chart table. "Now to figure out which way to go," he remarked. "I'd hate to wind up in Cuba." He studied the chart for a few silent minutes. Then he moved the wheel and unchained it. "Look," he said, "think you can hold this wheel on one-eighteen when I get her on that course?"

"Sure," she said, still the adventuress.

"I'll have a look around," Frost said. He went to the side of the box and yanked at the control. From somewhere in the boat's depth a bell tinkled. It slowly gained speed. Frost spun the wheel and held her circling until she was on the course he had determined upon as most likely to intercept the cutter he had summoned. Frost reached into his shoulder-holster and took out his other pistol. He laid it on the table beside her. "That's a .38," he said, "fitted with a silencer. And it's ready to blast." She nodded and he went out.

Frost noted that the *Catherine B* was holding steady at about half speed. He went to the rail and unloosed the rope that anchored his plane, snubbed it along the rail and finally tied it off the stern. Then he walked for'ard and went below through the fo'csle.

Helen Stevens, left alone on as weird an adventure as any newspaper woman ever had, gripped the wheel, her teeth clenched, and stared into that disk of white light that held the magic number, 118, wavering across a red line.

Some time later Frost emerged from the shadows of the deck-house and came forward into the wheelhouse wearing a wide smile.

"We're all alone but for the engineer," he said. "Now I'll take charge of that." He took the wheel, and she stood beside him and shivered.

"You might as well get comfortable," he said.

"I'm all right," she said. "I think this is a good time to begin that belated interview. Born?"

"Yes?"

She laughed. "Where?"

"I'd rather talk about you," Frost said. "How long are you going to be around Texas?"

"That depends."

"On what?"

"How long it takes to get this story."

"In that case—" he smiled.

And she smiled.

THEY PROBABLY WOULD have been talking yet had not a siren sounded off the port side some two hours later. Frost rang the signal for power off and went out of the wheelhouse.

"Ahoy, there!"

"Who's there?"

"U.S. Coast Guard!"

"Okey! This is Frost—Texas Rangers!"

The cutter pulled up alongside, its fenders bumped and they lashed on. Half a dozen huskies vaulted the rails. The leader shifted his pistol to his right hand and came forward fast. Frost could see in the half-light he was some sort of an officer.

"Frost?"

"Right!"

"I'm Al Bennett." They shook hands. "We picked up your message. I radioed Clay in Corpus that I'd located you."

Thanks," said Frost. "Can you send a man over to take the wheel? I've got somebody in there who's just about washed up."

"Sure," said Bennett. "Bucko—on the wheel!"

The man saluted smartly and preceded Frost and Bennett into the wheelhouse.

"Miss Stevens this is Mr. Bennett, of the Coast Guard." Bennett nodded his head. "So you're the little girl who's been leading us such a merry chase?"

"I'm afraid so," she said. She took Frost's arm.

"Bennett, there's three of the crew in the hold—one winged. For'ard there's a man dead and beside the sky-light there's another one in the same fix. There is a woman below I had to tie up."

Bennett looked at him, his eyes wide.

"Say," he said, "is it possible you took this baby all alone?"

"It was a cinch." Lightly.

"Yeh? Well. I don't mind telling you the whole Coast Guard has been trying to land this bark for weeks."

"Will you," asked Frost, disregarding the praise, "see that we get into port okey?"

"You bet." He went to the door and spoke to the crew who had come over in the recent boarding. "Pass the word along for the cutter to shove off. You men stay aboard with me. We're going to Corpus." He came back to the wheel.

"We'll go below," Frost said. "Er—"

"Sure," said Bennett, grinning.

"Business," Frost went on. "She's getting—"

"Sure—"

But Frost, self-conscious, refused to let Bennett be diplomatic. Helen Stevens finally had to rush to the rescue. "I'm interviewing him," she explained.

Bennett laughed, full. "That's okey with me, Miss," he said. "But you'd better shove off. Ox Clay and Jimmy O'Neill are on their way out here."

Frost and the woman walked out—close together.

The moment they disappeared Bennett turned to the man at the wheel and said: "Ever hear of anything like it?"

"Beats me."

Bennett looked aft at the shadowy form that rose and fell behind like a phantom. It was Frost's battle plane.

"I guess," said Bennett, soberly, "a guy has got to be a little goofy to try something like this. It wouldn't work once in a hundred times. They must be right about that guy, Frost. I've read of those one-man cyclones, but I never saw one before."

"You said it," contributed the man at the wheel.

The *Catherine B,* in the firm hands of the Coast Guard, slipped on towards Corpus Christi with a grim greyhound of the Gulf for a convoy, and another on the way.

In four hours they would be in port.

Somewhere in Mexico

The Texas Air Patrol Smashes into a Border Gang

THREE AIRPLANES, INDISTINGUISHABLE against the blackness of the night, their presence revealed as fitful air currents permitted faint motor dronings to reach the vicinity of the ground, sailed out of Mexico across the Rio Grande shortly after midnight. They passed over Espinard at something like 20,000 feet and veered sharply northwest in a line almost parallel with the river.

Flying through the Border country at midnight is, to say the least, a suspicious business: here of all places legitimate missions are not conducted at such hours or at such altitudes. The pilots of the three ships had, it seemed, selected the hour when they thought most of the countryside was likely to be under wraps and fast asleep.

As a matter of fact most of the countryside was. But there was one man awake and it so happened that he had taken a twenty-year course in the intrigue of the Border and was therefore skilled, nimble-witted—and curious. He was George Stuart, veteran captain of the Texas Rangers, who for no particular reason, was walking slowly along the main street of Espinard to his quarters.

The dronings were, at first, so faint and so vague they did not definitely register on his mind. His boots clanked on the only short strip of pavement Espinard possessed, interfered with the sounds and very nearly drowned them. But gradually he became aware that something was going on up above; and his natural instinct warned him it was irregular.

Suspicious, he stopped, slanted his head and listened attentively. For thirty seconds he was a graven image. He was now certain he was not mistaken. Those were airplanes—airplanes lost somewhere in the blackness of that ebony ceiling. Strange country, the Border land; the sky like the earth, had learned to hold its secrets.

An officer younger and less experienced than George Stuart might have dismissed this as an episode worthy of only cursory interest; indeed a younger officer might have thought nothing of it. But the score of ebullient years George Stuart had put in along the sluggish boundary had impressed him with the resourcefulness and daring of criminals, and of late he had become particularly familiar with the Black Ship gang, a syndicate of lawlessness which employed all manner of science to beat the Border patrols.

Stuart stared into the night in a desperate effort to penetrate the black curtain, but still could see nothing. The faint roars of the motors continued to roll.

"Funny," he said to himself.

He briskly resumed his march and a block down the street stepped on the porch of the building which served as his office, and fumbled at the door. He threw the latch, went inside and snapped on a shaded light above his desk. He picked up the telephone, spoke tersely to the operator, lighted a cigarette and for two minutes smoked uninterrupted. Ninety miles northwest a wall telephone jangled in headquarters room of the Texas Air Rangers, the base of Hell's Stepsons, a quartet of daredevils banded together in a crack patrol under Captain Jerry Frost.

The bell rasped stridently in the little room, and Frost came alive fast. He flung back the cover and got up, pajama coat open and feet bare, and went to the telephone.

"Hello," he said. He paused a moment to clear his head of the sleep stupidity, and went on: "Yes, this is Frost... Hello, George.... No, you aren't troubling anybody.... You did?... How many?... More than one—huh?... I get you.... You only heard 'em.... Headed this way.... Are you sure?... I say, are you sure they're coming this way?... Okey.... Yeh, we'll have a look... s'long."

He muttered a soft, "Damn!" and went back into the bedroom. He clicked the switch and contemplated the four men sleeping before him—Hell's Stepsons.

He grinned, stepped to one of the beds, and shook the form roughly.

"Hey, Hans!" he said. "Hit the deck!"

A bland oval face came into view, blinked its eyes and then opened them wide. The blanket fell away and Hans Traub, phlegmatic ex-Bavarian, once commander of a squadron of Maltese crosses on the Piave, sat up.

"What's the big idea?" he mumbled in rich Americanese.

"Stuart 'phoned from Espinard and said he'd heard airplanes. Didn't know how many—guessed there were three. They were headed this way, so I thought we'd take a look."

Traub clawed fiercely at his hair to satisfy a sort of primitive complex which always asserted itself when he first was awakened. "Hell," he snorted, "you *would* pick a moment like that to get me up! I was back in the old country with a stein of beer in each hand and a million—"

"*C'est la guerre!*" Frost said. He passed by the beds and slapped the other three men on that spot calculated to rouse them quickest. They stirred, yawned, and flexed their arms.

Frost said crisply to them: "The Black Ship gang or somebody else, is loose! We're going up!"

He went back to the telephone and spun the lever. Three long and one short. Rural custom. There was no answer; impatiently he spun it again.

"Hello!" he yelled. "Hello!... Johnny?... Get our ships out and check the ammo! Then douse all the lights!"

Eddie Giles grunted and reached under the bed for a woolen sock. He missed it and reached again; then gave up in disgust. "I say now, that's rather odd! Mr. Hinsdell, have you got my sock?"

Skipper Hinsdell sighed. "Lissen, Limey—who the hell was your nurse during the war?" He tossed the sock over the bed. "Ever try undressing on your own side?"

"Not a bad idea," Eddie Giles approved. "Not bad at all. Where're we going in such a rush?"

"To a movie, you sap!" fired Rowdy Perry.

"How lovely!"

"If you ask me," interposed Hinsdell, "it's a lousy night to go anywhere! So damned black out there you can't see your hand!"

"Yeh—we ought to get you a job in some refined girls' school somewhere," grumbled Traub.

"I want one too," said Giles. "Talk about heaven—"

"Nobody," went on Hinsdell, "has got any right to be joy-riding around this time of night. Maybe one of those deer-hunting private flyers who thinks it's smart to go somewhere at midnight."

Frost had dressed and had slipped on a pair of coveralls over his clothes. "Joyriders don't flirt with the ceiling," he said soberly. "Nor do deer hunters. If they were too high for Stuart to see, too high to be heard distinctly—they were way up there. Better not expect a picnic." He picked up his helmet. "Ready?"

"Righto!" said Giles.

Frost said: "Let's push off."

They walked two hundred yards across a barren strip of land to the hangar which lay like a tired monster in the darkness. Within a single light glowed, revealing two men busy around the trim battle planes.

"There ain't no sky at all," remarked Hinsdell, and there was no answer to that observation. Hell's Stepsons were silently contemplating another mysterious sortie, one of many. Words were meaningless, good-natured, even rough, repartee was poor surcease. They were willing—yea, anxious—to oppose a definite objective in the full spread of the day, but opposing a phantom at night was something else again. It was pretty grim business.

Johnny Rosenfield, the head mechanic, addressed Frost. He had been with Frost through a part of the war—and had attained that envious position where he could talk familiarly with a celebrity.

"Everything okey, Chief," he said. "What's up?"

"I don't know, Johnny. Somebody headed this way from Espinard. They came from below."

Johnny Rosenfield puckered his thick lips and whistled. "That gang, you reckon?"

"I don't know," Frost said. "Anyway, we're not taking any chances after all that's happened."

He moved his eyes to his battle plane. In its cockpit he had spent many long hours, through its blade he had fired innumerable shots, to its instrument board he had spoken countless words. That plane had ceased to become a thing of steel, spruce and linen—had become, instead, a living companion; his weapon against the Black Ship gang.

The Black Ship gang. For months it had gone on. Hell's Stepsons had wrecked a counterfeiting plant at Lamaraz, gone through dogfight after dogfight, captured a rum-boat and a woman who once had stood high up in the ranks. Nearly all the Air Rangers bore scars as mute evidence the gang respected no law—and yet Frost's men had been able to make only negligible progress in the struggle to get the higher-ups.

Who was behind the great fleet of airplanes and rum-boats and reaching into more than one police department? Who was the Black Ship gang anyway?

Frost had resolved to find the answer or die in the attempt. Hell's Stepsons had left the movie lots of Southern California to join him in that resolution... four former aces... courageous beyond question... reckless beyond wisdom... groping...

Johnny Rosenfield stood by Frost's side and the commander

spoke to him as a man in a limitless dream. "Wheel 'em out, Johnny, and douse the lights."

"Yes, sir," Rosenfield replied, turning away. There was no more curious person alive than this fat mechanic who had learned all there was to learn about airplane motors on the test blocks at Romorantin in '17 and '18, and outside of the immediate circle there was none who could ask questions faster. But Johnny Rosenfield tempered his curiosity with admirable diplomacy. And he knew that when Frost stared dreamily and his voice came out flat and faraway it was no time for him to indulge his curiosity.

The A3's were soon on the tarmac.

"Well?" said Traub.

"We'll wait," Frost said. "We won't ride until we know where we're going."

They moved to their planes and sat down in the darkness, their ears strained and alert. For perhaps twenty minutes they sat there.

Then Traub said: "Lissen!"

There was a thin humming down the river.

"Ships!" exclaimed Perry. "Two—no, by God, three! You can hear the break!"

You could. A trained ear could catch the slight lulls in the sounds as they cascaded down, could almost estimate the revolutions.

"Righto!" said Giles. "Three!"

"They aren't twenty thousand feet up now," said Traub. "They're about five thousand."

"Looks like deviltry," said Frost. "They couldn't lose that much altitude and not know it!"

The humming grew more and more distinct. Frost dashed to the side of the hangar and switched on a powerful searchlight. He cut it across the sky in a penetrating path like the finger of an accuser.

"There they are!" yelled Perry.

Frost had them centered a moment later—caught in the wide ray—three black planes.

"I'll give 'em a chance to get down," Frost muttered.

"To hell with giving them a chance," yelled Traub. "Let's get up!"

"Wait, Hans!" said Frost quietly.

The ex-Bavarian flared up heatedly, an astonishing thing for him. "Damn it all, Jerry," he rasped. "You see who they are. They aren't entitled to—"

"Hans!" It was the voice of authority.

Traub quieted somewhat, glared, and strode impatiently to his plane.

Frost moved the light in short, quick jerks in order not to blind the pilots, and at intervals dropped it to illuminate the flying field—the challenge of the Border patrol at night; a challenge forever respected by the peaceful.

But the three black ships thundered ahead, the roar of the motors filling the night.

"Well," said Hinsdell; "that's plain enough!"

Hans Traub, beside his plane, turned and yelled: "For God's sake, Jerry—let's get up!"

Frost turned and shouted: "Johnny! Johnny!"

The short legs of the mechanic brought him up beside the commander.

"Take the light and keep 'em in it!" Frost cried. "And don't blind us any more than you can help. Let's go, men!"

They trotted to their ships, motors barked and snapped into a deep concert of life. Frost's machine trembled and crept out, immediately followed by the impatient Traub. Behind were Eddie Giles, Skipper Hinsdell and Rowdy Perry. They pulled down their goggles, reached for their throttles and got away in a rush. Five ghoulish moths suddenly gone in the night sky. Their echoes clattered across the flatlands.

From somewhere above, the blackness was vividly cut by the flame of a gun that rattled angrily, the insolent barking of a terrier disturbed at play by a mastiff. A warning to stay away. Hell's Stepsons only laughed.

Climbing with their motors barking wide open to reach the source of gunfire, their eyes were suddenly drenched in a blinding bath of white light from below. Frost swore testily and thought at first that Rosenfield had let the searchlight beams strike them. Then a choked crash throbbed suddenly and died. The country was lighted in an eerie silhouette. Hell's Stepsons' planes rocked, then steadied; and the searchlight went out.

Frost's throat tightened and he knew. "Hell!" he muttered. "They dropped a bomb!"

His jaws snapped shut and his hand swept forward to his throttle. The engine whined quietly on a rising note until it reached its full pitch—a tremendous, screaming monotone that burst fiercely into his eardrums and stayed with such insistence that presently there was no sound at all. His ears itched under his helmet. He felt of the rudder bar cautiously as an organist about to begin an overture. He turned slightly and read the story of his instrument board. Motor—warm! Air speed—right! Revolutions—right! Altitude—twenty-four hundred! Cross bubble—center of tube. Longitudinal bubble—slightly forward. Then he decided to look out and stuck his head into the sharp scythe of the slipstream.

Ahead and slightly to the right he made out the form of one of the enemy, his presence definitely revealed by the yellow exhaust which trailed back like a frayed ribbon. Frost poked his nose up and felt for the trigger.

An ominous saber of light jutted forward for an instant and then died as a burned-out roman candle dies. "Atta-baby!" he said through his teeth, rolling over to center his prey. The black ship rolled too; Frost stood on his rudder bar and shoved forward on his stick.

"Hang together!" he screamed at his wings. There! Straight ahead! The black ship! Frost squeezed the trigger furiously; his guns chattered. The traction was knocked out from under the black ship. Frost squeezed his trigger again. His guns roared. The black ship wavered and slipped off on its wing, downward.

"Cinch!" he murmured. Sometimes a dogfight was tough and you got all shot up, and sometimes it was easy. He remembered, parenthetically, Lufbery had the same experience once over Etain, and when they got to kidding Luf, he shut them up with a, "Whatthehell—a good flyer don't need but one bust." Right!

He looked out and saw that Traub and Giles had another black ship in a bad pocket and that Perry and Hinsdell were cutting loose at the third invader. So he loafed along to let his men have the kill.

A steel-billed woodpecker close at hand broke his reverie. Bits of wood flew in his face. Something black streaked past above, so close Frost could almost feel the draft of air it had made in passing. One of the ships had got loose from Hell's Stepsons in a maneuver, and was streaking away.

Frost swore softly, marked this one for his own, and came over in a quick climbing turn and flattened out for the chase. The wind whistled through the struts; the night was black and the visibility poor, but the fire of battle was in his blood and a grim confidence in his heart.

He brought the nose of his ship over in line with the enemy, marking it by the flame from the exhausts. He settled down and took a look through his triplex windshield and discovered it had been cracked into a thousand lines. Moreover, his compass had been hit; it hung a ball on a broken pendulum. He could find no other damage in a hurried glance. Odd. Those bullets surely had some little brothers...

When he brought his eyes back to the front he learned that he was being outdistanced. Those flames by which he marked the enemy were now farther away. Frost eased his throttle forward and swore softly.

"Damn!" he said.

Below he saw the lights of Torcazas, and knew the enemy was heading for the interior of Mexico. "Me and you!" he yelled ungrammatically. He pushed his throttle to three-quarters.

After a while he was forced to realize he was being led a losing chase. The more distance he lost the more temper went with it. Soon he was biting at his lip in anger, and then he slapped his throttle full open. His ship quivered under the strain, and the motor shook as if every revolution would be its last.

Frost was enough of an airman to know this couldn't be kept up. Something had to crack sooner or later—wide open. So he decided to get in a burst now. His cold fingers sought the trigger, pressed it. His guns coughed spasmodically. Cold!

"Damn!" he swore again.

Again he pressed the trigger. Flame this time—reluctant flame. Cautiously, as he would touch a baby's cheek, he pressed the trigger again. Careful now. No use blowing your guns off the cowl. Damned nonsense! Stupid! This time there was a roar and a belching that soon settled into a rhythmic flow. Frost grinned, and maneuvered to let a burst get home.

He gave not a thought to his men, to the damage caused by the bomb, nor to the ship he had knocked down. That was the past; he was concentrating on the enemy ahead to the exclusion of all else. He had his head up, now in the slipstream, now out the side, fighting back the film that spread over his eyes from dilated lids.

As a matter of cold fact, Captain Frost was being outrun, but he wouldn't admit it. Subconsciously he thought he heard a faint noise that seemed to tell him his enemy was developing more speed, but he choked back the idea.

He ripped forth a savage burst that amounted to no more than a pot shot, and a moment later he plainly caught the black ship in his ring sights. He swore again and used up a venomous burst, but it failed to mar the serenity of the enemy pilot. For all the concern he exhibited he might have been on a short cruise over a flower garden. That indifference caused Frost to writhe. And it was cold—the thin cold that tightens about the heart.

He lost all sense of distance, time—everything. The ghost ahead lured him… became a mirage. Often he unconsciously reached for his throttle to find it already was open. Often he whispered: "Stay with me, bebby!" to his motor. Often he let his guns go.

To no avail. But there was no turning back for him.

Then, after a long time, he thought he detected a lapse of distance. The black plane seemed suddenly to hang before him, out of nowhere. Frost held his trigger long and affectionately.

He saw the black ship drop and lose distance. His heart leaped with the discovery that his enemy was vulnerable. For a long time he had thought the black ship magically protected, and the chase had been so keen, that a better fate was merited. The black ship seemed to fold its wings and glide slowly to earth. Frost cut his gun and looked down, listening for the crash.

None came. He brushed back his goggles and looked out over the fuselage. Presently he discerned the faint outlines of what he thought was a ship on the ground, but he could not tell if it had cracked up. He pulled his body back in the seat and twisted the tip end of his cold nose. Still, that failed to help.

Well, that was that. All I can do. Better get home. Cold. Cold as hell. Hope the boys—

His glance fell on the board and he saw his compass was smashed. What the deuce? Oh... remember now... the Black Ship's first burst... No compass, eh?... Silly to think you could fly without a compass... about a hundred miles from Torcazas... but in which direction... No compass... Hot, what?...

His mind reeled and the devils of anxiety crawled in his throat.

He was four thousand feet up in a black night over a strange country.

Jerry Frost was given to quick decisions. They were characteristic of the man. Instantly he decided to land, motivated by the desire to know where he was, and the more important knowledge that his fuel supply was low.

He threw out a flare and nosed over.

The countryside lighted, a great space in pale white, and Frost saw the black ship safely down in a wide field. A short distance away were the roofs of a white house, a long, rambling structure, impressive in its loneliness. Frost picked out a likely looking strip of ground and carefully pancaked down.

His wheels struck the ground, his plane bounced up, then settled and glided to a stop. He was down less than a hundred feet from the black ship. He leaped to the ground, his legs stinging at the sudden impact, and from their long cramped position in the cockpit. He reached over the board to cut the switch.

"Get your hands up!"

A sharp voice rose above the hum in his brain and he turned quickly. Two tall men stood there, their business revealed by two revolvers along the barrels of which gleamed the dying flare. Frost lifted his hands.

"Get his guns!" barked one of the men. The other unbuttoned Frost's coveralls and took his automatic.

"May I ask who the hell you are?" Frost said evenly.

"None of your damned business!" the man spat out. "Turn around and march!"

"But—"

"I said—*march!*"

He rammed his gun savagely into Frost's ribs. It was more of a short blow and Frost whirled, his face livid in the pale light. He looked upon a tight-lipped man of middle age, also garbed in flying suit and helmet. It dawned on Frost that this was the pilot of the ship he thought he had knocked down. Despite the situation he was rather surprised.

"I got to hand it to you," he said. "Anybody who can get a ship down on a night—"

"Never mind!" the man cut in. "Move on!"

Frost moved slowly off towards the house, the two men following silently, pistols ready. They reached the gate of a wall about eight feet high which surrounded the house, and pulled a cord.

A bell tinkled somewhere inside and a moment later the gates swung inward. They stepped through and the men spoke in low tones to the one who had let them in. Then the gates swung shut again, almost noiselessly.

Then Frost had his first view of the house. It looked neat and mysterious. The walls were bleak and depressive: the many windows were shaded by drawn blinds, and no smoke issued from the chimneys. There was no sign of life; the whole aspect of the place was uninviting. Frost's mind leaped back to the days of his boyhood, and now he knew how Poe's narrator must have felt that night when he looked upon the sinister house of Roderick Usher.

The man who had opened the gate now joined them and stepped in front.

"Keep moving!" brusquely said the man with the pistol.

They walked on slowly, the gravel crunching beneath their feet. They stepped on a long porch whose one door opened into a corridor as deep as the porch was long. Frost went inside and stopped.

"Go ahead!" the man rasped again, poking him with the pistol. Frost obeyed silently, treading upon a rug that was thick to the degree of muffling their footsteps. They passed four doors, then the man stopped and knocked.

"Come in," a voice bade.

The man swung open the door but did not enter. He stepped back and permitted Frost to cross the threshold first. The flying Ranger went inside and stopped, mouth wide.

He was in a low-ceilinged room, rectangular, brilliantly lighted. He made a mental note that this light did not show from the outside. Built-in bookcases were around the walls, *objets d'art* were everywhere, in the corner were two fine globes—terrestrial and celestial, on the walls were framed antique maps, and in the center of the room was a long table.

At that table sat four men.

If Frost was surprised, the men were dumfounded. They got to their feet in a single motion, highly wrought up, a question—one question—on their lips.

The two black ship pilots stepped into the room.

"Who is this, Waldman?" one of the men at the table managed.

The pilot called Waldman lowered his pistol and said respectfully: "I don't know, sir. One of the Rangers—he followed us."

"So!" the man ejaculated. He sat down. The others also sat.

"How did it happen?"

"He simply followed us, and shot all the way down here. We were the only ones to get through."

"Did you—" suggestively.

"Yes, sir," the man called Waldman nodded. "I think we got their hangar. Crites and Warwitz were—"

"Oh, yes," the man said.

"We landed," Waldman went on, "and about the time we got down this fellow—" indicating Frost "—threw out a flare. Then he came down. That's all there is to it."

"Oh, yes," the man said again. "A gift."

Both flyers grinned. "Something like that, sir," said Waldman.

"Very good. That will be all," the man said almost curtly.

Waldman stopped at the door and said, "We took his pistol, sir, but I'd suggest—"

"Care?" The man smiled as he intercepted the question. "Oh, yes—we know their reputation."

Frost was not a little awed by the crispness of the discipline. There was no doubt in his mind that he had, after weeks and weeks of arduous search, finally stumbled, through no fault of his own this time, upon the genuine higher-ups in the Black Ship gang—if not the leaders then the men only one step removed from the leaders.

Frost stood there, every nerve in his body tingling, but still fighting a mad, impulsive desire to laugh. It couldn't be, he told himself fiercely, it couldn't be real... he was asleep in his barracks... bad dreams...

A vision moved before his eyes. The man was getting up again. He was speaking in a flat, colorless voice.

"You may sit down, sir," he said as if he were bestowing a decoration.

Frost snapped out of it. "Thanks," he said coldly, pulling a chair to him. He scrutinized the quartet at the table.

The man who had been doing the talking must have been all of fifty years, thin, sallow-faced, with penetrating black eyes and a sharp nose. He wore silver-rimmed glasses and Frost reflected there was an air of the continental about him.

Frost spotted the man at his left for a Mexican the moment he saw him. He was given to obesity, swarthy, eyes distrustful. Beside the Mexican lolled the indolent form of probably,

Frost thought, the youngest man of the group, but his affected nonchalance was belied by his quick, nervous gestures. "A tough egg," Frost mused.

The fourth member of the assembly was thick-lipped, his hair a flaming red; not at all immaculate. He was a sprawling, fat figure who looked like a drunken portrait painter's conception of Genghis Khan.

An odd quartet…

The elderly man was speaking again. "You will tell us," he said in a tone not accustomed to refusal, "your name and position." His eyes glinted behind his glasses.

"You go to hell!" Frost said impetuously.

One man smiled at the other with a semblance of a threat. The Mexican moved his bulk in the chair as if he would be delighted to handle such a belligerent guest.

"You may as well understand now," the younger man cut in, "that your position is not improved by such an attitude." The others nodded approvingly. "Your best chance is to come clean."

Frost said nothing.

"Who are you besides being a Ranger?" the elderly man interposed again.

"Suppose," Frost said, for want of something better, "I should ask you that question?"

He said it bluntly, but not a man of the quartet seemed even a little disconcerted. It might even be truthfully reported they smiled as if they had encountered a private and amusing thought.

The elderly man got up with a flourish. He seemed delighted at the opportunity. Psychiatrists agree this is common to the mental attitude of crooks.

"My name, sir," he said, "is Franz Weisberg, and I am no

nonentity in Europe. This—" gesturing to the Mexican "—is Señor Jose Garza, quite an artist with the knife—" he paused to smile in, Frost thought, sardonic pleasure "—and this—" leveling his finger at the younger man "—is Floyd Knight, who is familiar with every reef from Koolau to Batavia, and the unimpressive gentleman is Red Jacobson—not recommended for children." Weisberg smiled broadly, still standing, and went on: "Did you expect us to be so candid?"

Frost smiled at the display of grandiloquence, smiled in spite of himself.

"No," he honestly admitted.

"Have you no idea why I talk so freely?" Weisberg went on. Frost looked up, but said nothing, and Weisberg continued: "We have good reason to believe you will be careful with our secrets." The suggestion was unmistakable.

"Where am I?" Frost asked.

"Somewhere in Mexico," Knight responded promptly. "Which is as much as you will ever know."

There was a rap at the door and Weisberg said, "Come in."

It was Waldman again. "Beg pardon, sir," he said, "but I've just looked over this fellow's plane. His name is printed on the fuselage. He's Captain Frost, sir!"

The only reaction was a slight widening of the eyes.

"Oh, yes, Waldman. Thank you."

"Yes, sir," said Waldman. He saluted hurriedly and closed the door behind him.

Not until then had Frost realized he was in a tight corner. He was inclined to let things shape their own ends before he started interfering, but in this case it appeared, more and more, that he was going to have precious little to do about it.

"So," Weisberg said slowly, "you are Captain Frost. The *Great* Frost," he emphasized.

Frost nodded. No use to worry now; no use to try to bluff it any longer. "Guilty!" he said with a short laugh. "Rather theatrical, isn't it? Ranger captain captured by enemy and all that sort of thing." He laughed again. "If I were in the movies now, I should finally turn the tables."

"Yes," Knight mused, his hands under the table. "And if you should make a funny move I would drill a pretty little hole right in the middle of your head!"

"I suppose, gentlemen, there is no use demanding the usual courtesies due a prisoner of war?"

Jose Garza's fat head bobbed up and down.

"Quite correct, *Capitan.* There are no courtesies!"

"I wonder, Frost," Weisberg went on, "if you'd ever thought how valuable you'd be to us. Soon now we shall be in Chapultepec Castle—"

"Easy!" hissed Knight.

Weisberg looked at him, then checked himself abruptly. "If there is any price…" His voice trailed away suggestively.

"There is none!" Frost flung in his face. "Not for a million."

"That, sir," Weisberg said softly, "is unfortunate. You are signing your death warrant." He seemed a little sorrowful.

He regarded the Ranger close up. Big. Tall. Rugged. A fighting chin. Clear eyes. A warrior such as must have been in the front ranks of the Crusaders' legions when they marched against the infidels. Looking at him thus he could believe all he'd heard about Jerry Frost… world war ace lieutenant in the Kosciusko squadron… Latin-American *soldado de fortuna*… admittedly one of the finest air fighters who ever stood on a rudder bar…

"Too bad—too bad," he mused again, stroking his chin. Franz Weisberg's sorrow was not all simulated. Some of it was genuine. He saw fine material going to waste.

"May I smoke?" Frost asked.

"You'll please," Knight cut in quickly, "remember what I said and keep your hands on your lap!" He got up and went to the Ranger. He took a cigarette out of a silver case, tapped the tobacco down, and put it between Frost's lips. Then he flicked a lighter and shielded the flame. "Please do not put your hands under your clothes," Knight repeated. "Keep them—" he smiled "—ah, in full view."

"Certainly," said Frost. He inhaled deeply. He slid forward in his chair and crossed his long legs. "May I ask, gentlemen," he said, "what you intend to do with me?"

They all smiled at that. Jose Garza answered him. Answered him succinctly, typical of the man himself. "Kill you!" he said almost reverently.

Franz Weisberg nodded. "Yes, Frost—we must kill you. I don't mind telling you that you and your men—particularly you—have delayed our plans long enough. With you out of the way—"

There was no humor in his tone now; he was sincere in his brief admiration of his enemy, but nonetheless grim.

"Permit me to say," Frost went on, "you have quite an organization."

Weisberg smiled slowly. "Give us time, Frost—give us time." His vanity had been touched. "Soon Mexico shall—"

"Easy!" hissed Garza, leaning forward anxiously.

Weisberg checked himself again and laughed nervously, plainly nettled at the interruption. "But, surely, there can be—"

"Careful!" snapped Knight.

"Oh, very well, then," retorted Weisberg, crestfallen. "I don't see how—"

"Forget it!" interposed Jacobson.

That ended it. Whatever Weisberg might have said in that moment of bloated vanity was forgotten, and Frost reflected on the few words he had been able to catch… Chapultepec Castle… Mexico… and was able to get no satisfaction. It was apparent however, that these men were copartners, and that although Weisberg was the accepted leader he was closely watched by his associates.

So, Frost mused, this was the Black Ship gang. Dreaming of conquests… Then like a thunderbolt it hit him. Chapultepec. Mexico. They were plotting a revolution! It was too absurd. And yet— Nothing had been too absurd for them thus far. Would they dare? He didn't know…

The Black Ship gang… held back by five stout-hearted flyers…

Five? Frost grinned. Four. That was more like it. He was in a bad way; he saw no avenue of escape. He wouldn't go without a struggle, of course, yet—

Weisberg pressed a button and far off in the cavernous depths of the house there was a faint buzzing. A moment later there was a rap at the door and Weisberg said, "Enter!"

A man entered—the one who had answered the outside bell when Frost first was made a prisoner.

"Pedro," Weisberg said, "lock this man in the strong room and take no chances with him."

"*Buena,*" said the man.

"Captain Frost," Weisberg went on, "you will go with him.

I am sorry to dismiss you but we have important business."
He glared and Frost knew what the "important business"
concerned—the fate of a Ranger captain.

"May I," Frost asked politely, "have a few cigarettes?"

"You may not!" Weisberg retorted.

"Take him away, Pedro—and be careful!"

"Oh, come now," said Frost irritated for the first time. "What
can be the harm in my having a few cigarettes?"

"Take him away, Pedro!"

Frost stared at him fixedly, his lips tightly pressed. He was
seized with an insane desire to throw himself across the table
and bash their faces. Only by supreme will did he control
himself. Such a move, he knew in a sane moment, would be
fatal. He would never live to reach his objective. Four men were
watching him through narrow-slitted eyes. At least three of
them had pistols out of sight waiting for him to make a break.

He nodded stiffly and went out.

DAWN THE FOLLOWING morning broke over the Rio
Grande and found Hell's Stepsons, haggard and weary, beside
their planes on the flying field at Gentry. Yesterday there had
been a great hangar there, and across its top the vivid orange
colors of a longhorn's head, insignia of the Air Rangers. And,
too, there had been, puttering about the place, a short-legged,
grinning mechanic who would have gone to hell and back for
his masters; who knew every whim of the Rangers' motors.
There had been. No longer was there either.

The Black Ship gang's bomb had done it.

The once capacious hangar had been reduced to a mass of
twisted iron and wood, and on a slab in the mortuary, his body

torn by the explosion, lay the mechanic, Johnny Rosenfield.

Hell's Stepsons contemplated the wreckage with something that approached awe. All night they had been in the air seeking some trace of their leader.

"It's no trick," observed Rowdy Perry gloomily, "to believe we're back on the front. This place looks like the field at Dieloulard after the Gothas got through with it." He lifted his eyes to the heavens, now being lighted in a greatburst of color by the early sun. The sun comes up like a red and orange comet in the Rio country.

"No trick at all," agreed Hans Traub.

"I wonder—"

"What the hell?" exploded Eddie Giles. "Don't we all?"

"—— it!" gritted Skipper Hinsdell. "If I could just level off at the dirty louses once—just once—"

"I'll bet," Traub mused, "he gave 'em a fit before they got him!"

Rowdy Perry whirled on the big ex-Bavarian, his face twisted with anxiety. "For God's sake, Hans," he rasped; "why keep on in that damned tone? 'Before they got him! Before they got him!' That's a hundred times you've said that. Cut it out, or I'll—"

"Rowdy's right," said Hinsdell. "Lay off that funeral stuff. How do you know they got him? How, I ask? Hell!" He gave up in disgust.

Hans Traub shook his head. He didn't think Hinsdell believed what he was saying. They all felt the same way he, Traub, did, but they wouldn't admit it. Frost was down. There was no other explanation. And they were whistling to try to keep their courage up.

"Hell," said Giles, "I'm going to shove off! I'll go batty waiting around here."

"Just a minute," Traub put in. "Don't forget the Old Man's on his way down here. And I could take on some coffee."

"Now I ask you what good that'll do." Giles frowned. "The Old Man—"

"Hey, Eddie," Traub blazed. "Cut that! I guess he's just as worried as we are."

"Hell!" said Giles.

They left their planes and went into the barracks for coffee. A percolator was kept handy for just such emergencies. Skipper Hinsdell got busy.

Hans Traub, nominally the leader of the squadron in the absence of Frost, deposited himself in a wing chair—the only wing chair—and reflected. Johnny Rosenfield was dead. Two pilots had been killed in the dogfight with the black ships. The hangar was smashed. And Frost was missing. That was the big thing—Frost was missing.

There was a void in the pit of Traub's stomach that he knew coffee wouldn't fill.

The thunder of a motor reverberated, and simultaneously the men started to the door. Had they but paused they would have known it was not the motor of Frost's ship they heard, but they were keyed to the point where they reacted subconsciously. Instead of the ship they had hoped to see they glimpsed a flat-winged monoplane bearing the shield of the sovereign State of Texas.

"The Adjutant-General," Traub said, and went out to meet him.

The monoplane skimmed the ground, bounced to a landing

and then turned back towards the barracks. Traub viewed the landing kindly, and well he might, for the Adjutant-General was his personal pupil. The monoplane wheezed to a stop and a tall, lean individual leaped out. He lifted his goggles and viewed the wrecked hangar; then struck off to meet Traub.

They shook hands perfunctorily. "Rotten business, Traub," the Adjutant-General said.

"Yes, sir," Traub said.

"Rosenfield dead?"

"Yes, sir."

"No identification on either of the pilots who were killed?"

"No, sir."

"Nothing from Frost?"

"No, sir."

The Adjutant-General's lips compressed and his eyes narrowed. "Damned rotten business," he said again.

"We are pretty worried, sir," Traub said. "The others are in having a slug of coffee. They're about washed up."

"Of course," was the abstracted reply. The Adjutant-General looked at the wreckage of the hangar again. He shook his head slowly and walked towards the barracks, Traub by his side.

"I've asked Kelly Field to help up," the executive went on. "But they've got some red tape to cut first."

"Yes, sir," said Traub. He didn't know what else to say. He opened the door of the barracks and the Adjutant-General entered the room. He nodded to Hell's Stepsons in a preoccupied manner and sat down.

Eddie Giles proffered him a cup silently, which was taken.

He took a sip and said, "There's no doubt about those ships?"

"Not a bit," Hinsdell declared. "It's the third or fourth time we've had a look at that gang. No mistake."

"Um-m-m. What happened?"

They looked at Traub to do the talking and the ex-Bavarian lowered his cup.

"Last night," he said, "Jerry got a call from Stuart at Espinard that some ships were coming across the Border—from Mexico—pretty high. Stuart said it looked funny to him, and Jerry waked us and said we'd have a look. After a while we spotted them with the light, and I tried to get Jerry to go up, but he insisted on giving them a chance to get down. They told us in so many words to go to hell, and so we went up. Then they dropped their bomb, and the next thing I knew we were mixed up in a dogfight.

"I saw Jerry's guns get going over to my right, and I thought he was all okey. After it was all over we missed him."

"Um-m-m," said the Adjutant-General, raising his cup.

"My opinion is," Traub went on, "that Jerry chased the other ship trying to get in a burst and was outrun. He's pretty hardheaded about some things, and he probably kept on."

"There's just one clue," Perry supplemented. "About two o'clock this morning the sheriff at Torcazas telephoned that he heard two planes pass over. That was a little while after we had come down."

"Going which way?" asked the Adjutant-General.

"South."

"Mexico?"

Perry nodded.

"Um-m-m," mused the Adjutant-General. "Do you—er— suppose he's down?"

"Undoubtedly," said Traub. "But the thing that worries us is how he's down."

"As bad as that?"

"Yes, sir," Traub went on glumly. "Jerry isn't the sort to keep us in suspense. If it was possible, he'd at least telephone."

"It's damned rotten, men," the Adjutant-General finally said. He put down the cup and lighted a brown-paper cigarette. His lean face was clouded with doubt and worry. There was a pause during which none of the flyers said anything. There was nothing to say. "I hate like hell to be beaten," he went on. "I thought perhaps that woman Frost got off the rum-boat might tell something, but so far she hasn't. They're trying to get her out on bond. God knows what it's all about," he said finally, stamping his cigarette on the floor. "Well, I guess I'll run down to Espinard and see Stuart." He stretched his gaunt form. "Good luck."

"Thanks," said Traub. He put down his cup and saucer. "Ready, men?"

They went out again to take the air.

Four such days passed, and the search had enlisted the interest of the whole state. The papers played the story up. Frost was a colorful figure and his exploits had caught the popular fancy. Local radio broadcasts helped out the papers, and everywhere people were on the lookout for some news of the lost flyer.

In the air, Hell's Stepsons were not alone. It seemed that every type of plane, whose pilot had the opportunity for it, joined them in their tireless search. But at the end of the four days not a trace of his whereabouts or fate had been discovered.

FROST, UNAWARE OF the furor his disappearance was

creating, thought every day would be his last. For four days he had been prisoner in the hacienda somewhere in Mexico, and since the first night had had no direct conversation with his captors. He had overheard snatches of talk and had learned three things of tremendous import:

That this quartet practically was the brains of the Black Ship gang, although not the final word. There was another man yet higher.

That the gang was planning a revolution across the Border which would establish their position there.

That the hangars adjacent to the hacienda were so skilfully camouflaged they were almost indistinguishable from a normal cruising altitude.

But he may as well, for the good he derived, have known the secret of life. Held *incommunicado*, in a house he had glimpsed only briefly, in a country he did not know, his position was very nearly hopeless.

And yet, strangely enough, he did not indict himself for landing that night when he was captured. He had no regrets. Always he had been the sort of person to invite strange events, whose life had been violent. He had evolved a system of philosophy from which he often had drawn inspiration and consolation—yet it must be admitted that left something to be desired in the present situation. No corner in which he had ever been seemed as devoid of hope of escape.

Once he heard the thunder of airplane motors overhead, knew in an instant they were the motors of his men, that they were riding directly above him. He beat the walls with his fists and screamed at the top of his voice.

Then they passed and he went to sleep.

His disappearance and the presence of so many planes about had had the effect of deterring the gang from any semblance of activity. It was something they had not counted on. It may, too, have had an influence on their plans regarding him. Indifferent to consequences as they were, the disappearance of this one man had stirred up a hornet's nest that demanded consideration.

The man called Pedro was Frost's keeper. Three times a day he brought food, brought it openly and unafraid. Weisberg had relied on Frost's intelligence, and knew the flyer would take no unnecessary risks. As far as that deduction went it was perfectly correct. It didn't go far enough.

On the afternoon of the fourth day Weisberg himself paid his prisoner the honor of a personal visit. He was, as Frost had first seen him, immaculately groomed. Accompanying him were Pedro and Waldman. Weisberg sat down on Frost's bed and said by way of introduction, rather fatuously, Frost thought: "Captain, your disappearance is causing quite a stir."

"You didn't expect them to turn handsprings, did you?" he replied acidly.

Weisberg frowned darkly. "You don't seem very cordial, sir!"

"Why the hell should I be? Have you come to turn me loose?"

The lean face before him bore the faint suggestion of a smile. "Not exactly," he admitted, "still, I have a proposition." He was silent, obviously hoping Frost would interpose a question, or at least register interest. He did neither, so Weisberg went on: "There are so many airplanes looking for you that we—er— find our style is rather badly cramped. We have—er—decided that you shall call them off."

It dawned on Frost what they meant. "I see," he said dryly.

"You want me to stop the search so you can carry on with your business—whatever that is?"

"Exactly! Exactly!" beamed Weisberg pleasantly. "We have something that must be done at once, and we thought you might send a message that because your life was endangered by the search, you'd suggest they—"

"Call off the planes or I'd be killed."

"That's the idea!"

"And then I'd be killed anyway."

"No," said Weisberg deliberately. "We'd agree not to do that, although of course you would have to be reasonable in other matters as they developed. I've given you our suggestion, and we shall expect your answer in the morning. There is an alternative that might be as effective for our purposes. Your body dropped across the Line would stop the need for further search. We shall decide these matters definitely tomorrow."

Weisberg strode from the room, followed by Pedro and Waldman.

Frost was alone again—alone with the tiny light in the wall bracket, his four-day companion.

It is rather strange how confinement and hard thinking have a variety of effects on a variety of persons. Frost paced his room for a while then fell across his bed and went to sleep.

How long he slept he had no idea. He suddenly came awake. And his mind was no longer chaotic; it was rational and calm. Artists know how that is.

His first impression was that he was cold. He had not yet opened his eyes, although he was awake—a trick of his. He lay motionless for a long time… slowly raised his lids. He was conscious of sounds.

There was a quiet rustling that he classified as the wind, and then he remembered there were no trees around. He lay there and pondered over the strangeness of that. Queer that the wind should rouse him. Damned queer. Then he heard other sounds—the sort that always exist in old and mysterious houses. It seemed between a moan and a sharp sputtering, a kind of mixture of some fantastic noises.

They seemed to issue from the side of the room and he carefully got up and made his way there. He placed his ear against the wall and listened.

Had his hearing been at fault? He listened again, more intently. He balanced himself against the wall with his hand and turned his other ear against it. Amazement quickened his pulse-beat.

That sputtering was the jumping of a wireless spark.

Fully alive now, he tried to make out the message. He knew the international code backward and forward, but he realized this message was in private code. He could not understand it.

Did it concern him?

Suddenly all the wild scheming of his four-day confinement welled in an inspired thought—that was the way out. He had to get in that radio room.

He reasoned there was no chance backward, but there was a fighting chance if he went forward. Anything that could happen would be an improvement.

He had to get into that radio room!

There was but one way—a big gamble. He would have to lure the operator into his room first. To hold the scheme off at arm's length and view it makes it fantastic, but Frost was in the exigent position where nothing mattered. To fail meant death.

He listened closely and after a while the sounds ceased. Then there was a faint scraping sound such as a man would make when he arose from a table. Frost visualized the scene, timed it. He heard a door close and moved across the room to his own door. He stood back to the wall with a heavy chair poised in his hands.

Footsteps came softly down the hall…

"Waldman," Frost chanced the name, "I've decided to call them off. I've got a message for Weisberg."

The footsteps stopped and Frost's heart bounced into his throat.

"I'll give you the message," he repeated, trying to make his voice casual. "Take it to your master."

He felt the door creak slightly as a form bent against it.

A key grated, and the knob turned. Frost stepped out from the wall, still concealed, and tensely poised the chair.

A head and a pair of shoulders appeared. Frost did not recognize them, did not try to. This fellow expected no trouble; Frost had been docile… Crash!

The chair fell and the man groaned and clutched at the door for support. Frost lifted the chair again.

Crash!

With all the strength he could muster he brought it down. The chair splintered, and the man gurgled and fell prostrate to the floor. One ear hung by a shred of skin.

Frost grabbed him by the collar, pulled him inside, and removed the key and shut the door. He dropped on one knee beside, he saw now, the man known as Waldman. Frost glowed at his guess in the name, his luck.

Quickly, precisely, he went through the pockets. From the hip-pocket he took a bone-handled .38 automatic, from the vest pocket he took a long slender key—the one, he knew intuitively—to the radio room.

He got up and dragged the body into a corner. Then he opened the door cautiously and looked out, saw nothing, and locked it. He tip-toed down the corridor to the first room on the left, inserted the key and pushed back the door. There was a short flight of steps downward, and from the hall illumination he could see the switch on the wall. He pushed it and shut the door, locked it, and went down.

He was in another small room, although this one was lower than his, why he knew nor cared not. There was a long bench along one side and on the other a huge cabinet with wires and keys and dials. A battery of wires disappeared through a conduit in the corner.

Satisfied there was but one door, and that trouble could come but one way, he sat down at the cabinet with a reminiscent smile on his lips. He was remembering what Red Grace, an old instructor, had told him when he first took his flying lessons.

"It never hurt anybody," Red had said, "to learn the wireless code. It's good stuff to know."

Well, Red had been correct. But—his heart poised for the drop—did one forget the code...

He reached over and cut on the switch. There was a faint humming sound. His anxious fingers reached for the key.

He tapped out his call. He remembered... dash-dot... dash-dot... dash-dash-dot-dash...

"CQ... CQ... CQ... CQ... CQ..."

He clamped on his headset and listened. There was no sound save the faint humming of the motor. He twisted his set open farther. Again his fingers found the key.

"CQ... CQ... CQ... CQ... CQ..."

Was that right? Fear gripped him.

"CQ... CQ... CQ... CQ... CQ..."

The motor hummed on at top speed, throwing off the distress call from somewhere in Mexico. Still there was no response. God...

His headset crackled and he jumped in wild exultation. Somebody was listening. His message had gone through!

But the sounds were jumbled. Too fast. Much too fast.

He tapped again.

"Slower... slower..." he spelled out, every letter a stab in his heart. Time was precious. He might have all day and then again he might have but a moment...

The crackling came again. Slower.

"CFR... San Antonio... USA... who are you..."

His fingers were humming now.

"Frost... Texas Rangers... CQ... CQ..."

He cut his key.

"Where?"

He cut it in again.

"Prisoner... one hundred miles south of border... mark straight south from Torcazas... white hacienda alone on plain... hangars camouflaged... rush aid... get word through to Ranger patrol at Gentry..."

There was a pause; then a reply.

"Message through O.K... this is Kelly Field... are you injured?..."

Frost grimaced.

"No... rush help... desperate..."

Many an amateur wireless enthusiast, unskilled in catching the thirty-five-words-a-minute message of practiced senders thrilled to the exchange of communiques between Captain Frost and Kelly Field.

No less thrilled was the operator himself who intercepted the first flash. He copied the messages on a flimsy, and when Frost quit his key, he handed them to an assistant who got in a sidecar and rushed to post headquarters.

A major read them and went to the telephone. He called the Ranger headquarters at Gentry.

Later: "Hello.... This is Eldred.... Kelly Field... I want to speak to Adjutant-General.... Hello.... Major Eldred speaking.... My compliments, sir.... Our wireless station has just received a message from Frost... yes, sir.... I'll read his flash to the post.... 'Prisoner... one hundred miles south of Border... mark straight south from Torcazas... white hacienda alone on plain... hangars camouflaged... rush aid'... Hello... did you get it, sir?... I'm coming right over..."

He hung up the receiver, telephoned again: "Hello... Hangar Five... Major Eldred... get my plane out..."

The Adjutant-General was reluctant to leave the telephone, but finally replaced it and turned to the group of flyers. His harried face was illuminated by a single light, and it can be called only—hope.

"They've located Jerry," he said excitedly.

Hell's Stepsons got up with a clatter, their faces eager and their eyes shining brightly.

"Where?" they fired.

"He's a prisoner in a hacienda one hundred miles south of Torcazas in a straight line... a white house. Says the hangars are camouflaged—"

Hans Traub grabbed his helmet off the table and snapped it on.

"Major Eldred is coming directly over," said the Adjutant-General. "He'll be able to give us better directions."

Hell's Stepsons followed Traub. Giles ran into the bedroom and emerged with two submachine-guns.

"Major Eldred—"began the Adjutant-General.

"Sir," said Traub, "we will not wait! We can handle this. Let's go!"

They ran through the door before the Adjutant-General could reply.

Two minutes later they were in the skies.

The fighting Air Rangers were riding.

SOUTH OF THE Rio Grande some one hundred miles, in a cellar-like room, the wiry form of Jerry Frost was squared behind a bench, his eyes fixed on a door at the head of the short flight of steps. In his hand he held an automatic pistol.

He knew, of course, that sooner or later the gang would learn he had invaded the radio room. That would be all right. He had thought it all out. There was a bare possibility that he might have escaped through the house on to the desert, but his situation would not have improved by that.

Now he found himself praying for the thing to come to a showdown. Anything was better than the torture of waiting…

It seemed ages later he was conscious of excited noises in the hall and a loud banging at the door. Daylight was showing. "Tomorrow" had come, and he was ready for it.

He smiled grimly and pulled himself closer to the bench he had turned over as a shelter.

"Pedro! Pedro!"

Frost recognized the voice of Weisberg.

"Pedro! Pedro!"

The hammering was more insistent; then it stopped altogether. Footsteps arrived and more raucous voices. A dull thump as if a shoulder had been hurled against the door. Another. The door groaned.

Frost leveled his automatic and waited for the door to be torn off its hinges. The first one through died.

Bloom! Bloom! Bloom!

The door creaked and almost bent under the impacts.

Bloom! Bloom! Bloo-oom!

It parted with a tearing, ripping sound. Forms scurried back out of the light.

"Pedro! Pedro!"

That was Garza's voice. He poked his head inside, and his foot felt for the stair.

"Another step," Frost said to himself—"just one more step!"

Garza, unknowingly, took it.

Crack!

Frost's gun spat a livid flame.

Garza gasped, threw up his hands, and fell forward down the steps.

The forms in the corridor faded into shadows, and then the shadows disappeared. The steps in the hall were hurried; presently all was silence.

Frost crawled forward and felt Garza. His hand touched something cold and he took a revolver from his coat pocket. He satisfied himself the man was dead and retreated, inch by inch, to the upturned bench.

There was another noise in the hall, but no form appeared.

A voice: "Frost?"

Weisberg. Perfectly calm.

"Frost?"

"What the hell do you want?" Defiantly.

"I want to talk with you."

"Come and get me!"

The Black Ship gang had an answer for that. As if anticipating such a reply, two pistols came around the door facing and blasted in the general direction of his voice. Their volleys emptied into the bench and the wall behind Frost.

The Ranger drew himself up on his elbow and took a bead and pulled the trigger.

There was a scream of pain, a muffled oath, and a pistol clattered on the steps.

And again the footsteps went down the hall, this time with high conversation.

Frost pulled himself forward to the steps and retrieved the pistol. Then he went back to his corner. Soon he heard blows and thuds on the other side of the wall, and the wireless set on the table moved slightly. They were wrecking the plant.

"Too late," he grinned. "Too late."

He settled down to wait for the next move. He wondered about Hell's Stepsons. Had they got the message?

AT THAT MOMENT four silver battle wagons were ripping through the skies with their motors throbbing; Hell's Stepsons on the way—as relentless in the saddle as death itself.

Hans Traub was leading the formation—a mile ahead and four thousand feet lower than his mates. He had ordered them to remain higher and behind to look out for a trap. The stolid ex-Bavarian saw no reason to be foolhardy.

He was flying by compass, straining his eyes at the ground below. He had flown thus for an hour and had seen nothing. He knew he should be close to his objective, and each moment his heart got heavier with anxiety.

Then he caught a movement on the ground. A black spot against a white background of sand. An airplane! A black airplane!

Then he saw the house. An innocent-looking hacienda. Two wireless towers at the north side. Antennae.

"My God!" breathed Traub. "This is it!"

The black ship pilot saw him, and was coming aloft to duel. There was another ship being wheeled out… another… The first one got away.

Hans Traub gunned his motor and looped high, flattened out, waggling his wings to Hell's Stepsons for help. He could see, far behind, black rings popping from their exhausts as they opened the throttles…

Traub dived to attack and caught the black ship at less than five hundred feet. His tracers cut a livid path into the fuselage, but the black ship zoomed and got out of range. Traub slid by in a roar, kicked at his rudder and his stick to slide around.

Rowdy Terry, Skipper Hinsdell and Eddie Giles, flying in a straight line at close to a hundred and twenty, saw the black ships struggling to get up and dived at once after them. They cut their guns open in what amounted to an enfilading fire and the ships never had a chance to get away. It was a massacre. One of them managed to get up a hundred feet where it took a full burst head-on, and it folded its wings and fell backwards as a kite the first moment when the string breaks.

Meantime Traub had come out of his skid and was up again

after his man. He rolled over and pulled up on his tail and let go, a withering blast, and the plane jumped forward. The pilot threw up both hands and slumped downward. His plane turned over slowly and drifted down…

Skipper Hinsdell came over the hacienda and dropped in a long fall and pulled on his toggle. Half a dozen tiny missiles sped downward.

He repeated the procedure, half a dozen more dropped downward.

Gas bombs.

Traub and Giles dropped their consignment, and then came down a quarter of a mile from the camouflaged hangar. They bounced along and came to a stop.

When they got out of the cockpit they brought their sub-machine-guns with them. Giles and Perry came running over. They gave not a thought to the black ships they had knocked down. One of the pilots had been caught in the debris and was crying for help.

"Squawk your head off!" Traub gritted.

"Looks like we'll have to fight 'em!" Hinsdell said grimly.

"Right!" said Giles. "Thank God for that wall! They can't snipe us!"

"Let's be going before the gas wears off," said Traub.

They went slowly across the field, running a few yards and then dropping after the manner of an infantry advance. They were close enough now to get an occasional whiff of gas.

"Ugh!" said Traub. "Tough stuff!"

Soon they had reached the gate and Traub cautiously went through. They crept along the outside to the window of the first room and Traub set up his gun and took aim at the top.

It barked and the glass shattered to the bottom.

"Come outta there!" he cried.

There was no response.

Traub turned up the machine-gun, put his helmet on it and slowly raised it. It drew no fire. Finally his head went up slowly. He saw a form inside, moaning and waving.

"Get your hands up!" he barked.

"My eyes! My eyes!"

"Get 'em up!"

The man's hands raised slowly and he turned, momentarily blinded.

"Get through there, Eddie," Traub said, "and put the cuffs on him."

Giles piled through the window and snapped the handcuffs on the moaning man.

"Who else is here?" Traub demanded.

A groan.

"Let's go!" Traub said. He cautiously entered the hall. He moved slowly down the corridor, his gun ahead and Hell's Stepsons behind.

He lifted his voice: "Jerry! Jerry!"

There was a voice from below somewhere.

"Hans! Here! Here!"

Traub dashed recklessly past the broken door, looked and stopped abruptly.

"Jerry?"

"Down here! Look out for the steps!"

Traub plunged downward.

"Where?"

"Right here beside you!" Frost reached out and got his leg.

"Well, then, I'm glad," cried Traub, relieved. He bent down and lifted Frost to a sitting posture.

"This stuff is tearing at my sockets," Frost said. "You must have dropped a boatload. Get me out of here!"

"Right!" said Traub. "Hurt?"

"Not even scratched."

Traub helped Frost up the stairs into the corridor. The captain was blinded and he had to be led.

"Jerry—you old son of a gun!" Giles cried, rushing forward.

Frost tried to open his eyes. He couldn't. They stung. "Skip... Rowdy?"

"All present and accounted for," said Skip.

"I wish to hell you could see yourself," Perry said. "Damned if you don't—"

"Cut the comedy, Rowdy!" Traub cut in. "Jerry, how many men here?"

"I dunno—four or five. How many have you got?"

"One!"

"Well," lightly, "there's more than one. Some of 'em are pilots."

"We know about that," said Giles.

"I know you do," Frost said. "I heard you boys leaving your cards. Were they hard?"

"Pushovers," Traub said contemptuously.

"Well, I got one of the big boys square through the heart," said Frost. "He's down in the cellar."

"Look!" said Traub. He followed a thin trail of blood with his finger. It disappeared behind a door at the end of the corridor.

Traub moved there quickly and banged on the door with the butt of his pistol.

"Come outta there or we'll blow off the hinges!" he yelled.

There were groans from the inside.

"Coming out?"

No answer.

Traub counted slowly: "One—two—three—"

He dropped on one knee and leveled his machine-gun at the door lock. *Put-t-t-t-t-t! Put-t-t-t-t-t!*

He moved the gun around the lock in a circle.

"Wait, for God's sake!" came an agonized voice.

"Hurry up! And keep your hands high!"

The door opened.

A fusillade of shots came through the air.

But Traub was too wise. He was not in front of the door. He was behind the wall.

"——'em!" Hinsdell exploded. "Give it to 'em!"

Traub stuck the muzzle of the gun in the door and pulled the trigger. Lead sprayed the room. He couldn't miss. There were oaths and groans…

"Come outta there with your hands up!"

Frost blinked his eyes again and opened them carefully. There was a film over them that he tried to brush away. His sight was slowly coming back.

The first man out of the room was Floyd Knight. He was followed by Red Jacobson. Jacobson was winged slightly and was swearing like a sailor.

"Anybody else in there?"

"One—but he's dead," said Knight. His eyes were tear-stained.

Traub poked his head inside. The room was a wreck. The machine-gun had chiseled the plaster off the walls, chairs were overturned and, face downward on the floor, was a body.

"Put the bracelets on these babies!" said Traub. He went inside, rolled the body over, grunted, and came out.

"A Mex," he said. "That doesn't count."

"Where's Weisberg?" Frost asked.

"He went up to shut the windows," Knight said. "That's the last I saw of him."

"Say," said Giles, "there's a bird up there we put the nippers on. Maybe—"

Frost went back up the hall and entered the room. The man was sitting in a chair rubbing his eyes with his manacled hands. Frost was able to see it was Weisberg.

"Well," Frost said, "this looks like the works."

Weisberg made a weak effort to smile. "Not at all," he said grimly. "You forget this is Mexico. We cannot be carried—"

"No? Well, my hearty, you've got a sweet surprise coming to you. You're going over—and how!"

Traub marched the prisoners back in the room. "What's next?" he asked.

"Take 'em outside and let Eddie look after 'em," Frost, back in command, said. "Then come back. I want to have a look around." He smeared the tears out of his eyes again.

Frost and Traub went out the door and down the hall to the room in which he had first seen the four Black Ship leaders. They found the door locked.

"Wanna get in?" asked Traub.

Frost nodded.

The ex-Bavarian balanced himself on his left foot and slammed his right foot against the door. It gave slightly. He slammed again and it burst open.

They went inside and Frost busied himself with the open

books which were on the table. He glanced through them hurriedly, and stacked them up. He crammed a handful of loose papers inside one of the ledgers, and placed it on top.

He looked carefully through the drawers for other evidence and then turned to his second in command. "Regular business, eh, Hans?"

"Looks like it, Traub replied. "How high up are these guys?"

"Pretty damn' high up," said Frost. "Pretty nearly the whole shebang."

When Weisberg saw Frost with the books he went off into the choice oaths of at least three nations. "You have no right—" he protested.

"Don't make me laugh!" Frost said.

It was the first time he had been in the full glare of the sun in days, and he carefully shaded his eyes until they could become focused. Then he saw the hangar of the Black Ship gang.

It was a long sheet of linen that had been stretched out on narrow poles for a hundred feet, and its sides were daubed with painted chaparral and cholla thickets—not bad work, he noted. It represented a clever piece of work, although, he knew, it would not long defy a windstorm.

He looked for his plane. "Hans," he said, "you see anything of my bus?"

Traub shook his head. "To tell the truth," he said, "I never thought about it. But—"

Frost looked inside the hangar, saw only a tiny black monoplane. Fifty feet away from the hangar he saw a pile of twisted wires and longerons…

He whirled on Weisberg in a burst of fury. "Did you burn my plane?"

Weisberg smiled. "Certainly. You think we are fools!"

The veins in Frost's forehead almost burst. He was seized, again, with a desire to smear the smirking face before him; again he controlled himself.

He walked over to the ashes of what had been his battle plane.

He came back and picked up the books, and went to the black monoplane. He looked inside and some of the shock at losing his own ship passed. A creation of speed and effectiveness stood before him. He laid the books inside and looked it over. He liked it…

"Lissen, Hans," he said, "I'm going to take this bus in exchange. Load those guys up! Hey, Eddie—gimme a twist!"

Giles came over and centered the prop.

"Contact!" he yelled.

"Contact!"

The motor of the little ship caught in a buzz that sounded unlike Frost's sturdy A3, but he could tell from its talk it was ready for business.

He eased it out, got his wind, and slipped across the field in a cloud of dust. He waved his hand at Hell's Stepsons and they moved their ships around.

Frost got off lightly as a feather, and, two thousand feet up, gunned his motor. It responded instantly. He touched the trigger on his stick: the machine guns spat a loud and vicious note.

"Whoosh!" Frost ejaculated.

Then he settled on his compass and headed for home, with Hell's Stepsons and their prisoners trailing behind.

The Gun-Runners

Strategy and bullets on the Texan Border

ACROSS THE RIM of the Texas plains country on a bitter night there flashed a monster of steel and iron: the luxurious Eastern Express, pride of the Lone Star and Lakes Railroad. It was speeding across one of the flattest and most desolate strips of land in North America—a veritable playground of the elements; and now, out of its vastness, a sharp norther had blown up and swirled a sheet of cold rain against the car windows.

Ahead, the engineer strained his eyes through the blurred glass of his cab to better follow the dancing beams of the headlight, his hand on the throttle, every muscle taut as a bow-string. His fireman closely regarded the multiplicity of gauges. Behind, the train crew sat, half-asleep, caps down over their foreheads, and passengers sank comfortably in their seats and silently mocked the bleakness outside.

The Eastern Express, the epitome of transcontinental travel, was pulled by a 900 type Baldwin locomotive and carried eleven all-steel coaches. In the first ten of those coaches there were calm and quietude: there was more than that. The Germans have a word for it—*gemüthlichkeit.*

But in the eleventh and last it was like a Poe tale come to life. Fear, horror and nausea followed the other in swift succession.

Riding there, handcuffed to each other, under the rigid surveillance of two veteran members of the Texas Rangers were four prisoners, who were, admittedly, the brains of the Black Ship gang. Their activities were so multifold, their vigor so reckless, they kept the state constabulary—all the constabulary—in a constant turmoil. No defenses could be prepared because nobody knew where the next blow would fall. Particularly had their unceasing war affected Hell's Stepsons, the air wing of the Rangers. Captured, finally, by Captain Frost in a stirring episode, they were on their way to Jamestown for safe incarceration and to face formal charges.

For six hours the prisoners had been on the speeding Eastern Express. They might have been, for all the trouble they caused, so many well-behaved children. They were docile, polite, courteous. They had, apparently, accepted the inevitable; they laughed a little, conversed a little, and laughed again. Already they had ceased to be objects of curiosity to the seven other passengers.

It was a few minutes to ten o'clock. The pitch and roll of the train had become a pleasant, sleep-inducing swaying, the noises had lost their irritating harshness and had become, instead, restful symphonies.

Suddenly one of the Rangers got the idea that the train was coming to a stop. Curiously he peered through the window, but saw only flurries of rain and limitless space. He sat back. He remembered the Eastern Express had no stops scheduled until dawn.

But coach eleven, despite the schedule, was, quite definitely, coming to a stop.

The Ranger lifted his eyes quickly, his alertness accentuated by the importance of his prisoners. His hand went to his hip in a purely mechanical movement and he stood up.

A pistol cracked; a sheet of flame lashed out. The Ranger spun almost around and fell in the aisle with a bullet in his head.

Bewildered, the other Ranger started up. He did not get on his feet. The same pistol exploded again; he gurgled and slipped back in the seat in a sitting posture. His head fell forward, giving the impression that he was sleeping. Only he had ceased to breathe.

The seven passengers in coach eleven could only stare. It was too weird, too grotesque to be real. The panorama unrolling before their eyes was only a bad dream. Things like this no longer happen…

"Just keep still, everybody!"

The voice came from the end of the car. Standing just inside the vestibule was a man of ordinary build. His face was covered by a mask, his hands held two squat pistols. He was unmindful of the gusts of rain and wind that beat around his shoulders from the open end of the car.

His eyes pivoted and he moved his head slowly. Over his shoulder he yelled:

"Come on!"

He pressed himself against the compartment and permitted three other masked men to get by. They passed quickly to the four who were handcuffed; the pistols in the hand of the speaker never wavered.

One of the prisoners, of professorial mien, slightly gray, wearing silver-rimmed glasses, rasped: "Drag him out of the aisle and get the keys. They're in the watch pocket of his pants!"

The masked men bent to their task, propped the dead Ranger to a reclining position and fished for the keys. One of them clucked triumphantly and held them up, laced with a string.

"Hurry, fool!"

The key was fitted to each handcuff in turn and one by one

they dropped to the plush carpet. Motivated by the same thought, the prisoners stood up and briskly rubbed their wrists.

One of them was fat, swarthy, obviously Mexican. He cried: *"Vamose! Pronto!"*

They moved out of the car without looking back, turned into the vestibule, dropped to the ground. The rescue, perfectly co-ordinated, had consumed less than three minutes.

The rain fell in sheets, the wind howled, it was cold and miserable. Unmindful, the rescued prisoner of professorial appearance smiled broadly. "Excellent!" he commended. "Have any trouble with the job?"

All-steel coach eleven, of the crack Eastern Express, stood alone in a desolate country, robbed of its motive power and left there for the elements to tear against. It had been cut off from the train.

"No trouble after we got the air line fixed," came the low retort. "But we'd better step on it now. It wouldn't be healthy…"

"Right!" broke in another voice slightly more resonant. It belonged to one of the rescued prisoners. "I'm damn near frozen!"

They stumbled across the right-of-way, two hundred yards to the highway; and walked, heads low, up the highway. One of the group emitted a shrill whistle through his chattering teeth. They stopped and stepped aside. An automobile, capacious and curtained, rolled up; the men clambered in. The gears ground and the car moved away. A moment later the headlights snapped on.

For five miles they hurtled over the road at a speed decidedly unsafe. The driver was constantly being admonished to have a care, to look sharply. The only other sounds were grumbles at the penetrating weather and the chill, soaked clothes.

They veered abruptly into a smaller road, skidded perilously, and from the tonneau there came a smothered oath. This road was graveled, tricky: no great speed was possible. Finally the car came to a stop beside a dilapidated gate.

One by one the occupants emerged. The last one out spoke hurriedly to the driver.

"Nice work, George! Be careful now! Good luck!"

The automobile turned around, aided by straining arms at the wheel, and departed. Seven men went through the gate and across the field to a phantom shape in vague silhouette against the stormy night.

It resembled a huge bird with wings outstretched. The men lowered their heads and entered its belly. A door closed and was locked from the inside. A starter whirred and a motor barked into life. Its lurid red and yellow exhaust stabbed the darkness.

The crescendo rolled in waves for a brief spell—an age to those inside—and the huge bird awkwardly lumbered out.

In some desperate, miraculous way it got off the ground.

The men who were prisoners less than an hour ago permitted themselves the luxuries of sighs. They had proved, again, the impregnability of their clan.

The plane climbed quickly, leveled off and gathered speed.

It was heading due south.

IT WAS THREE hours past dawn along the Rio Grande. The sun-baked countries that parallel the international boundary had come alive. The sting of the sun was beginning. In a short time it would be almost unbearable.

Thirty-five hundred feet above the river were three airplanes. Two silver monoplanes, not large as size goes, but large compared to the third one. It was small and its black fabric gleamed in the sun. Were they to come closer you could have distinguished those dots on the wings—orange longhorns' heads. They were the cockades of the Air Rangers—Hell's Stepsons. And those slim needles which lay over the hood were machine-guns.

At the controls were Captain Jerry Frost, Skipper Hinsdell and Rowdy Perry—three of the squadron. Skilled under fire, aces in their own right, companions in adventure, they comprised that technical detail known officially as the South Patrol.

Frost was riding the black plane. It was a souvenir of his last brush with the Black Ship gang, taken to replace his A3 which they burned. He rode with a nonchalance that might be called indifference.

At intervals he led them close to the ground, then soared back and with his eyes traced the line on his map. It was a short line traced with black india ink. It began in the Big Bend country and ran across the river in a wide curve.

Hell's Stepsons were following that line.

They followed it to the river, winged over and went back over the same route. Alternately they scanned the ground with heavy binoculars. There were occasional movements, closer inspection revealed a tourist or a native in a small car. To them that was uninteresting.

They were seeking traces of big trucks. It was a new cross-current in the turbulent Border country; but a cross-current so potent, so fraught with menace, that to disregard it would have been inexcusable stupidity.

The new cross-current was *Los Contrabandista*—gun-runners.

But the trail was so indefinite Hell's Stepsons saw naught but a country parched into a whisper. Trucks there had once been, along that line Frost had traced diligently. Those trucks had borne—heaven knows what! Mexico is the land of countless intrigues. But there were no trucks now.

Frost waggled his wings, caught the eyes of Hinsdell and Perry and dropped his forearm in a sweeping gesture. Hell's Stepsons ruddered over and started for home.

Thirty minutes later they swept into sight of great sheets of galvanized iron on the ground beside gaunt columns that reared above wreckage not yet wholly removed. Frost saw, remembered, and his jaws came together with a snap. The new hangar was under construction; Frost remembered a few nights ago when that wreckage had been their old hangar and shops, and major-domo of it all was little Johnny Rosenfield. Now there was debris; Johnny Rosenfield was no more.

A bomb dropped by the Black Ship gang had done it.

Frost dipped into the field, dropped down to a perfect landing and was followed at once by Hinsdell and Perry. They taxied their ships across the field, their backwash raising clouds of dust.

Frost's trim monoplane came to the line and he cut the switch and vaulted out. He unbuttoned his chamois jacket and took off his helmet. His shoulders were broad, his curly black hair lay close against his massive head, and his eyes were blue and unafraid.

He was smiling as Skipper Hinsdell walked up. Hinsdell was inclined to slight bulk, his hair was tinged with gray and he radiated peace and unconcern. But that was anomalous. Skipper Hinsdell was a bitter foe.

"It looks," Frost said, "as if we've run into another one of those damned things. This gun-running isn't my idea of a picnic."

"You said it," Hinsdell declared. He poised a cigarette at his lips. "Nothing to work on. Funny country—funny people."

Rowdy Perry, built like an all-American halfback, came up, his eyes twinkling. He chuckled broadly and said, "My motto is to let this country alone as long as it wants to be let alone— Say—have a look at who's here!"

Perry pointed across the field to a plane half-hidden by the material being used to construct the new hangar. Both Frost and Hinsdell recognized it at once.

"Whew!" Frost whistled. "The Old Man!" He regarded his pilots quietly. "I wonder—"

Hinsdell snorted, "Hell, he may be here to decorate you."

"And then," Perry broke in, "he may be here to give us a kick in the pants."

"That's more like it," Frost rejoined. "I'll take half of that bet." Neither Hinsdell nor Perry had moved. Both were puffing at their cigarettes in deep unconcern. "Well," said Frost, "let's shove off. If there's any trouble coming we'll all get it at the same time."

Silently they crossed the field to the frame building that was their barracks, stepped on the porch and paused briefly at the threshold.

"Hello!" boomed a deep voice as Frost's shadow fell into the room.

"Good morning, sir," said Frost. The others nodded and followed him inside. They scattered themselves about the room, awaiting the blow. That some sort of blow was coming was quite plain. The Adjutant-General of the State of Texas was wearing his most perturbed expression.

"If we'd known you were coming—" Frost began. He was silenced by a broad flourish.

"I didn't know it myself until a couple of hours ago," the Adjutant-General said. "Then I thought I'd better come myself. A telephone wouldn't do in this case." He grimaced, produced a sheaf of brown cigarette papers, a sack of tobacco and quickly rolled a smoke. He lighted it and sat down. He motioned to another chair.

"Sit down, Jerry," he said, "and take the weight off your feet. What I've got to say is pretty amazing."

Captain Frost sat down. He nodded slowly. He wondered what it could be. So did the others. Hans Traub, the rotund ex-Bavarian flight commander, looked at Eddie Giles, the kid out of the old R.A.F., and Giles looked at Traub.

"Well," said the Adjutant-General, "those four ringleaders have escaped."

"Impossible!" Frost gasped.

"Sir!"

"Escaped—beat it. All of them. And," he lowered his voice a trifle, "the State of Texas is out two damn' good Rangers."

"You mean—" Frost exclaimed.

The Adjutant-General nodded. "They killed Nettleton and Galloway. Plugged one of them through the head and the other through the heart. They used two bullets—*just* two."

"When? How?"

"They cut the coach off from the train. Four men took part in the rescue. Nettleton and Galloway didn't have a chance—damn!" The thought of the murder of his two officers caused the Adjutant-General to grind his palms together in impotent rage.

"No trace, eh?" asked Frost soberly. The first shock had passed, and with its passing came the sober realization that all of their work had gone for nothing. Weisberg, Garza, Knight and Jacobson—the big four of the Black Ship gang gone? It was incredible.

"Not even the faintest trace," he said. He spread his hands in a helpless gesture.

He puffed again at his cigarette.

"And such facts as you have, I presume," said Frost, "are merely the stories of the witnesses?"

"Yes."

Frost was smoking now. He bit his lip and contemplated the ashes on his cigarette. "They had an automobile, of course. Maybe they had an airplane."

"Undoubtedly," said the Adjutant-General. "If they had men planted on the train they most certainly had an automobile following them."

"And a plane stowed away somewhere."

Hell's Stepsons nodded.

"It had to be perfect to work," observed Giles moodily; "and it seemed to work."

"Yes," said the Adjutant-General. "Those fellows have a habit of pulling perfect things."

"And to think," put in Traub, "I had a wide-open shot at them the other day. I should have given 'em the works on the spot!"

Frost knocked the ashes off his cigarette and went to the window. He stared out at the turgid Rio in somber reflection, and beyond into the fastness that was Mexico. Then he turned back.

"Well," he said, "they're gone. It doesn't matter a damn how they got away—they're gone! And again we're holding that well-known sack." He came back into the group and stood beside the Adjutant-General. "What's your idea, sir?"

The commander of the Texas Rangers shook his head and closed his eyes wearily. "To be plain, I haven't got any ideas. I came down here because I wanted to tell you this first. I confess when I first got the news from Jamestown I was dumfounded. It seemed too big to actually happen. But happen it did, and since we're all in this together I felt—"

He broke off and regarded the flyers before him with something that approached affection.

"Of course, sir," Frost said hurriedly, generously, to cover his commander's display of sentiment. "But it comes at a bad time. We got a pretty good tip yesterday that the Tento crowd is alive once more. Somebody is running guns to Coahuila again."

"Tento?"

"Yes— Madero's old colonel. I thought"—he grinned—"that

when we knocked over the Black Ship outfit we had just about washed up the country."

"Gun-running, eh?"

"Well, we think so. The stuff is coming through from San Antonio. We don't know what it is—but it's something. Something they carry in trucks at night."

The Adjutant-General sat up slightly, ground his cigarette under his heel and rolled another one.

"Federal men know anything about it?"

"A little," Frost said. "Tony Casales was down yesterday afternoon from the San Antonio office of the Secret Service. You know Tony—was one time a Villa soldier. He said the other day he saw old Tento himself in Alamo Plaza and tailed him. Tento, he said, went to one of the wholesale houses which maintain a fleet of trucks for the Southern trade. A little quiet investigation developed they had almost a hundred large boxes of merchandise for a company in St. Alto, a town just outside Carrizo Springs."

The Adjutant-General exhaled the cigarette smoke. He looked at Frost. "Well—"

"Well, there isn't any company in St. Alto. The address was faked. Now Tony believes all the furor in the Gulf has stopped them from running them in a boat and that they're coming overland. We were asked to keep our eyes open—so we rode over the trail from Carrizo Springs to Coahuila today. We saw nothing."

"Tento has started half a dozen revolutions and has always been whipped," Hinsdell said.

"This time," said Frost, "he seems to have plenty of capital and influence."

The Adjutant-General looked up suddenly from under his bushy eyebrows.

"Do you suppose that gang—"

"That's exactly what I had in my mind," said Frost heartily. "At first I thought the gang leaders were in jail, or on their way, and discounted it. Now, I'm not so sure."

The Adjutant-General scratched his lower lip with his long forefinger. "It's a wild scheme."

"And yet," said Frost, "they're capable of such. The very fact that it is wild makes me all the more positive they are mixed up in it. Commander," he went on, a reminiscent look falling upon his face, "I studied Franz Weisberg the short time I was his prisoner. He's crafty and probably crazy, but he's no petty crook. It is not beyond him to dream of being something pretty big down there."

"And yet," replied the Adjutant-General in a tone that contained a faint hint of fatigue, "we don't know anything save that those men escaped. This other scheme—"

"Planned, maybe," said Traub, "before the capture."

"And," added Perry, "one of the main reasons for the escape."

"I suppose so. I thought we had concealed the movement of the prisoners perfectly. We should have flown them up."

"There's no use crying now," Frost declared. "They were all set for the rescue no matter how they were moved."

"What does Casales hope to do?"

"Capture them with the goods. Mexico City already knows about it. But that land is so barren the rurales are nearly helpless. In this case Mexico is looking to the U.S.A. for protection."

"And Texas," said the Adjutant-General.

"Yes," Frost said quietly, "and Texas. We have a perfect right to pitch in now. It is ours as much as the Secret Service Department's."

The Ranger chieftain nodded. "Challenge all planes along the river. The prisoners maybe are in Texas now, but eventually they'll try to get back to Mexico."

Hell's Stepsons nodded. They well knew their task. They were, in truth, pawns in the game of the law. Another group was reaching across the wilderness to plant an empire in that tropical, fabulously wealthy land which has long lured the master schemers. What if those gestures previously had been ill-starred, futile? Ambition ever beckons and always there will be men who will follow the will-o'-the-wisp of power...

Yet Hell's Stepsons were an arrogant lot. They had tasted adventure, danger and war—and had come through safely. They drew their inspiration from obstacles. Their arrogance, perhaps, was well-founded.

"Yes, sir," said Frost. But he meant a great deal more than merely that.

"Descriptions of the men have been sent to all corners of Texas, New Mexico, Arizona and California. Jerry, I leave it in your hands. I must be off. The Governor probably is wanting to see me now."

He stretched his length, shook hands with the flyers and went through the door with Captain Frost. They moved across the field side by side.

FROST CAME BACK presently. He said, "Well, the Old Man is shot up about this business."

"He looked it," said Traub pointedly.

"But," Frost interposed swiftly, to intercept any stray, careless thoughts, "don't any of you babies get the idea he's ready to quit. He's a bulldog! He said we could have all the National Guard we wanted."

"That's out!" snapped Perry. "We don't want any guard!"

"Speak the truth!" said Hinsdell. "We'll handle these double-tough guys without any help!"

Frost's lips went white from the pressure of his teeth. It suddenly seemed to him that this feud had been going on forever; was an age-old thing, something that had been handed down through the generations.

"I guess," he said quietly, grimly, "we've got to start all over again. The next time—"

Hell's Stepsons sensed Frost's emotions. They knew what was in his mind and, in a measure, underwent the same chaos of thought and passion.

"The next time," echoed Hans Traub, "will be the last time!"

"I hope so," said Frost suddenly. "You know—that Weisberg outfit is behind that gun-running as sure as there are little apples. I was never so sure of anything in my life. If we bag those *contrabandista* we'll know something. The only question is: are they running guns?"

"Why, hell, yes," Perry said bluntly. "What else?"

"We can look for business to pick up, too," interposed Hinsdell. "I know a little about that fine art of smuggling rifles—and they move 'em all at once—bang! like that. They've got sense enough to know they can't keep it up."

"If Weisberg's party is involved, it'll get busy without losing any time," Frost said. "I've got my serious doubts about them being in Mexico. They know the Border is being watched—and they're somewhere in Texas."

Frost moved to the door and picked up his helmet off the table. "Meanwhile," he said, "we're leaving the dear old river all by its lonesome. Let's have a look-see up and down."

"I could take on a little air," said Traub. He ran his arm through his leather jacket.

"Want Skip and me to take a crack at the north?" asked Perry.

Frost shook his head. "Nope—we'll stick together. We don't know what may happen now. I want to get low over Carrizo Springs. Maybe we can see something."

"Away—Landing Force!" boomed Hinsdell. He made a move to go and was joined by Traub. Frost and the others fell in a pace behind. They walked briskly, seriously; and yet Eddie Giles hummed a few bars of a well-known popular song.

Traub glared at him over his right shoulder. He took many liberties with young Eddie Giles. There was a strong attachment between the two. He said to Hinsdell, audibly enough for Giles to hear, "Ain't it wonderful what the radio does for these youngsters?"

"Go to hell, squarehead!" Giles barked. He made a pass at Traub with his foot.

"Lissen—Cupid!" Traub rasped. "Another crack—"

"Pipe down!" said Frost. "This is no tea party!"

Traub grumbled: "All right, serious!" He stopped beside his plane. "Hey, Cupid! Turn 'er over for me!"

Hinsdell moved around to the propeller. "I'll spin her."

Giles stepped in front of him and reached for the blade. "I'll do this," he said. "Bad luck for anybody else to twist it."

Hans Traub smiled and slipped into the cockpit. "*Coupez!*"

sang out Giles. *"Coupez!"* came the echo. Giles moved the propeller, centered it and cried: "Contact!"

He gave it a yank and it blasted loudly, roaring its message. Soon the four other blades were spinning in thin circles of light.

Frost pulled out and was the first one off.

Hell's Stepsons were back in the air with work to do. They had a new problem—*Los Contrabandista.*

THEY SWUNG SOUTHEAST over Maverick County in a straight line with Carrizo Springs.

The country between Gentry and the Springs, across the tip ends of Maverick, Zavalla and Dimmit counties is desolate, but, even to an eye unused to the beauty of ruggedness, never uninteresting. There are flatlands, arroyos, sharp acclivities and cañons whose sides are steep and sharp. Over a period of ages the weather has played queer tricks with the Texas badlands.

Frost had never found this land stupid. It always had fascinated him; the prospect of man matching his elements with a nature so unrelentless held for him an almost irresistible appeal. There was no middle ground—you conquered or were conquered.

Now it was particularly interesting. It was breeding an intrigue that must be stamped out at once, permitted to nourish it would send flames into another country. Somewhere below him that *coup* was being carried to execution. And it was no longer far-fetched to presume the scheme was being financed by the Black Ship gang.

He dropped lower than a thousand feet and peered through his goggles. Occasionally there was something on the ground to attract his attention, but for the most part it might have been another world so destitute was it of travel.

It was difficult to perceive how the innumerable little hamlets close to the Border existed. From the air one got the impression they were toy villages dumped off somewhere in a fit of temperament and, in some inexplicable measure, taken hold. They were isolated, unneighborly, and seemed to find contentment in solitude.

Carrizo Springs was such a village. There were, to be sure, other villages much more monotonous—but not a great many more. It was, as its chief claim to fame, the southern terminus of the S.A.U. and G. railroad, thirty miles removed from the Border. St. Alto was but ten miles from Carrizo Springs—twenty miles from the Border. That is an hour's run with a loaded truck.

Directly opposite St. Alto is Coahuila—as impenetrable as any state on the face of the earth. It literally festers with bandits and all manner of evil, and Mexican federals are powerless to interfere. There are passes in Coahuila which a company of infantry, properly accoutered, could hold against an army. The gun-runners had selected their destination with extreme care.

Frost led his flyers over Carrizo Springs and St. Alto in what might be called an intimidation program, and St. Alto saw nothing which would arouse the curiosity of even the most suspicious. It was a tiny village that sprawled across the road, helpless in the grip of a noon sun, and which didn't choose to do anything about it.

Back towards the Border Hell's Stepsons flashed, and halfway between St. Alto and the river Frost picked out a flat strip near the road and gestured to his companions. He floated his black ship close, observed the topography, rose to get his wind-age, and then swooped in to a landing.

Like eagles coming to rest, the Rangers followed him down. They left their motors idling, got out and walked to where their leader stood.

"I want to take a look at that road," Frost said. "If it's been traveled lately it ought to show it."

"Ought to," said Hinsdell. He fished for a cigarette. Rowdy Perry unhooked his helmet and cast a glance at him. "Make it a pair," he said.

Skipper Hinsdell grimaced. "Don't you ever buy—"

"Make it three," said Giles.

At that Hinsdell exploded. He grunted and buttoned the flap of his jacket. "Damned if I smoke!" he said. "Every time I reach for a cigarette it costs me three or four. Take time out next pay day and buy your own smokes!"

Hans Traub interposed his frame into the picture. "Skip, I haven't asked for a cigarette since—"

"Since we landed!" Hinsdell turned to Frost who was smiling at the byplay. "What about the road, Jerry?"

"Let's have a look."

They came under the barbed-wire fence into the dirt road. It bore traces of travel. Frost looked at it closely. Then he straightened.

"I can't tell," he confessed.

"Nobody else can," said Giles. "Now if you ask me—"

"Which nobody did, smart feller," said Traub.

"If you ask me," Giles continued unperturbed, "I'd say this was a great place to waylay 'em."

"Whatdya mean—waylay 'em?" Frost demanded.

"Well, have a look at that cañon," Giles said, pointing to a narrow roadway a few hundred yards south.

They did. They followed Giles' finger and saw, a scant few hundred yards ahead, the roadway sink between two ominous bluffs fifty feet in height. Those bluffs were natural barriers, and at the crest they had been eroded into serrated, grotesque spires that resembled the points of dozens of giant needles. The cañon continued for a quarter-mile, and then emerged on to the tableland.

"We could come out here at night and pen 'em up in that gap," Giles said. "It looks pretty simple to me."

Frost surveyed him critically.

"See, Jerry," Giles went on, "in that way we'd soon find out whether these guys are running guns or not. See?"

"Sure, I see," Frost admitted. "That'd be great—*if* we knew when they were going to take them over."

Skipper Hinsdell produced a cigarette and lighted it. "Well," he said slowly, "there's this much I know: unless they've got all the guns they want, they'll lose no time in getting them across the river. Gun-runners have got to move fast."

Eddie Giles was watching the face of his commander for some sign of approval. The idea with him had been, first, entirely spontaneous; as a matter of fact he had not weighed its possibilities at all. He had thought it and said it in the same breath. But now, after a few seconds' reflection, he rather liked it.

Frost looked up quickly. Giles beamed proudly. He knew what was coming—they all did. Their commander was a commander in title only. Frost always put extra-duty missions, hazardous assignments, to a vote.

"What say? Game to come back here tonight and take pot luck?"

"Sure," they chorused. Hans Traub added in an undertone, "I've got insomnia anyway."

"We'll have to get machine-guns," Frost went on moodily. "And help from somewhere."

"Help?" snorted Giles. "We won't need help!"

Frost looked at him with tolerant benignance. "Ever try to capture gunrunners, Eddie?" he asked, a trace of a smile about his lips.

"No—but—"

"Then," said Frost, "you can't appreciate the size of the job. Policemen don't get fat trying to capture those guys with paper-cap pistols and without help." And as if to settle the question, he added, gravely, "We'll get all the help we can muster."

"I only hope," said Hinsdell, "there'll be something doing."

That brought a smile of genuine amusement to the lean features of Jerry Frost.

"If they come," he said, "there'll be plenty doing."

The drone of a motor overhead broke their conversation. As if they were marionettes and the puppeteer yanked the string, they looked up. A biplane loomed in the north.

"Let's go," said Frost.

They crawled back under the fence and ran to their planes. They trundled out and soared away. Frost climbed to a thousand feet and winged over. The biplane still was several miles off. Frost turned the nose of his black monoplane upward and touched the trigger to warm his guns. They chattered through the roar of his motor.

"Maybe yes, maybe no," he said to his instrument board. "You never can tell."

He leveled off and headed straight for the approaching plane.

Hell's Stepsons flanked him. As they came closer to the plane they gauged its altitude and climbed above. At four thousand feet Hell's Stepsons ruddered over and loafed.

Frost could make out the markings now. A commercial plane. It seemed to be heading straight for him. He swung away to the left, prepared for battle. The Rangers had dropped in single file. The plane was almost on them. They could see an arm waving from the rear cockpit.

Hell's Stepsons were at attention when the plane slithered by at a ground speed of better than a hundred miles an hour. At four thousand feet the wind was blowing great guns. Frost, allowing for this wind pressure, flew in a circle, or rather an ellipse.

As the plane went by a man stood up in the cockpit, his helmet off, and waved. He had recognized the fighting forces and plainly was taking no chances on an attack.

It was Tony Casales, the Secret Service operative. He was motioning for Hell's Stepsons to follow him.

The Rangers kept their eyes on Frost, who gestured for them to fall in. They rolled into the wake of the commercial plane and let it set the pace.

Casales' ship flew to the landing field at Gentry in a straight line. Hell's Stepsons dropped in immediately behind him. Something was up.

Casales and another man climbed out of their plane and came over to Frost. Casales was tanned to a dark brown and his voice was deep and pleasant.

"Hello, Jerry," he said warmly.

"Hi, Tony," Frost returned.

Hell's Stepsons came up and Casales nodded. Then: "Jerry— Colonel Pablo Benito y Rafari, of the Mexican Army."

Colonel Rafari bent his body in the middle and bowed graciously. He was all of six feet, with a breadth of shoulder and a litheness in his muscular body that suggested the latent power of a panther. He was alert, physically and mentally, and it required no powers of observation for Frost to realize this man would be a worthy foeman for anyone.

"*Muy Capitan,*" he said softly. "*Salud!*"

"How do you do?" said Frost, nodding. "Colonel Rafari— my squadron: Messrs. Traub, Giles, Hinsdell and Perry." He indicated them with his hand and they each nodded. Again Colonel Rafari bent his body.

"What's on your mind, Tony?" said Frost. "You came slipping out of the north and we almost got a hot reception ready."

Casales grinned broadly. "I told Colonel Rafari we might get such a greeting." His grin faded. "Jerry, let's go over and sit down." He obviously was deeply concerned about something, and they went to their barracks.

They seated themselves; and Hell's Stepsons registered high interest.

Casales said, "Colonel Rafari is out of the regular Mexican army and was in San Antonio to investigate those revolution reports. I think things are moving to a head."

"Oh, yeah?" said Frost.

"Yes. Tento is planning to get the rest of his guns into Coahuila tonight. That much is a fact."

Frost was studying Rafari. His eyes were a blue-gray and they had the steadfast look of a man of courage; his hair was straight and black and a black mustache failed to hide resolute lips. A vague idea came to Frost that he had seen him before; even his voice seemed faintly familiar.

Rafari intercepted the attentive glances. "There is a question in your eyes, *Capitan*," he said.

"I was just wondering," Frost said, "if I had not seen the Colonel before?"

Rafari smiled in a shadow, his eyebrows lifted and he lightly shrugged his shoulders.

"*Quien sabe?*" he said. "*Puede ser!* Perhaps! The world is not so large."

Casales sensed a challenge and rushed to the relief. "The colonel is anxious to co-operate with us," he said. "He realizes, as I hope we all do, the value of numbers in this."

"*Si, si,*" the Colonel purred.

"Well," said Frost, "we personally have considerably more at stake than the capture of gun-runners. We have good reasons to believe that some men in whom we are deeply interested are involved in this young revolution."

Colonel Rafari nodded vigorously. "*Exactamente!*" he said. "The government of Mexico has taken notice of those men. They are a desperate lot."

"So you see, Tony," Frost went on, "we're anxious to stick our oar in this. How straight is your dope on the party tonight?"

"Damned straight!" said Casales emphatically. "We took a look at that warehouse in San Antonio this morning. It's empty!"

"That means they've moved the boxes to St. Alto?"

"It means they've moved them somewhere. I guess it's St. Alto. They'll start across tonight."

Colonel Rafari said, "We have been advised that Tento has quartered several thousand troops in Coahuila, and that he also has cavalry. Señors," he said in a rush of passion, "these revolutionists must be stamped out! It is impossible for me to get help, but I shall be glad to offer my life if necessary."

"Spoken like a true soldier, Colonel," said Casales.

Hell's Stepsons only looked, but their looks belied Casales' words.

"You, *Capitan*," Rafari went on, "surely have some plan?"

"Yes," Frost admitted. "Tony—how many men can you supply?"

"Oh-h-h-h—half a dozen."

"That'll make twelve then, including the Colonel. I was thinking we could get them south of St. Alto—although the real idea belongs to Eddie Giles. There's a deep cañon there through which they've got to pass. We can bottle 'em up."

"Say," put in Traub, "how about Stuart and a couple of men from Espinard?"

"Right," said Hinsdell. "We want to be ready for those guys. And I got a snappy hunch they'll be tough and then some."

Frost thought that over and nodded. "All right. You and Rowdy pick them up this afternoon on the patrol and get 'em back here by five o'clock. There won't be anything doing before dark. That'll be around seven o'clock." He was looking at Rafari again. Something was turning over in the back of Frost's brain. He had an indefinable feeling that Rafari and he had met somewhere before, and looking at him he rather felt he was one of those men who must always hold the advantage or be broken. Many are like that.

Rafari dropped his eyes before Frost's cold stare and Frost felt a vast relief sweep over him at the realization that he had matched and beaten the Mexican at nerve. It was a little thing, a fleeting thing, to be sure, but the Ranger felt it was tremendously important.

"This is a big job, Tony," he said.

"I know it," Casales returned heartily. "Of course, there is little reason to think it'll be successful. The *Federalistas* have taken every precaution on the other side."

"But," Eddie Giles finally spoke up, "we don't want them captured on the other side. We want them on this side."

"You mean—we'll *get* 'em on this side!" corrected Perry.

"We win or lose in one effort," smiled Rafari.

Skipper Hinsdell chuckled. "Just like a parachute jump—it's got to be perfect the first time."

Colonel Rafari looked at him frigidly as if he could not understand levity in such a moment. Hinsdell did not see the look of disapproval.

Tony Casales got up to go. "Jerry, I'll be back here at five o'clock with some men. It'll probably cost us some money to get them hauled—but we'll be here. Ready, Colonel?"

"Surely," said Frost swiftly; "surely you aren't going to take the Colonel?"

"Of course," said Casales. "That is—"

Colonel Rafari nodded. "Unfortunately, yes." He stood on his feet and balanced his weight on his toes like an athlete. "It is regrettable to leave such charming company, but I must. I always feel perfectly at ease with fighting men." He directed the last remark to Captain Frost. But Frost gave no sign that he heard.

"So long," said Casales.

"*Adios,*" said the Colonel. He bowed again.

When they had gone off the porch, Traub exploded: "There was something about that bird I didn't like. I think he made a dirty crack as he went out."

"You *think* he did?" cried Giles. "You *think* he did? Lissen, Kraut—I'm an expert on dirty cracks. And that was one he made."

Frost smiled wanly. "It's funny," he mused, "that you should get the same impression I did. You know, I've seen Rafari somewhere before—only that wasn't his name then."

"Can't you remember?" asked Perry.

Frost shook his head. "Not for the life of me. But I've seen him before."

Skipper Hinsdell wrinkled his face in deep cogitation. "This is no lawn party we're having tonight," he observed after a while. "It's got a lot of funny angles—and I want to be behind a machinegun when it starts. I always feel safer there."

"Don't worry," Frost said. "We'll all be behind them."

SHORTLY AFTER FIVE o'clock there gathered in and around the barracks of the Air Rangers fifteen men. Eight of them were in the service of the Texas Rangers, five air pilots and three of the Border staff from Espinard: George Stuart, Jack Marvin and Zeke Grimes—old-timers of the Rio campaigns.

Five had come down from San Antonio with Tony Casales in a cabin plane—five members of the Secret Service, and they looked every inch as hard as the popular conception of Secret Service men. They were equipped with .45 automatics—Casales had a brace. Colonel Rafari was the only one of the group unarmed.

Frost, Tony Casales, Rafari and two of Hell's Stepsons were in the main room of the barracks. The rest were outside, some distance away, looking over the planes.

Frost was speaking: "It isn't necessary for me to tell you these men are a violent bunch. There'll probably be a lot of shooting. I've got ten Thompson machine-guns and a thousand rounds of ammunition each. That," he smiled, "ought to be enough."

"May I," asked Rafari, "be allotted a machine-gun?" There was a proprietary confidence in his tone that brought a flame of anger to Frost's eyes. Rafari's voice stirred him, spoke out of the past. That voice! Desperately he struggled... his jaws came together with a click.

He remembered! Years ago in Rio Rita... Maranga's minister of finance... who sold him out and joined the rebels... his name was Rod... Roder... Roderiguez... now he called himself Rafari.

It came back to Frost in a flash. Rafari's question had hardly died. What manner of deviltry was afoot now? Rafari could not exist without his schemes and plots...

"Of course, Colonel," Frost smiled. "Are you familiar with their mechanism?"

"Perfectly," purred Rafari. "Perfectly."

Frost said, "Very well," and got up. Rafari was also on his feet. "Shall I help you?" he said.

"Please."

They went into the adjoining room and Frost handed him one of the guns. Rafari examined it closely.

"Wicked looking," he commented.

"Yes," said Frost.

Rafari spun the disk and leveled it at Frost.

"Now, Señor," he said softly, "you will please get your hands up!"

Frost turned, surprised, but lifted his hands.

"Back into the other room!" Rafari commanded.

Frost slowly moved back into the room. At the threshold

Rafari paused and barked: "Your hands up! Hurry!" He trained the muzzle on the others.

The hands of the man-hunters slowly went up.

Rafari's eyes were narrow and the gun seemed held in a vise so unwavering was its barrel.

"Come forward one by one," he said; "and leave your pistols on the floor. There will be no other movement or I shall chop you down where you stand!"

Tony Casales was closest the Mexican. He had begun to recover from the amazement visited upon him by this move, but was still a little bewildered.

Frost said: "It's all right, Roderiguez! Your voice trapped you. Remembering the trick you played on Maranga I gave you an unloaded gun. The drum is empty!"

For just a second Rafari's stern front collapsed and gave way to wild dismay. But that was enough.

Crack!

A sudden explosion filled the room as Frost's automatic barked.

"Ugh!" exclaimed Rafari, reeling. He grabbed his shoulder and would have fallen to the floor had not Casales caught him. By that time Jack Marvin and George Stuart had burst in and were beside him.

They laid him on a table.

"My shoulder," said Rafari. The other men had come running in and were crowded around him. And there was little confusion. It had happened so quickly there hardly was time for a clear thought. "Who shot me?"

"I did," said Frost. He surveyed the reclining form superciliously."

"Gee, Roderiguez, you had a lot of nerve to try one like that! You might have got killed!"

"Jerry," said Casales, "who is he?"

"A rat," supplied Hinsdell tersely.

"Well," Frost said, "it's a long story and you haven't got time to hear it now. But his name isn't Rafari and I doubt if he is a Colonel."

"But," Casales insisted, "I know he is."

"How do you know it?"

"I've known it a long time. Three weeks."

"Did you meet him or did he meet you?"

"Why, he came to see me—"

"Take the trouble to investigate him?"

"Well—no—"

"That's it exactly," Frost said. "That guy's name is Roderiguez and he's a snake." He paused briefly. "Hans, drag out the guns and let's shove off."

"What are you going to do with that egg?" Giles asked.

Rafari rolled on the table and groaned.

Frost answered that question by moving closer to the wounded man. "Listen," he said, "things look pretty bad for you. Want to help yourself a little?"

Rafari moved his head and stared. He grunted.

Frost bent closer. "If you'll answer a few questions you might get off. Interested?"

"What—" he managed, "are they?"

"They running those guns tonight?"

Rafari hesitated, grimaced. "Yes," he said finally.

"Tento with 'em?"

"Tento is in Coahuila."

"How many trucks?"

"Five."

"How many men?"

"Ten."

"Um-m-m-m. Know a guy named Weisberg?" Frost repeated.

"Yes."

"Know where he is?"

"No."

"How about the rest of that outfit? Know any of them?"

"Knight is with them. He's coming over with…"

His voice faded, obviously from pain.

"That's all," Frost said. "Eddie—go get Lunsford to come over here." Lunsford was the mechanic.

"Okey," sang out Giles. He left.

"Men," said Frost, "Knight is one of the four of those leaders who escaped from the Eastern Express. I want to bag him tonight for the sake of two good Rangers who are no longer among the living!"

His voice rang like steel. There was a silence, disturbed only by the click of the metal as Traub handed out the machine-guns.

"It's still an hour until twilight," Frost said. "We'll go over there and dig in. And you can look for plenty of hell—because they tried to make doubly sure by sending their fake colonel down here to interfere. Tony, did he have any communication with anybody this afternoon?"

"No," said Casales. "He hasn't been with anybody but me—and my men."

"Think hard, Tony. It's important."

Casales shook his head firmly. "He hasn't seen anybody at all."

"All right," said Frost. "In that case I don't suppose they're expecting action tonight. Still, this business is damned odd. I don't see how the hell this Rafari guy could help them much. It looks to me like his best bet was this afternoon. The idea of trying to cover a mob like this is foolish."

"Since I come to think about it," Casales said, "he has been acting queer. But I never thought—"

Eddie Giles returned with a six-foot husky who wore the smeared coveralls of a mechanic. His name was Bob Lunsford.

"Bob," said Frost, "I want you to take my gun and stay right on top of that bird on the table. He's been winged in the shoulder. Nothing serious, but he'll try to make you think he's dying. Don't pay any attention. He's slick as an eel. If he makes a crooked move I want you to let him have it right between the eyes. You haven't forgot how to shoot, have you?"

"No, sir," said Lunsford, grinning at an active part in the drama.

"All right. You're responsible for him. Did you set those bombs on Mr. Hinsdell's ship?"

"Yes, sir. All set; toggles checked."

"Fine. Tony, we're going to tear up the road just this side of the cañon. Of course, the good county of Maverick is going to have one of its senators get up in Austin and swear at the Boy Scouts who drop bombs on their fine roads. But there's no other way. I guess," he added, lower, "a couple of shell craters will stop 'em."

"Right," said Hinsdell. "I can drop bombs like nobody's business."

"About twenty feet the other side of the cañon, Skip. The side nearest the Border. Got it?"

"Right."

"Okey. Let's shove off."

They went through the door and across the field lugging their guns. George Stuart got in Frost's ship, Grimes got in with Traub and Marvin crawled in Giles' bus. None of the passengers had helmets. They got in courageously and put their hats in the seat beside them. Grimes and Marvin clenched the rim of the fuselages until their hands went white before the motors were even started. Traub and Giles smiled in honest amusement. Casales and his men got in their cabin job and whirred the starter. The A3's of Hell's Stepsons were soon popping and they followed Frost off the ground. The cabin plane was the last one to get into the air.

Frost purposely set and held a slow pace, his mind altogether intent on the capture of the gun-runners.

He was, therefore, surprised when, looking out a little while later, he saw the silver ship of Skipper Hinsdell's flash by. It was, to say the least, a strange procedure; but he looked up in time to check an angry exclamation.

Less than half a mile ahead were two black ships.

Frost at first was loath to believe they were the enemy. The thought of an enemy ship being in the sky, so close to the Ranger headquarters, after all that had happened, was preposterous. But there they were.

Unmindful of his passenger for the moment he sent his ship into a climb and timidly touched his trigger to warm the guns. They belched a short burst and George Stuart's head popped up like a jack-in-the-box. Frost never forgot that look.

It wasn't fear exactly and it wasn't bewilderment. It was something between. George Stuart knew he was fighting at another man's game. But he was cut out of the fighting pattern.

He braced himself and laid his gun in his lap.

Frost perceived the resoluteness of Stuart's move, paid him an unseen tribute, and wheeled into fighting front. At five thousand feet one of the black ships cut loose with a burst at Hinsdell. The flame was easily perceptible although a great blob of sun still hung on the rim of the world.

Hinsdell slipped over and ruddered around and Frost, having got his altitude, nosed over in a dive. He looked back quickly and saw the other planes were loafing along. Giles and Traub were at six or seven thousand set to spring, and Hinsdell was turning in a wild splitair to get back to Frost. He was trying to take the game away from his comrade.

Stuart, gripping the rim of the cowl, suddenly saw the two slender pieces of steel over the hood burst into flame. Stuart thrilled to that. The wind was in his teeth. Those guns ahead of him were spitting death.

The black ship slid under Frost's dive by a fraction, and as if by prearranged signal the other black ship veered sharply out of Hinsdell's line of fire. But it had put itself into a perfect pocket.

The black ship Hinsdell had missed was caught unaware by Frost; had not, as a matter of fact, seen him. It afforded an unmissable target; was full broadside. It loomed in Frost's ring sights and he squeezed the trigger. It was a long, ripping burst and the black ship fell out of control.

Frost zoomed and rolled over to go to Hinsdell's rescue. But Skip needed none. The black ship, seeing it was trapped, tried to straighten out in a frantic maneuver. Hinsdell was on it like a hawk, both guns in a venomous burst. The black ship seemed to hesitate, as if its nose had been stopped by a giant impediment, then dropped down a trifle and flipped over on its back.

It fell in that fashion without ever righting itself.

Frost was down now seeking a landing place. He was eager to have a look at his victim. He picked out what seemed to be a flat strip and glided in, but it was anything but smooth. He bumped along and finally settled. He came to a stop fifty yards from the wreckage of one of the black ships.

George Stuart was on the ground when Frost got down. He was slightly ill at ease, but was forcing a smile.

"Sorry, George," Frost said. "But somebody had to get it. I'd rather it would be him."

"It's all right," Stuart said. "But, believe me, I'll walk to the next party." He became conscious that he was still holding his pistol and, what was infinitely worse, that Frost was looking at it. He laughed nervously and slipped it in his holster.

"I notice," Frost smiled, "you weren't taking any chances with my marksmanship." He started to the plane with Stuart beside him.

The black ship was a wreck and a bad wreck, but it had, in some miraculous fashion, escaped flames. It was smashed as if a pile driver had caught it dead center. An arm protruded from the cockpit and Stuart and Frost moved the plane and dragged the body from it.

Frost unbuckled the helmet and looked into a young face.

"A kid," he said softly. "What a pity!"

The boy—he could have been no more than twenty-three or four—was riddled through the chest and arms with a direct burst. He probably never knew what struck him. Frost went through his pockets but found only a few coins. There were no marks of identification.

"Too bad," he mused. "I'd like to know who he was." He

straightened up. "Well, George, we've got to leave him, and there's no use going to look up that other guy either. We've got some business ahead." He stepped back a few paces and waved his arms across each other as a signal to the planes above.

"Come on, George." They went back to their plane without a word and got into the air.

Frost led the ships to the cañon and slowly circled the south end. He pointed downward and Hinsdell waggled his wings that he knew. Frost then slipped away and Hinsdell floated over at two thousand feet.

He pulled on the bomb toggle and a blunt speck flashed downward to explode with a loud boom and fling dirt and debris high in the air. Hinsdell went back and dropped another one.

Underneath him two great holes opened in the road. He raised his hand to Frost, and Frost signaled him okey. Then Frost dropped into the field and pancaked down.

He cut his switch and let Stuart get down. Then he handed over the machine-gun. Stuart was still silent. Frost knew what was eating him.

"Look here, George," he said. "You're an old-timer and tough as a boot. You aren't thinking about that smash, are you?"

"Well—"

"Forget it, George. It's foolish."

Skipper Hinsdell came up lugging a machine-gun and Frost looked at him with undisguised admiration and affection. "Sweet work, Skip," he said. That was all. Casales and his men were getting out. Giles and Traub marched up with Grimes and Marvin.

Zeke Grimes surveyed Stuart enviably. "How you feel?" he asked.

Stuart grinned in spite of himself. "You go to hell, you smart boy," he said.

They gathered around Frost. "There's nothing to do but sit out there and wait—just like Sandy Claws was coming. The knoll will hide the planes and we'll take up a position there"— he pointed— "and Tony and his men there. When they run up to that crater, they'll stop."

"If," said one of Casales' men, "they don't fall in."

"Yes," said Frost, "if they don't fall in. Remember the advice I gave that lad back in the barracks goes here, too. We'll take no chances. I'd like to get these bimboes alive—but we're going to get 'em dead or alive. That clear?"

"Good and clear," said Casales. "I'd like to have a couple of them to show the chief in the morning."

Frost smiled. "Well, unless I miss my guess you'll have more than just a couple. Now, Skip, if you've got the cigarettes, we'll go over and get set."

"Suits me. Only," he said triumphantly, "I've stopped smoking! I'm fresh out of cigarettes."

TWILIGHT WAS COMING up when they moved into position, and Frost noticed, with a feeling of gratification, that the moon was promising effulgence. He placed Hell's Stepsons in front and Casales and his men behind.

"Now," he said, "there's only one thing missing—the trucks. We may as well get comfortable."

Two—four—six hours dragged by. It was shortly after midnight when the rumble of a truck was heard in the distance, sweeping across the countryside like the thump of a tank, and soon a pair of headlights were discernible.

"Get set," Frost called.

Hell's Stepsons scattered themselves on the slope of the cañon and the Secret Service men went to the opening of the gorge.

"Don't hesitate to let go if things look bad," Frost said.

The trucks crawled onward. There were but four of them. Four pairs of headlights scattering their rays about the road, only one pair visible all the time. The others could be seen only at intervals.

They rolled slowly into the cañon, still entirely oblivious of their danger. Hell's Stepsons waited with bated breath for the first truck to come to the rim of the crater made by the bomb.

Finally it did. It pulled up with a screech of brakes and at that same moment a man jumped out of the driver's seat and ran into full view of the headlights. He looked at the yawning gap and for a moment seemed at loss for an explanation.

The trucks followed in close order and they came to a stop one by one. Two other men joined the first at the rim of the hole. Quite plainly they didn't know what to make of it.

Then it dawned on them that this was an unnatural occurrence.

One of the men wheeled and yanked out a pistol; looked around carefully.

Lying on his belly not fifty feet away was Frost, the muzzle of his gun poking ahead. His fingers were on the trigger.

"Get your hands up!" he screamed at the top of his voice.

The man wheeled and fired in the general direction of the words.

Frost squeezed the trigger and a rattle broke above the chug of the idling motors. The man who held the pistol leaped into the air two feet and pitched forward on his side.

The other two men ran back behind the truck.

"We've got you surrounded," Frost yelled again. "Get out there and put your hands up or we'll blow you all to hell!"

For emphasis he pulled the trigger again and the bullets beat a tattoo against the wooden boxes in the truck.

"Come on!" Frost barked.

No other had fired. Only his gun had spoken, but the others were taut and tense awaiting the signal.

Three or four men came out in the light of the truck. One of them had his hands up, and the others followed suit.

"Where are you?" came a question.

"Keep those hands up—and get the others!" Frost boomed.

The man turned and yelled something behind him which Frost didn't understand, but presently several other men gathered on the edge of the shell crater. Frost counted them. There were nine.

"All right, men," said Frost to the Rangers. "Take it easy."

They went forward by feet, their guns still leveled.

Frost faced the prisoners across the hood of the truck. "Tony," he yelled, "cut those switches."

One by one the motors gasped and died.

"Anybody else in this cargo?" Frost asked.

"We're all," came the sullen retort.

Frost spoke out of the side of his mouth. "Skip, you and Rowdy frisk 'em."

Casales and his men had gathered around.

"Step out there one at a time, you birds!" Frost went on. "Any monkey business and you'll lose part of your heads!"

Hinsdell, Perry and George Stuart quickly searched the men. They took a pistol from each, and from three men they removed two guns. The guns were thrown in the shell hole.

Frost missed Floyd Knight. "Where's Knight?" he demanded.

"Who?"

"You heard me—Knight! Where is he?"

"He didn't come."

"No? Zeke, take a couple of men and look underneath those tarpaulins."

Frost laid his machine-gun on the running-board and climbed in the first truck himself. It held four large boxes, manifestly guns. He lifted the tarpaulin carefully and saw nothing.

The second truck was devoid of humans. But the third gave up its secret.

"Hey," yelled Casales, "I've got somebody else!"

Frost ran a few feet and stopped behind the third truck. Casales had his gun leveled at a form which was stretched prone on the differential housing.

"Come outta there!" he ordered.

The body finally moved and backed out. When it straightened up, Frost recognized Floyd Knight—one of the four ringleaders of the Black Ship gang who had escaped from the Eastern Express.

"By Gad, Knight," he said. "You fellows need somebody to direct you. I never saw a lousier mess than this in all my life. I'm ashamed of you. An amateur could have done better."

Knight tried to grin. His hands were by his sides.

"Stretch your arms up," Frost said. "I want to take your gun."

He moved forward as Knight's arms went up and removed an automatic from a shoulder-holster.

"Now," Frost continued, "go on ahead. And I just hope to hell you try to make a break. I'm laying for a good chance to shoot your ears off."

Back in the group which stood there, hands high, Knight was disheveled and not at all the immaculate daredevil Frost had first seen when he was a prisoner at the hacienda in Mexico.

"You drivers get back under the wheel. We're going to Carrizo Springs. Men, split up and ride with them. George, you and I will bring up the rear. We'll leave the ships until in the morning."

The drivers got back in their seats and after a tedious process, the trucks were backed up and headed back towards Carrizo Springs.

It was an hour's run, and the tiny jail was that night crowded to capacity. Hell's Stepsons, three Rangers and the Secret Service men aided two town constables in guarding them.

Casales telephoned his chief at San Antonio and Frost telephoned the Adjutant-General at Austin. He put through his report and was told to come on as soon as possible—something important.

At dawn the following morning the prisoners were handcuffed and put on the San Antonio train. The Secret Service men were given charge of them.

Frost and Casales had an argument about Knight. Frost said he wanted him on a previous charge and Casales finally conceded. The trucks were left in charge of the Carrizo Springs constables until the proper disposition could be effected.

Hell's Stepsons saw Casales off. Then they went back to the jail and crowded into the rickety flivver that was the property of the city.

Thus six of them returned to the cañon. Frost loaded Knight into his ship and they turned back to Gentry.

At the landing field Frost sent Skipper and Perry back in

one ship to get the cabin job the government had pressed into service.

"You bring it back, Rowdy," he said.

He went into the barracks and found Bob Lunsford and the man who called himself Rafari engaged in a polite conversation. Rafari wore a bandage over his shoulder.

"How's tricks, Bob?" Frost asked.

"Great, sir," the mechanic grinned. "He isn't a bad guy at all."

"No, I suppose not. We brought him a playmate. Come in here, Knight."

Knight came in, saw Rafari and his face went purple. He spluttered: "So you spilled the works, eh? Damn you—" He would have thrown himself at the wounded Mexican had not Frost intervened.

"No sense in you guys scrapping," Frost said. "You two are bagged, but there are more to come before we're through."